"Finally, we can put the past behind us, yes?"

"Soon." I drummed my fingertips on the countertop. "I have discovered some information about my parentage."

"And?" Luca took a seat. "Why does this concern me?"

"Because my real father killed Trace's parents."

"I see. And who is he?"

I played with the stem of my wineglass. "You wouldn't believe me even if I told you. I need more proof than someone just telling me. I need to catch him."

Luca nodded and took a tentative sip of his own wine. "You mean to catch the fly."

"I mean to make such a damn good web that everyone within forty square miles will know he's a rat, but it's complicated."

"Our business always is."

"Right."

Luca pulled out a cigar and sniffed it. "Let us speak plainly. What can I do for you, Nixon?"

My heart hammered in my chest as I looked into his eyes and said, "I need you to kill me."

ELECT

Other Forever titles by Rachel Van Dyken

Elite

The Bet Series

The Bet

The Wager

ELECT

RACHEL VAN DYKEN

FOREVER

NEW YORK   BOSTON

Forever
Hachette Book Group
1290 Avenue of the Americas
New York, NY 10104

www.HachetteBookGroup.com

Printed in the United States of America

RRD-C

Originally published as an ebook

First trade paperback edition: December 2014
10 9 8 7 6 5 4 3 2 1

Forever is an imprint of Grand Central Publishing.
The Forever name and logo are trademarks of Hachette Book Group, Inc.

The Hachette Speakers Bureau provides a wide range of authors for speaking events. To find out more, go to www.hachettespeakersbureau.com or call (866) 376-6591.

The publisher is not responsible for websites (or their content) that are not owned by the publisher.

Library of Congress Cataloging-in-Publication Data

Van Dyken, Rachel.
    Elect / Rachel Van Dyken. — First trade paperback edition.
        pages ; cm — (Eagle elite)
    "Originally published as an ebook."
    ISBN 978-1-4555-5421-8 (softcover) — ISBN 978-1-4789-5544-3 (audio download) — ISBN 978-1-4555-5422-5 (ebook)
    1. Organized crime—Fiction.   2. Man-woman relationships—Fiction.
I. Title.
    PS3622.A5854845E44 2014
    813'.6—dc23

                                                    2014028072

To all those girls out there who want to see the bad boy redeemed...
And to my amazing, amazing group of readers who make what I do the
best job in the world! I love you all!

Acknowledgments

First, I have to thank God—He is totally the reason I am able to do ANYTHING—and I'm so thankful every morning that I get to wake up and do what I love.

Husband—I'm sorry I keep bringing my computer to bed, but thank you for being awesome enough to kiss me anyway and turn out the lights even when I'm typing away at two a.m.!

Also, I feel terrible...In my last acknowledgments, I never once said thank you to Erica Silverman, my amazing, amazing agent. She's like the soldier you want on your team during Capture the Flag—she's that awesome. And I'm THAT competitive, so it works.

To Grand Central Publishing—I heart you guys big. You've been so amazing in this process. Words can't even begin to describe how amazing my experience with you guys has been!

Lauren—friend, editor, fellow Tom Hardy fan...Your input on my last two books has been incredible! I've never had such a positive editing process, so thank you for not only making me better, but making it so fun!

To my street team, beta readers, and all the bloggers: To thank each and every one of you individually would take page and pages. Just know that I appreciate your love and support so much. I would be nowhere without you guys and I'm so thankful and humbled that you not only keep reading—but keep encouraging me! Love you guys!

ELECT

Prologue

I hid in the shadows hoping he wouldn't see me as he hit Ma again. He'd promised Ma he'd stop drinking. He'd promised he wouldn't be mean anymore, but he never kept his promises—not anymore.

"You stupid bitch! I know you were looking at him tonight! You think I can't tell?"

"I wasn't!" My mom wiped her eyes and tried to reach for my father's hands, but he pushed her to the ground and kicked her stomach with his foot.

Afraid, I looked around the room for help. Chase was right next to me; I could see his knuckles turn white as he clenched his hand into a fist. He was just as helpless as me. I swallowed as my eyes fell to Uncle Tony; slowly he shook his head at me. He stood motionless in the corner, his gaze without emotion. Did he want me to sit there and watch? Watch while my father killed my ma? Weren't men supposed to protect those they loved? I felt my nostrils flare in silent outrage. Someone had to do something.

I heard another shriek and then the sound of glass hitting the floor. I turned just in time to see my mom hit the ground, blood spewing from the side of her face.

"Ma!" I ran toward her, pushing my father out of the way. I had to save her, I had to protect her. "Ma!"

"Nixon." A hand reached out to stop me. "Don't."

I looked up into Chase's sad eyes. "I have to save her."

"You can't."

"But I can! I have to—"

"Nixon, you're my best friend in the whole world, but Dad said if you make your father angry again he's just going to turn on you. The way I see it, is he's gonna pass out soon anyway."

"But..." I looked over at my mother. She gave me one terrified silent nod before my dad landed a final blow to her face. Her eyes fluttered closed as her head hit the ground. I watched for her lips to move so I could tell she was still breathing.

Her chest rose and fell.

Alive. She was alive—this time. Paralyzed with fear, I kept watching, counting the seconds between each weak breath, hoping, praying, that it wouldn't be her last.

"Nixon, come on." Chase tugged on my arm and led me outdoors. The minute my feet touched the grass I took off running.

I pumped my legs until they hurt, finally stopping at the tree on the farthest edge of our property.

"Nixon." Chase was behind me, out of breath, but still behind me. "I'm sorry, Nixon. I'm so sorry."

I nodded. I knew it was the right thing to say, that he was sorry; I was sorry, too. Sorry that I wouldn't listen to Chase and that one day, I would kill my father for what he was doing to my ma. I would kill him and I would go to Hell for it—but I didn't care. Dad said I was going there anyway.

"Let's make a pact." Chase put his hand on my shoulder.

"A pact?" I sniffled and turned to him. "What kind of pact?"

"One that's forever. One that protects people rather than hurts them."

"How do we do that?" I was suddenly interested. What if I could make all the hurt go away? What if I could save everyone!

"We do this." Chase pulled out his pocketknife and cut open his hand, then nodded to me to do the same thing. Without pausing I cut open my hand and handed back the knife. "Blood brothers. We're never gonna hurt each other and we're gonna save those like your ma, Nixon. Ones who can't save themselves. We're going to protect them."

"How?" I watched as the blood dripped from my open palm.

"Rules." Chase shrugged. "They keep people safe, right? At least that's what my mom says." He smiled. "We make rules and we start our own club. That way, we don't have to listen to anyone but us."

I liked it. I chewed on my lower lip. "What do we call ourselves?"

"The chosen?" Chase offered.

"No, that sounds lame. We have to sound...more powerful than that."

My eyes flickered to the road, and a sign poked into the ground. It said election. "Elect." I pointed. "Let's call ourselves the Elect." It made sense; after all, the president was elected, wasn't he? We weren't exactly chosen, but we were making the choice, we were electing ourselves protectors. That's what we were.

"Who else can join?" Chase asked.

"Tex and Phoenix. They'll want to." A weight suddenly felt like it was being lifted off my twelve-year-old shoulders. "Should we shake on it?"

"Yeah." Chase smashed his hand against mine as our blood mixed. "No going back, Nixon."

"No." I shook my head. "No going back."

*　　*　　*

I pressed my fingers to my temples and watched, replaying that moment over and over again in my head as the outline of Chase and Tracey flickered in the moonlight. Would he really do this to me? After all the shit we'd been through?

I gauged her reaction, hoping that I would be wrong. Praying to God that Trace would just this once listen to me. Her eyes flickered with interest for a few brief seconds before she looked down at the ground.

"Shit." I waited in the shadows. A part of me knew this would happen. The part that told me to damn my feelings to hell and ignore all the warning signs that I'd been seeing. But now it seemed like it was too late. I stayed, planted where I was, watching, waiting.

"Chase, you can't…" Trace shook her head. "You can't be like this. We can't do this!"

"We aren't doing anything," Chase said in low tones, reaching for Trace's hand. "Don't you?" He looked directly at me, although all he saw was a shadow. I knew I was well hidden. "Don't you feel the same way?"

Trace jerked her hand away from Chase's. "It doesn't matter what I feel. It's not about me, Chase."

"But it is." Chase reached for her again. This time her hand grasped his in such an intimate embrace I thought I was going to vomit all over the ground. The outside air was cold as hell as little pieces of ice tried to find their way into my wool coat.

"It isn't." Trace sighed. "It never was."

Chase jerked her toward him. She fell against his chest and looked up into his eyes. "What are you doing?"

Chase sighed. "What I should have done a long time ago." He grabbed the back of her head and pulled her in for a kiss. Their lips touched.

I had to look away.

The only sound in the night was that of my soft footsteps as I walked away...leaving my heart in broken pieces where I'd last stood. She was lost to me; it wasn't even the Sicilians that had taken her, but my best friend.

A gunshot rang out loud and clear in the night air. I turned back around just in time to see Trace collapse into Chase's arms.

Chapter One

Nixon

Three weeks earlier

C hase," I growled. "Do your damn job."

My cousin rolled his eyes and saluted me as he jogged off to Trace's side. We'd all decided it would be best if she stayed in school. After all, the security at Eagle Elite was tight. And nobody would dare try something during the day.

Really, it was the nights that had me going insane. I didn't know whom to trust. I wasn't even sure if I could trust myself. If anything happened to Trace again, I would never forgive myself. The way things stood, I was having trouble even looking in the mirror after the way I'd treated her over the past few weeks.

Raped. She had been so damn close to being raped by someone I'd once called friend. And now...now her grandfather was in hiding—again. You can't just shoot a mafia boss without a damn good reason and he didn't have a leg to stand on. It was crucial that we find out who'd killed Trace's parents, because if it was the De Langes like I suspected, at least her grandfather wouldn't get shot—or worse, tortured for doing what was right.

I couldn't shake the feeling that it had been my fault in the first place. If I would have just stayed away like her grandfather had asked. She would have been safe. Instead, the pull she had on me was so magnetic I found myself falling. Before I knew it, I was ready to start an all-out family war against the Alfero boss in order to have his granddaughter. Hell, I was ready to kidnap her.

I groaned as I watched Chase run to Trace's side and grab her hand. Okay, I could handle a lot of things. Guns, violence, people who didn't know their place in this godforsaken world, but my best friend kissing my girlfriend's hand? The same girl I'd been in love with my whole life? Yeah, I was going to freaking murder him if he did anything to mess that up.

She was the only thing I had going for me. I mean, I had my sister, but both my parents were gone. My mother died when I was younger—at the hands of my bastard of a father, and my father, well...I would dance on his grave if it wouldn't make me look like a genuine ass. The fact was, I needed Trace; she wasn't just a girl to me, she was my lifeline. I was terrified that if I lost her, I would lose myself—lose everything that keeps me grounded and sane.

"You okay with this?" Tex asked next to me as he ran his hands through his dark red hair and nodded toward the happy couple.

I shrugged, trying to look nonchalant. "Are you challenging my judgment?"

"Whoa." Tex lifted up his hands in surrender. "I was just asking a question, Nixon, not challenging you. Take a sedative. Seriously."

"Take a—" I bit down on my lower lip and sucked on the metal of my lip ring. "I'm fine."

"Right. I'm fine, you're fine, everything's fine. Oh, look, I think a rainbow's sprouting out of your ass."

"Remind me why you're here again?"

Tex grinned and shoved his hands into his pockets. "Oh you know, to make your life miserable. That and because your hot sister promised she'd meet me before her first class."

"Please don't use 'hot' and 'sister' in the same sentence."

"Sorry." Tex cleared his throat. "I'm here because your *sexy* sister promised she'd meet me before her first class."

"And I'm leaving." I rolled my eyes. "Tell my not-sexy, not-hot sister that she needs to answer her damn phone."

"Will do!" Tex saluted. "Don't trip over the rainbow, sunshine!"

I flipped him off and jogged in the opposite direction to the business building. I was technically a senior in college, though I truly only had three credits left before I'd be able to leave. I'd enrolled in electives so I could stay a student for the rest of the fall semester. I was seriously thinking about failing my last few classes so I could stay spring semester, too. I had to do something—no way was I going to be the only one not at Eagle Elite, not with the Sicilians rowing their boats across the Atlantic at this very moment.

I'd only been given control of the school because my family owned it. Clearly it was all a front. I needed access to everything, and therefore the dean had looked the other way when I enrolled in certain classes and dropped others. I'd been working for four straight years trying to discover who had killed Trace's parents when she was six. And after all those years of trying to clear my family name, it just seemed like now everything was going backward and spinning out of control. The last thing I needed was the Sicilians breathing down my neck for raising hell these past few weeks.

"Mr. Abandonato," my senior seminar professor announced the minute I stepped foot into the classroom. It was a tiny class of only about fifteen students, all of them too engrossed in talking and texting to care that I was late. None of them even noticed that I looked like I'd just gotten back from visiting the seventh circle of Hell and had a meet-and-greet with Satan himself.

"Yes?" I tried not to appear as irritated as I felt. As it was, I knew I was only about five seconds away from losing my shit. "What can I do for you?"

My words held a double meaning. My asking what I could do for him. He knew who I was; he knew what my family did. I always chose my words carefully for that very reason. Most people asked for favors in public—not in private. So the art of deception was my specialty. If he answered that he needed something taken care of, then I'd know he wanted to deal with Nixon Abandonato, mafia boss. If he laughed and started spouting out nonsense instructions about school, then he just wanted to talk to plain old Nixon.

Sometimes I wondered what normal would be like. For example, what does it feel like to wear jeans without hiding a gun on your leg? Or not feeling leery about every single person that looks at you cross-eyed? Sleeping was overrated, and now I was running on pure adrenaline.

"We have a new student." Mr. Ryan's gaze flickered to the front of the room. My eyes followed his. Rage mixed with that very same adrenaline, making my hands shake as I balled them into fists.

"Shit." A few students looked in my direction, then gazed back at

their phones as my eyes slowly took in the new student. I could probably scream "fire!" and their asses would still be firmly planted in their
seats. Idiots, all of them.

"Pardon?" Mr. Ryan said. "Do you know one another?"

"Oh," a hiss of air escaped my lips as I marched over to the desk.
"You could say that."

"Well," Mr. Ryan said from behind me. "If you could show him
around, it would be much appreciated. After all, you are senior class
president."

"That I am," I answered. I stopped in front of the new student's
desk and whispered, "How the hell did you get in?" I was so close to
his face that I could see the faint bruising across his nose—telling me
one thing. He wasn't there by choice—he'd been forced; not that he'd
ever admit defeat. My nostrils flared as he licked his lips, taking his
time in answering.

He leaned back in his chair, his long dark hair covering part of his
face. "You think you're the only one with connections, Abandonato?"

"Of course not." I gripped the sides of his desk and leaned in
until my face was inches from his. "I just didn't think you'd be stupid
enough to pick a side."

"I didn't pick. I was chosen. They want someone to investigate.
Somebody trustworthy needs to be on the inside. It's not like they can
enroll in college."

"Really?" I reached into my pocket and pulled out my knife, slid-
ing it across the desk toward his stomach. "And I'm not?" I tilted my
head to the side. "Careful how you answer, Faust. I wouldn't hesitate
to slice you open where you sit."

Ever since Faust had accused Trace of *asking for it*, when she was nearly raped, he'd been on my shit list. He was from one of the Original Sicilian families and a big giant pain in my ass.

He leaned in so that my blade was literally poking a hole through his white cotton shirt. "Do it. Then Trace won't have anyone protecting her, or her grandfather. The Alferos are officially at war with the rest of us. Pick a side, Nixon, or I'll pick for you."

"Class!" Mr. Ryan clapped his hands. "Everyone take their seats."

I pulled the knife back and hid it in my hand. "This isn't over."

"Of course not." Faust smiled, his eyes darkening with smug satisfaction as he nodded toward me and answered, "It's just begun."

Chapter Two

Nixon

The minute class was over I walked over to Faust's desk. I should have seen this one coming—which was another reason Chase was Tracey's bodyguard instead of me. I wasn't thinking clearly—and it was all because of her. My focus was on protecting her but in the process I was losing my touch.

Which meant only one thing.

I needed to put the fear of God into Faust before he went back and reported to whatever family the Sicilians had sent.

The door shut. I slowly turned the lock on it. I removed a poster from the wall and used it to cover the small window in the middle of the door, then turned back to face Faust.

He was leaning against his desk. "You can't kill me."

I smiled as adrenaline pumped through my system. I clenched my hands into tight fists and relished the feeling of blood soaring through my veins. "Oh, I wouldn't dream of it."

Faust's smile fell from his face as I charged him from the side and slammed his body against the brick wall. His arms came up to stop me but I had him pinned with the weight of my body. Knife in hand I held it to his throat. "Who did they send?"

Faust swallowed against my metal blade, causing his skin to catch slightly on the edge. A trickle of blood fell from the small cut his movement had made. He stilled.

Faust wasn't answering.

Fine. I'd play.

I threw the knife behind me and punched him across the jaw. His head made a cracking noise as it slammed against the brick wall. I didn't want to knock the guy out, so I pulled him away from the wall and threw him into the desks. Cursing, he fell to the ground and then got up.

"Is that all you got, Nixon? Losing your touch?"

Oh, hell no. I lunged for him. Just as he moved out of the way, I caught his foot. He tripped, slamming his body against the floor. I dragged him by his heel to the closest window I could find and opened it.

We were on the second floor. The fall probably would do a lot of damage; maybe if he landed on his feet we'd be lucky and he'd break both legs on his own. Either way, I just hoped nobody was on this side of campus. I figured most people would already be in their next classes.

With a grunt I lifted him onto the windowsill and grabbed the front of his shirt. "Here's how this is gonna work." I smirked. "You either tell me who sent you, or we participate in a physics lesson. How fast would you fall from twenty feet, you think? And how many bones would you break, *if* you survived the fall and all that."

"You wouldn't kill me."

"I would." I blinked. "In fact, the idea gets more and more enticing the longer I look at your shit-eating face."

Faust's nostrils flared. Impatient, I punched him in the nose and grabbed his shirt again before he fell. "Think, Faust."

"Nicolosi," he spat. "The Nicolosi family is investigating. They arrived two days ago."

Stunned, I could only hold him in place. Forget killing him; I wanted to jump out the window myself.

Any family but the Nicolosis. I'd thought they'd send one of the original Sicilian families, but not *the* original family.

Not the family that Trace's grandfather had singlehandedly forced out of America—when they had enough money and power to have a say. What was worse—our family had helped them do it. Granted that was all before the Romeo and Juliet drama had exploded onto the scene with all of our parents, but still.

Son of a bitch.

"I can tell by your horrified expression you were hoping for someone else," Faust grunted.

I pulled him back into the classroom and punched him so hard in the jaw that he fell into a cold heap on the floor. I wiped my bloody hands on my jeans and walked out of the room.

Mr. Ryan was waiting in the hall. "Do I even want to know?"

"Nah..." I shook my head and offered him a smile. "That may just get you killed."

"Is there a body in my classroom?" His tone was calm, as if he were asking if I wanted a drink of water or a can of soda.

"I couldn't say." I shrugged. "But maybe cancel the rest of your afternoon classes."

Mr. Ryan nodded and pulled out his phone. "Sending the e-mail now. I'll put a note on the door, too."

"Thanks." I'd made it halfway down the hall when Mr. Ryan's voice rang out.

"You, uh, have a knife sticking out of your leg."

Shit. I looked down. So that was why Faust was smiling. Didn't feel it. I was so used to getting the crap beat out of me that I rarely reacted when attacked. When you react out of pain or fear, you pause, giving your enemy time to kill you. "So I do, Mr. Ryan. Have a good day."

I reached down and pulled the small knife from my thigh and wiped the blood on my jeans. I needed to change before Trace saw me. She would flip.

Chapter Three

Chase

I seriously needed to stop pissing Nixon off, but it had been a knee-jerk reaction, kissing Trace on the hand. If he didn't want me playing friendly with his girlfriend, he shouldn't have ordered me to be her personal bodyguard every freaking day of the school week.

I was in a living hell and nobody knew it but me.

"Can we skip?" Trace asked as we walked to her third class of the day. It was a KI class, one I knew she hated because it was all about self-defense. To be honest, she needed that and more, so I put my foot down even though her gorgeous smile was killing me inside.

"Nope." I put my arm around her. "Just imagine Phoenix's face when you're punching Spike."

Trace shuddered beneath my arm. "Yeah, when I imagine Phoenix I have a knife to his balls. Pretty sure that would either scar Spike for life or get me kicked out of Elite."

"Fair enough." I pulled her closer. "He's taken care of, Trace. Nobody's seen him in two weeks. He's either in hiding or across the Atlantic. He's not stupid enough to attack you again. Let Nixon do his job. We may not be able to kill him for what he did to you—but we sure as hell can make his life a bitch."

Trace nodded, but didn't say anything. I knew she was still traumatized over the whole ordeal. Shit, I was still traumatized and I'd done my fair share of dirty work in the name of the Abandonato family. Finding her on the floor with her clothes bloody and ripped from her body was one of the most horrifying experiences of my life.

I still wanted to kill Phoenix.

But Nixon wouldn't let me.

It had to do with some sort of code about killing off direct descendants of mafia bosses and them being next in line. Considering Phoenix's dad got a bullet to his head a few weeks ago by Trace's grandfather, our hands were literally tied.

Didn't mean I couldn't dream about his death every freaking day. It seemed unfair that the bastard could breathe the same air as Trace, let alone walk around as if he hadn't tried to kill her.

"You're late," Trace's professor announced when we walked in.

"My fault," I lied. "My shoe was untied, I fell, pulled Trace down with me, got her shirt all—muddy, and she had to go change."

Professors hated me. Nixon was the golden boy, kind of like a god around this place. I was just the assistant, the one who did the dirty work. Didn't help that my grades were less than stellar ever since I'd been trying to get homework done while Trace slept. It was the only free time I had.

Keeping her safe was a full-time job. Not that I was complaining.

The professor's sharp eyes focused on me with chilling indifference. "You're wearing boots without strings, the sun's shining, and one more tardy and your grade falls, Tracey."

"Ouch," I mumbled next to her, "I can order a hit on any professor you want, just remember that." I patted her back and winked at the professor.

Trace rolled her eyes, but it did make her smile.

"Your partner has fallen ill, so you'll be working with Chase today." With that, the cranky professor walked to the front of the room. "Now, today we're working on footwork and self-defense techniques. Instruction packets are on the desk; be sure to work through every scenario before you leave."

Trace grumbled beside me and went to fetch a packet. Her face fell when she read the first page. "I-I can't, Chase. I can't..."

Suddenly, the Trace I was used to was a shadow of her former self. Shaking, she wrapped her arms around my neck like I was her lifeline, her savior, her everything. As much as I hated seeing her freaked out—my body responded to her proximity like she was my gravity. She gave another shudder. I gently pulled her away and looked into her fear-stricken eyes.

"What the hell?" I grabbed the papers from her and quickly scanned the first scenario.

A guy and girl alone in his apartment. He tries to take advantage of her, she gets away but he's able to grab her wrist and overpower her on the ground. What do you do?

Freaking hell.

I reached for Trace's hand and squeezed it. "It's just you and me, Trace, okay? You'll power through this, and you know why?"

Her hand shook inside mine.

"Because you're an Alfero." I gritted my teeth and pulled her closer to me. "Do Alferos back down?"

"No," Trace whispered.

"I'm sorry; what was that?"

"Hell no." She nodded.

"Do you let people walk all over you? Do you let people attack you, Trace?"

"No." Her nostrils flared as she jerked her hand away from mine and glared.

"Good girl." I nodded. "Now, try not to forget that it's me, not Phoenix. I'm really partial to my anatomy, and I'd like to, you know, in the future have kids someday."

Rolling her eyes, she took a stance next to me. I muttered up a prayer as I quickly tripped her and pushed her down against the mat. She struggled against me, but I held her wrists firmly above her head—just like Phoenix had. Shit, it was killing me. Her face contorted in pain as she closed her eyes, and shook her head back and forth. I waited for the fear to pass—waited for the moment when her body would switch from being terrified to being pissed. But it was hard as hell.

I could shoot a man twice my age in cold blood.

I've buried more bodies than I can count.

I've grown up around drugs, prostitution, and the gambling underworld.

Nothing—and I mean nothing—had ever been harder to do than forcing Trace to relive one of the worst moments of her life. Nothing was more necessary than that she do it, so I held her. I held her and I leaned in.

"Fight back."

She squirmed beneath me, I could see the panic welling in her eyes. Maybe I was wrong, maybe she would crumple under the pressure, but she had to learn how to defend herself. As much as I wanted to be—I knew I wasn't part of her future, I wouldn't always be able to protect her. I gripped her harder. Trace's nostrils flared as she took in a few deep breaths.

"Trace," I whispered hoarsely as her body moved against mine. Shit, I wasn't counting on my physical response to her, to being so damn near...Swearing, I tried to focus. "Think, Trace, think about how to move my weight, or use it to your advantage."

Her eyes narrowed, and then she wrapped her leg around me and pulled my body tight against hers, making it so I couldn't gain any leverage. It was a smart move; most people wasted their energy on trying to get the person off of them, then they gave up.

It was always wise, when in such a situation, to not fight against but fight with. Trace used her other leg to swing it around my body and then slowly pushed me so that I was on my side and she was on top of me. She wasn't able to gain quite enough leverage, though. In seconds I had her flat on her back again.

In that moment, seeing a bit of sweat pouring down her face, I hated Nixon all over again.

Because he knew he was torturing both of us. He knew how damn difficult it was for me to keep my paws off what wasn't mine to touch, yet he trusted me enough to put me in the damn situation every day.

Her body felt so right underneath mine, I could almost forget that it wasn't real—that we weren't just friends, that we were more. My chest tightened a bit as Trace wrapped her arm around my neck and jerked me down; my mouth hit her cheekbone, not hard, but that touch, that one sizzle of my lips grazing her skin, was enough to send me over the edge.

I wasn't just teaching her anymore.

I was fighting myself.

I was living in hell—and she had no idea.

"That's it," I said hoarsely. "Now, use your leg again."

Trace tried again; this time she was able to push me onto my back before I flipped her again.

Exhausted, she closed her eyes and sighed when I was back on top.

"I'm tired...I think I got it..."

"Hell no." I gritted my teeth and leaned down so that the full weight of my body was on her. "You don't got it, you don't have it yet. So help me God, I will keep you pinned to this damn floor all day if you don't fight me like your life depends on it. Go again."

Her eyes flared with anger as she wrapped her arms around my neck again. Our mouths were inches apart, both of us breathing hard from exertion.

Correction; *she* was breathing hard from exertion. I was breathing hard from the supreme self-restraint it took for me to keep my lips off of hers and my clothes on my body.

She groaned in agitation.

Son of a bitch.

She groaned again, and really, I wondered, in that moment, would death be worth it? Was a lifetime of friendship with Nixon that meaningless that I would just toss it away for one chance with this girl?

Tracey must have felt me pause. She took her chance, swung her leg around me, and with a loud shout pinned me to the ground.

"Well done." *Shit. Shit. Shit.* I needed to get a girlfriend or find a distraction. Anything. So close, so damn close to ruining everything.

"I did it!" Her chest rose and fell with exertion; her sweaty white t-shirt was pressed tightly against her body.

"Yup." I reigned in the lust. "You were a regular Tito Ortiz."

"Who?"

I chuckled. "Never mind. Now get off of me before I throw you against the ground again."

She laughed.

I didn't.

I was damn serious.

Hanging by a thread. Huh, never understood that expression until now. Fantastic.

Chapter Four

Nixon

I sent Chase a quick text to meet back at our hangout on campus, or as Trace referred to it, the Bat Cave. I had exactly ten minutes to wipe the blood from my body and change my clothes.

On a more positive note, I'd been wiping blood from my hands for the past ten years of my life, so it wasn't a new experience for me.

I grabbed a beer from the fridge and reached for the salt and baking soda. I jerked off my jeans and held them under the cold water, then made a paste with the household stuff. After rubbing everything together I went and tossed them into the washing machine.

I was clad in only my boxers.

"If only it would wash away your sins…" a voice said from behind me.

"Ah, the bastard returns. Tell me, how was Women's Studies?" I turned around to see Chase and Trace setting their bags on the couch.

"Awesome," Chase said dryly. "I learned exactly how not to piss Trace off, so that should come in handy one of these days, or like in the next few seconds."

"Hilarious." Trace pushed him and then held out her hand to me. "I missed you."

Was it wrong that I hated how much I missed her, too? I sighed and pulled her into my arms. God, she smelled so good. It always calmed me to hold her. Having her in my arms was the closest to heaven I would ever get.

"How was your day?"

"Better than yours." She pulled back. "At least I kept my clothes on."

Chase groaned from the couch.

"You okay?" I looked above Trace's head.

"Splendid. Ask Trace about her KI class. She kicked my ass."

Trace wrapped her arms around my neck and kissed me softly across the lips. It still made me feel—unbalanced—when people were touching me. Trace never knew the real reason. I swore I'd take it to my grave. But it always reminded me of his hands, of being strangled within an inch of my life, of being locked in my room without food. It just...it was damn difficult. And although she calmed me down—when she wrapped her arms around me, or when I felt like I had no escape—I panicked.

I slowly undid her hands from behind my neck and kissed her fingers. "I'm liking this conversation. So you kicked Chase's ass? About time, I'd say."

"I tried." Her shoulders hunched as her brows furrowed together.

I tensed. "What the hell happened?"

"Why did something have to happen?" Chase asked behind her.

"Because she's all...stiff."

"Me too," Chase grumbled.

"Excuse me?"

"Never mind." Chase got up from the couch. "Look, I need to

go"—he pointed to the door—"take a break from security detail. I'll come back and get her for her last class and you and I can chat, okay?"

"Fine." I watched him leave. Nervousness was making a damn hole in my stomach. I walked Trace over to the couch.

Her eyes were glued to my bare stomach.

"Not my face, Trace." I tilted her chin up. She blushed and then closed her eyes.

"That was embarrassing."

"Not for me." I grinned. "Now, stop objectifying, and tell me what happened in class."

"It wasn't a big deal. I mean, it was but—"

"Why the hell are you shaking?" I gripped her wrists, probably harder than I should have, and told myself to calm down. "Trace, tell me."

She was closing herself off, the way she sat on the couch, crossed her legs, and primly placed her hands in her lap—everything was off. That wasn't the Trace I was used to being with. It scared the living hell out of me.

"We had to act out scenarios."

I felt my eyes narrow. "What kind of scenarios?"

Trace played with the edge of her shirt and shrugged. "Ones where people get attacked, broken into...raped." Her voice trailed off.

That particular professor had just sealed his retirement.

"Trace, look at me, are you okay? Did Chase—"

"Chase was great." Her face lit up. Damn it. "He talked me through the situation and, well, it ended up being fine. I think I'm just a bit shook up. He forced me to do it. Basically threw me against the mat and gave me hell."

It took me exactly five seconds to decide that I was going to murder him on the spot for putting her in that position. Ten seconds after that, I was feeling such insane jealousy that his body had been pressed against hers, I almost grabbed my gun and took off after him.

"So…" A few pieces of hair fell across her face as she bit her lip. "Chase gave me some tough love, said to buck up, and I did it. I actually pinned him to the ground." Her face lit up like a damn Christmas tree. No wonder Chase left; he didn't want me to shoot him in the ass.

I snorted. "I'm sure he loved that."

"What?" Trace tilted her head. Was she really that clueless?

"Do you really have no idea?" I tucked some of her dark hair behind her ear and sighed. "No idea at all?"

"Idea? Help me out, Nixon. I don't speak crazy."

Cursing, I pulled her into my lap and wrapped her legs around my waist so her body was pressed against mine. "You. Are. Gorgeous." Her body shivered in response to my touch. A hiss of air escaped through her lips as her legs tightened around my body.

I braced her hips with my hands and slowly moved them up. I looked at her perfect body as it fit like a missing piece to my puzzle. "Any guy would be an idiot not to have a problem keeping it in his pants around you, Trace. And that's the truth."

"You don't seem to have a problem with it?" She winked.

I growled and jerked her head toward mine, crushing my lips against hers. I slipped my tongue past the barrier of her lips and promised myself she'd forget Chase had even touched her today. "Right," I growled low in the back of my throat. "No problem whatsoever. I'm basically a saint." I brought her hands down the front of my chest and lower, to my boxers. "You need to know one thing, sweetheart."

"What?" Her hands froze on my abs.

"I would kill my own cousin."

"What?" Her expression turned horrified: Her eyes widened and her mouth dropped open.

"I would." I shrugged. "He knows you aren't his to touch, you aren't his to want."

"And I'm yours?" *Oh great, now I've pissed her off.*

I gripped her face between my hands and kissed her mouth softly. "Yes. Whether you like it or not, we belong to each other. I'm as much yours as you are mine—I don't share. I want to freaking murder anyone who even so much as looks in your direction, or at your shoes, and damn if I don't hate those boots that Chase got you. I want to consume you. I want to be the one that puts a smile on your face. I want to be the one that teaches you pleasure—me. Not anyone else. Sharing you—even by way of my cousin, who I trust more than anyone in the world—has to be one of the hardest things I've ever done."

"Nixon." She sighed against my mouth. "I love you. You have to know that."

"That's the problem," I said.

"How is that a problem?"

"It's a problem because I'm consumed with you, Trace. Are you hungry? How are classes? Do you need your space? Are you scared? Can you shoot a gun? Shit. I can't even sleep at night because I'm so terrified, and I've literally been sharing a bed with you for the past two weeks."

A pretty blush stained her cheeks.

"Sharing a bed isn't sex; stop blushing." I winked when she smacked me on the shoulder. "Not that I'm opposed to the idea…"

"You're a guy. You're never opposed to it."

"You're not ready, therefore I have to be." I pushed her away gently and cupped her face with my right hand. "I'm not telling you all of this to get all sappy and freak you out. I just want you to know what's at stake."

"What do you mean?"

"Faust is here."

"WHAT?" Trace stumbled out of my embrace and stood. "The same Faust who accused me of asking for it when I told him Phoenix raped me? That Faust?"

I chuckled. "Yeah, though he may be unrecognizable right about now."

"Nixon, you didn't…"

I shrugged. "He's alive."

Trace pressed a shaking hand to her temple. "What does he want?"

"What does anyone want in our world? Leverage? Money? Your guess is as good as mine. But he basically wants me to pick a side…"

"By you not finishing that sentence, I'm guessing it's not the Alfero side he's wanting you to stand on."

"Smart and sexy. How did I get so lucky?"

Trace sighed and closed her hands. "My grandfather—"

"—is fine." I knew we were alone, but…a person could never be too careful. "Drop it."

I hated that I had to be rough with her. I hated that it was necessary in order to protect her. If she knew where he was, she was making herself a target. I knew, and that was enough.

"So what happens now?" Trace grabbed my hand and traced a small circle next to my newest scar.

"We wait it out. The Sicilians are here. I know the family well. Business goes on as usual and you try to graduate."

"Without getting killed," she murmured.

"Nobody is going after you." I released her hand and got up. "Besides, they'd have to kill me first and I don't die very easily."

"Right."

"I'm going to go put on some clothes so you stop staring at my ass."

"I'm not—" Trace closed her eyes as her face flamed bright red.

"You are." I walked over to the spare room, where we kept clothing and took naps in between classes. "But I forgive you because I have a really nice ass. It would be kind of cruel to hold that against you."

"Wow, cocky and a killer. How did I get so lucky?" she said dryly.

I laughed and went into the room to find something without blood on it. Not that I would ever be free from the stain. After all, it was like my marker—blood.

*　　*　　*

Once I was dressed, I went back to find Trace laying facedown on the couch, her breathing deep.

I checked my watch. She had class in exactly ten minutes. I sent a quick text to Chase that I was going to steal Trace away for the rest of the afternoon. He responded quickly, saying he didn't mind and that he was going to go find a hot chick to make out with. As long as it wasn't my hot chick, I was fine with that.

"Trace?" I nudged her awake. She groaned aloud and mumbled something that sounded nothing like English. "Trace." I kissed the back of her head. She moved her arm toward me, hitting me directly in the stomach. Hard.

I smacked her ass just as hard and laughed as she fell off the couch and glared. "What's wrong with you! You can't just go waking people up like that! I could have . . ."

"What? You could have what?" I crossed my arms and smirked. "What could you possibly do that would bring me to my knees?"

Trace licked her lips and eyed me up and down. "Oh, I have a few ideas."

"Well played," I grumbled. "We're skipping class."

"Why?"

"Because I want to."

"Why?"

"Say thank you, Trace, and so help me God if you say why one more time I'm taking you into that back bedroom and having my way with you until you can't ask why anymore."

She seemed to actually think about it. Shit. I was kidding, I wasn't ready for that, not with her. It seemed too precious. And here I was joking about it.

"Fine." She yawned and stretched her arms high above her head. "Do I need to text Chase?"

"Nah, I just did. He said he's gonna go make out with some chick. Clearly you're messing with his mojo."

Trace's face fell a bit. "I guess I never thought about that."

"Don't feel sorry for him. The man could charm anything with a pulse and could probably use this time as a way to do some sort of cleansing ritual."

She nodded and reached for my hand. "So, where are we going?"

"Somewhere safe." I winked.

*   *   *

I pulled the Range Rover up to the large metal gate. After I pushed the intercom button, a voice came on the speaker. "Who is visiting?"

"Nixon Abandonato."

Lots of yelling and hushing and then, "Pleasure to have you, sir." The gates opened in front of us and I drove through.

"Doesn't that bother you?" Trace asked, pulling off her sunglasses.

"What?"

"'Sir'?" Her eyebrow arched. "It makes you sound so old and... just old."

"It's a respect thing." I shrugged.

"No," she argued. "It's an old person thing."

"What?" I pulled to the front of the mansion and turned off the car. "You'd rather they call me Dude? Or Homie?"

"I vote Homie. It sounds—"

"I'm an American-born Sicilian," I interrupted. "It sounds like an easy way to get shot; that's what it sounds like."

Trace rolled her eyes and unbuckled her seat belt. As she reached for the door, I grasped her wrist and pulled her toward me. "What would you call me?"

"You mean other than your name?" Her eyes narrowed.

"Yeah." I licked my lips. My tongue touched the metal of my lip ring. I could almost taste her hot mouth on mine.

"Perfect." She sighed. "I'd call you perfect." Her hands reached out to cup my face as her tongue touched my lip ring and then slipped into my mouth.

I groaned in frustration when our lips met in a frenzy. It really wasn't the time or place to be kissing her, or nearly exploding with frustration that I couldn't just jump across the console and maul her. Reluctantly, I pulled back.

"As much as I'd love to finish that…conversation…" I chewed hard on my lower lip and literally had to look away from her so I wouldn't say what the hell and drive her back to my house and lock her in my bedroom. "We're here for a reason."

"Oh yeah?" Her eyes were dilated as they looked me up and down. "What's that?"

I smirked. "You'll see."

Thankfully, the air was crisp, so when I stepped out of the SUV I wasn't still so aroused that I was ready to shoot something.

"What is this place?" Trace put her hand up as a shade over her eyes and looked up at the mansion. It was an impressive four stories, with over three hundred rooms. I'd loved this place, loved visiting. It had been my safe haven when my dad beat me. "My cousin Sergio takes care of the place while his father serves out the rest of his sentence." I led her toward the back of the house.

"Sentence?" Trace repeated. "As in prison sentence?"

"We like to think of it as an opportunity for a family reunion," a voice interrupted. I laughed when Sergio winked at Trace and held out his hand. "It's been a long time, Nixon." His dark wavy hair was tied at the nape of his neck. He was clean-cut, one of the rare sons who didn't rebel against the formality of being in the mafia. His blue t-shirt fit tightly across his chest as he stood in front of Trace.

"He doesn't call you 'sir,'" Trace interjected, then clapped her hand over her mouth. "Oh my gosh, I'm so sorry; it slipped."

"It slips often," I added.

Sergio laughed. "So I hear." He held out his hand. When she gave him her fingers, he kissed her knuckles and smiled. "Guess the rumors are true."

"Rumors." Trace pulled back her hand and rubbed it.

"Of your beauty…" Sergio stepped closer to her and sighed. "Too bad I did not discover you first."

"Yeah, that lament is already taken by another cousin." I slapped him on the back. "Don't make me threaten you, too."

Trace rolled her eyes and fell into step beside us.

"Sergio." My cousin cleared his throat. "My name is Sergio."

Trace examined his face. "Of course it is."

"Pardon?" He stopped walking.

She looked between us and shrugged. "The way I see it, every Sicilian name either sounds like something out of a mafia movie or a—"

"A…?" we said in unison.

"Never mind. So, nice house." Trace tried to change the subject.

"Oh no, sweetheart." I tugged her arm and made her stop. "Let's have it. Or what?"

"Promise not to shoot me?" she whined.

"He's threatened to do that before?" Sergio yelled.

"No." I rolled my eyes. "She's being dramatic."

Trace turned back toward Sergio. "I'm a girl."

"I noticed." His eyes darkened as he licked his lips and looked about one minute away from devouring her where she stood.

"Trace…" I nudged. "What do Sicilian names sound like?"

"I need to learn when to stop talking." She put her hands over her face. "A porn star name. Okay?"

Sergio and I burst out laughing. Damn, I loved that girl. The tips of her ears burned bright red as she covered her face in her hands.

"You know," Sergio said in a serious voice, "not to brag but you aren't too far off with your assumptions I—"

"No." I shook my head. "You're not going to finish that sentence. You. I will shoot."

Sergio chuckled and held up his hands. "So, everything has been set up. Just be sure not to kill any cows."

"Cows?" Trace's head jolted up. "Where?"

"In fields." Sergio cleared his throat. "Where they live." He looked at me and shook his head. "Where did you say she was from again?"

I opened my mouth to answer but Trace was running toward the field to the cows.

"She likes cows."

"I see." Sergio chuckled as we both watched Trace run up to the fence and stand on it.

"How are things?" I asked. "Any more news?"

"They want to meet." Sergio stuffed his hands in his pockets. "That is all I've heard. It's your call, Nixon. If you want to meet with them, test out your peacekeeping abilities, I won't keep you from it."

"But?" I crossed my arms and continued to watch Trace laugh like she didn't have a care in the world.

"But." Sergio cleared his throat. "I don't see this ending well. For any of us. You must be prepared to go into hiding. You must be prepared for the worst."

I swallowed the dryness in my throat. "I'm not afraid to die."

"I know." Sergio patted my back. "Your problem stems from the very fact that you've finally found someone to live for. It is not our death that we fear, but leaving those behind that we love."

"You sure you don't want to be the peacekeeper, oh spouter of wisdom?" I joked.

"No." Sergio kicked the grass at his feet and pulled a gun from the back of his jeans. "I'm here to counsel you in secret. I like my life. Being a made man? Jumping back into the limelight with you and Chase? No. I'm of more use doing what I do."

"A ghost."

"A damn good one." Sergio thumped my back with his hand. "Here, let her use this pistol. It was my mom's."

I took the gun from his hands. It was sleeker and smaller than mine; it would be a perfect weapon for Trace to learn on. "Thanks for this."

"I do what I can. Now, try to stay alive." His blue t-shirt fanned in the wind as he stuffed his arms into his jeans pockets and walked off.

"Nixon!" Trace yelled from the fence. "Come on!"

I walked over to her and sighed. The cows weren't used to people. Meaning she was most likely scaring the shit out of them.

"Nice." I pointed to the brown creatures and lifted her off the fence. "Now, we only have an hour or so, then we have to head back into town. Let's make good use of it, shall we?"

Chapter Five

Nixon

I suck at this," Trace said for the tenth time. "I don't understand how you can shoot something without falling down."

I braced her body against mine and wrapped my arms around her in order to help her position the gun. "That's why it takes practice."

"Why does it look so easy on TV?"

"Because it's TV," I whispered in her ear. "Now, focus on the target. Remember pistols always have a slight kick. Do you want the earplugs?"

"No." She breathed. "Because then I can't hear you and for some reason having you behind me, helping me, it's easier to concentrate."

Funny. I was just thinking the exact opposite. It was damned difficult to concentrate on breathing, let alone shooting an actual target with her body squirming in front of mine.

"Remember," I whispered. "You want to relax but also take a stance that allows you to breathe and take the hit."

"Hit?" Her voice dripped with dread.

"From the kick, not a bullet. I wouldn't let you get shot."

She straightened her shoulders and pulled the trigger, hitting a good foot away from the actual target.

"Not too bad," I lied.

Trace handed me the gun. "I can't be awful at this, not when we're still in danger."

"Hey." I took the gun and placed it on the wood stump next to us. "You're not terrible and it's not like you're supposed to know how to do this well. You're just a little rusty and used to shooting rifles on a farm. Not a smaller gun that doesn't have great aim."

"I know." She looked back toward the mansion. "I take it Sergio isn't going to join us at all?"

I cringed, thinking it best to keep most of the truth from her. The more she knew, the more in danger she would be. "He doesn't like to involve himself in the business."

Trace grabbed my hand and pulled me down to sit on the wooden table with all the ammo. "I don't understand. Why help you, then?"

"Sergio's what I like to call a ghost. He doesn't exist. He likes it that way. After his father was put in prison, well, it was easy for him to get out. The feds were sniffing around too much and the family basically let him go off on his own. Of course, he's still watched, but he's basically free to live his life as he sees fit. He helps me when he can; he's brilliant when it comes to computer hacking and research."

Trace squinted. She had that look on her face, the one that meant she was thinking really hard about something. "So if Sergio decided he wanted to just up and marry some normal girl and live a normal life out with the cows...he could?" Her eyes looked hopeful. Damn, but I hated being the one snuffing out that hope.

"In theory," I answered slowly. "But Trace, you're never really free from this. You're always going to be watching your back. You'll always carry a gun with you just in case, and you'll still never trust the other families or sometimes, even your own."

She exhaled. "Sounds kind of awful."

I cupped her chin with my hand. "It used to be. But now"—I kissed her softly across the lips—"not so much."

"Are you afraid?" Her eyelashes fanned across her high cheekbones.

"I've known fear twice in my life. Once when I was little and watched my mother get beat and then suffered at my own father's hands. And now..."

"Now?" she prompted.

"With you. Every damn second fear threatens to overtake my sense of peace. Because, in the end, I can't control anyone's decisions but my own."

"I'm sorry"—Trace laid her head on my shoulder—"for making you feel that way."

"Hey." I pulled back and held her head firmly between my hands. "You make me feel—incredible. I think of the fear as something healthy. It means I'm that much more careful with the treasure I've been given."

"You just called me a treasure." She sighed happily.

"That I did."

"Chase would say you've gone soft."

"Chase can kiss my ass," I grumbled. "And I'm not soft. I'm just..."

"Just?"

I kissed her forehead and laughed. "I'm in love."

"Who is she!" Trace jumped to her feet and yelled. "I demand to know the person who holds your affection."

"'It is the East! And Juliet is the sun!'" I jumped off the table. "'Arise fair sun, and kill the envious moon, who is already sick and pale with grief, that thou her maid are far more fair than she, but not her maid since she is envious: Her vestal livery is but sick and green: And none but fools do wear it. Cast it off!'" I stalked toward her and grasped her hands. "'It is my lady, oh, it is my love.'" I touched her face and whispered, "'Oh that she knew she were.'"

Trace's eyes fluttered closed as she leaned into my hand. "That was…"—a small smile played at the corner of her mouth—"the sexiest thing I've ever experienced."

I chuckled. "Clearly I've been slacking then. You know, all the shooting in my direction and keeping a sworn enemy in hiding."

"Excuses, excuses." She opened her eyes and wrapped her arms around my neck. "I promise I won't tell anyone you have scenes from *Romeo and Juliet* memorized if you say more of it to me."

"And if I say no?"

"Then I tell."

"Pretty sure that's bribery, perhaps bordering on extortion."

"I'm an Alfero; what do you expect?"

"Everything." I took her lower lip tenderly between my teeth. "From you—I want everything."

*   *   *

I hated how easy it was with Trace. When we were alone it was almost like we were actually alone and we could do whatever we wanted. In a perfect world things would be different; it just sucked that our world was as far from perfect as a person could get.

I jumped out of the SUV and opened Trace's door. It was getting late and I still needed the final confirmation that we were going to meet that evening with the Nicolosi family.

Trace and I walked into my house and found Mo drinking a glass of wine and reading a book.

"I'm gonna go shower." Trace got up on her tiptoes and kissed me on the cheek, then took off down the hall just as my cell went off.

Tonight. 7:00

After my afternoon with Trace, I knew she was more of a sitting duck than I'd care to admit. But I needed the guys with me for this meeting. I ran my hands through my hair and sighed.

Mo looked up from her book, her face pinched with worry. "What is it?"

"I have to steal Chase for the evening, okay?" I shoved my hands in my pockets and tried to look as if I was discussing the weather or a football game, when really I was stressed beyond belief.

Mo frowned. "And Tex? Is he going with you guys?"

"Probably." I shrugged. "No big deal, just business. Make sure you lock the doors, put on the alarms. I'll make sure Uncle Tony knows you guys are alone and have him send over some men."

"Great." Mo huffed and pulled her shoulders back tighter against her body. "More assassins. Sign me up."

"Sorry. You know the rules."

"I hate the damn rules."

"The rules—"

"Keep us safe," Mo finished. "I know. I just wish we could walk around like normal people without the fear of getting shot at. If Trace had any idea how bad it really was—"

"She won't find out." I felt my control snapping as I glared at my twin. "Right? Because I'm sure as hell not telling her."

"Nixon..." Mo swore. "Sometimes I really hate you."

Sometimes I hated me, too. Mo crossed her arms and scowled at the ground.

I cursed and rubbed my face with my hands. I didn't want to have to deal with family drama. Mo could act like a spoiled mafia princess on her own watch. "Get in line. Now, do what I say."

"Yes sir." She saluted me with her middle finger.

Cracking a smile, I patted her on the shoulder. "Love you, too."

Chapter Six

Chase

The only positive thing about the entire day going to hell—business was booming. Or so my dad said when I went home to get fresh clothes before I met up with Nixon.

"How is the girl?" Anthony asked. I never referred to him as "Father"—he'd never given me the impression that it was something I was allowed to do. And I wasn't about to disrespect him.

"The girl"—I stuffed some shirts into my bag—"is fine. She's going to school and safe."

"Thanks in part to you." Anthony laughed bitterly. "So Nixon's put you on security detail? How do you think that looks?"

"Hmm." I paused and turned to face him. "How do I think it looks that the boss entrusts me with the love of his life and nobody else, not even you? Pretty damn good, thanks for asking."

"He's young."

"He's the boss." I clenched my teeth and tried not to lose my cool in front of him but he really pissed me off.

"It should have been you," Anthony swore. "God knows it should have been you."

Had my father been spying on my mind during the day or

something? I mean, I know I wished it was me, but only because of Trace; not because I wanted the responsibility of a century-old Sicilian family hanging on my shoulders. No thank you.

"Yeah, well." I put my bag over my shoulder. "Sorry I wasn't born before him, sorry he's still alive. Just what do you want me to apologize for? I'm not going to apologize for being loyal, or for thinking he's what's best for this family."

"He may get us all killed."

I wasn't an idiot. My mind had come up with every worst-case scenario, every possible outcome, and I knew that we weren't exactly on the right side of the odds. Hell, we weren't even in the same universe. But I couldn't get myself to care about the family when all I really cared about was keeping Trace safe. I'd die before anything happened to her. Anthony could go to hell for all I cared.

"Not if I can prevent it." I pushed past Anthony and grabbed the keys to my Range Rover.

"You cannot prevent what is coming. It has been hanging over our heads for years," Tony said from behind me. I didn't know if he wanted me to answer him, but I chose to ignore him. Ever since Nixon's father had died last year—things had been in upheaval. Half the family thought it was good to have fresh blood leading the Abandonatos. After all, Nixon's dad had literally beat the shit out of Nixon and his ma on a regular basis when Nixon was little. And possibly, he'd killed Trace's parents out of a jealous rage because he'd loved Trace's mom more than life itself and she didn't choose him.

Shit, that hit way to close to home.

Whatever.

As far as I was concerned it was old drama and the rest of the family could either get on board or go screw themselves. Nixon was doing the best job he could at twenty-one. Shit, I'd probably be having a nervous breakdown if I had a few multi-billion-dollar companies underneath me.

Granted, Nixon had business associates that dealt with most of the money, but still. It was a lot of responsibility.

I drove the ten miles to his house. He lived on the other side of the city, where houses had gates and people had helipads in their backyards.

Our houses were pretty similar. Only mine contained just me and Anthony. My mom had died several years ago, just like Nixon's. I wondered if that was a bad sign, or some sort of prophecy. Women never lasted in our family.

Refusing to think about Trace and the life ahead of her if she stayed with us, I pulled into Nixon's gate, swiped my card, and honked my horn.

Nixon came flying out of the house with Tex.

Good. They were laughing.

"Dude, what took you so long?" Tex said from the backseat. "The girls were watching stupid chick flicks again."

Nixon snorted. "Right, and since they pulled each DVD from your collection—I'd probably stop complaining."

Tex grinned. "So, who we killing?"

My laugh was hollow.

Tex had always seemed so easygoing about the business. I, however, still hated doing the dirty work. I didn't mind watching others do it, but doing it myself? Let's just say I'm not as scary as people would like to think I am. No, that nomination goes to Nixon.

The things I'd seen that guy do would put nightmares into even the worst sort of prisoner.

"We have a meeting," Nixon said in an even voice. "With the Nicolosi family."

"Son of a bitch!" I slammed on the brakes in the middle of the driveway. "The Sicilians? We're going to meet them? Now? Are you freaking insane?"

"No." Nixon pulled out his cell phone. "We've only got twenty minutes to get to downtown Chicago. I'd hurry."

"Great." I blasted the accelerator and swore. "What the hell, Nixon? It's like you want us to die."

"They won't kill us." Why was he so damn calm! "They can't. We have too much money. Besides, by now Faust will have reported back."

"And just what do you think he said?"

"You mean before or after he shit his pants?" Nixon smirked. "They know where we stand. So now we negotiate. We tell them we've got it handled."

"Um…" Tex cleared his throat from behind us. "No offense, Nixon, but we have absolutely nothing handled. We have a crazy mafia boss in hiding and we still don't know who killed Trace's parents." I sighed in exasperation. Maybe it was Nixon's father—after all, he was capable of anything. We all knew that.

"Right." Nixon exhaled. "But they don't know we don't have answers yet. And I have a plan."

"Plan?" I echoed. "You want us to meet with the scariest family known to the Mafia because you have a plan? Are you insane?"

"God, I wish." Nixon laughed and bit down on his lip ring. He pulled off his leather jacket and checked a few of the guns strapped to his body. "We've got some old beef between us; they'll be curious, they'll want to listen."

I cursed and hit the steering wheel.

"Calm yourself." This from Tex. Did he seriously not know?

Once we were at the stoplight I turned around and glared. "Calm myself? You naive piece of shit. The last time they were in Chicago my mom was shot. She died, Tex. So help me God, next time you tell me to calm myself I will shoot you in the foot."

The light turned green and I sped off. Complete silence blanketed the car, and for once I was thankful that I didn't have anyone in my life that loved me. Because if it came to a shootout with those guys, I would take it, with pleasure. I would end them—for what they'd done to me and my family—without hesitation.

Chapter Seven

Nixon

I knew Chase was pissed. I also knew he wouldn't have wanted to come if I'd told him who we were meeting. And he needed this as much as I did. He needed closure. What they did to his mom...it was horrendous. It was never proven that she'd been murdered by the Nicolosi family but we had our suspicions. Strong ones. After all, each family had a crest, and the one left by the body had belonged to none other than the Nicolosis.

She was raped and beaten to within an inch of her life—and all because she'd talked to one of their wives. Confided in them about something to do with the family.

She'd been killed the next day. Left in a warehouse.

Adrenaline surged through me as we pulled up to the restaurant. It was a good meeting place, one of the chains we owned, known for its Chinese food which, frankly, I always found hilarious. Just because we were Sicilian didn't mean we only owned Italian restaurants.

The smell of sweet pork and fried rice invaded my senses as we burst into the restaurant and went to the back meeting room.

The first thing I noticed was that the lights were dimmed, dimmer than I remembered. The second was that the bartender's hand was shaking. He smiled and nodded in our direction, but his damn hand was having trouble pouring drinks.

I nodded back and showed him one of my guns—reassurance and all that.

The back room was usually reserved for out-of-town guests. But when I say "guests" I really mean out-of-town family who need a place to interrogate.

It was completely soundproof and had at least twenty cameras set at different angles up on the walls, just in case we needed to watch tape to see exactly who did what first.

I nodded to Tex. He shut the door behind us. I walked toward the table and had a seat, placing my gun in front of me for all to see.

"Nixon…it has been…a while. Tell me, how is your family?"

"The same," I said dryly. "Wealthy, powerful, pissed…"

Luca Nicolosi grinned. His glaring white teeth were like a bright light against his tanned skin. At forty-seven, he'd been taking care of the Nicolosi family since his father's passing ten years ago. The last time I'd seen him, he'd been a cocky piece of work. Now, well now he just pissed me off. Everything about him screamed indulgence, from his pressed silk suit to his combed hair. Hate did not even begin to describe what I felt toward him and his family.

I detested them—more than anything in the world.

At eleven years old, I had trusted them. I had run into their arms that night…

"Help! Help me!" My father had left the box unlocked this time. I hadn't realized it until I started kicking against the door. He was punishing me again. I knew it was my fault he was angry. He'd told me to spy on Ma again and I'd told him to go to hell.

So he'd put me in the time-out box.

It was really small and black. One time I'd been in there for the entire day.

Lately it seemed like just looking at him wrong earned me time in the box.

"Help!" I ran directly into the living room, where a few men were seated. Father wasn't anywhere to be found.

"Help? What do you need help with?" Luca stood in the corner, hands in pockets. His thick accent reminded me of my grandfather. He'd been kind to me, my grandfather.

"My father, he locked me in a box and I don't know where my ma went and—"

"Aww." Luca clapped his hands. "Family drama. It never ceases to amaze me how easily the families fall apart when we leave them to their own devices."

What was he talking about?

"Listen." Luca knelt down in front of me. "Do you hear that?"

"Hear what?" I could only hear my breathing.

"Exactly." Luca patted my shoulder. "Nobody cares that you were locked in a box, not even God. So run along and crawl back in before I give you a true reason to scream for help."

Frozen in place, I could only stare at him.

"Run along..." He sounded bored as I ran from the room. I was terrified for the rest of the night, terrified that he would make good on his promise and come get me. I even crawled back into the box.

My dad finally found me in that same position a day later, dehydrated and traumatized. It was the first time he beat me. He said I was an embarrassment to the other families.

It was also the first time I shot a gun and put his name on the target. He would die by my hands one day; he would die just like Luca.

"Why exactly are you here?" I asked, feigning boredom as I drummed my fingers against the table. "You have nothing to gain by your presence."

Luca laughed. "And that is where you are wrong. We keep the peace between the families. We've heard of some unrest. You know the rules, Nixon. You live by them. One cannot simply shoot someone because they have a grudge. Hand over Mr. Alfero and this will all simply be a memory. We'll leave on the first plane."

"I can't do that."

"And why not?" He leaned forward. "What do you have to gain by protecting him?"

"Nothing," I lied, "except a guilt-free conscience. How will his death wipe the slate clean?"

"A life for a life." Luca shrugged. "After all, doesn't he have a grandson or granddaughter next in line?"

So that's what they wanted.

Trace.

Over my cold lifeless body.

"How would I know?"

"Bring him." Luca motioned to someone behind him. The door opened and then closed again.

I tried to appear unfazed as I watched Faust bring Phoenix into the room. But damn if I didn't want to jump across the table and end his life.

Chase tensed next to me.

So it had come to this? We let him live and he tells all?

Phoenix took a seat, a shit-eating grin on his face. Holy mother of God, I was itching to end his life.

"This man seems to think differently. All I ask"—Luca cleared his throat—"is that you turn over Mr. Alfero, turn over the man responsible for De Lange's death. A life for a life. If not, I'll hurt those you love the most. After all, Phoenix is the leader of the De Langes now. Justice needs to be served."

"Noted," I said through clenched teeth.

"Do you doubt me?" Luca tilted his head to the side and placed his hands on the table as he pushed himself to a standing position. "Clearly, you do, otherwise you would be handing over the head of the Alfero family on a silver platter."

"Why in the hell would I hand over the head of the Alfero family, especially when the person calling for his head is nothing but a treacherous snake?" I looked at Phoenix and glared. "So you listen to me."

Luca's eyebrows lifted just slightly.

"I will discover who murdered Frank Alfero's son and daughter and when I prove what I've suspected all along, you will leave."

Luca leaned back on his feet and laughed. Phoenix briefly made eye contact with me and shook his head, just once. But it was enough to catch me by surprise. What the hell kind of a dangerous game was he playing? I was about five seconds away from pulling my gun out and opening fire on everyone in that damn room.

"I will hurt those you love most," Luca whispered. "Is that what you want?"

"I love no one."

Luca laughed and reached into his pocket. He pulled out an envelope and lifted a lock of hair out of it.

A lock of dark, silky brown hair. He held it to his nose and sniffed. "Coconut? Lavender? Do remind me to ask your little girlfriend what she uses. It's absolutely ... divine."

I gripped the seat until my knuckles turned white.

Chase burst out laughing and slapped me on the back.

What the hell was he doing?

"Phoenix, you always were such an ass. Luca, can I call you by your first name?"

Hair still lifted by his face, Luca looked between me and Chase. I remained emotionless on the outside, while on the inside I was praying for my cousin to pull his head out of his ass. What the hell was he thinking?

"And who are you?"

"I go by Chase Winter—my mom's last name and all that—but I'm an Abandonato. I'm the boss's cousin. I'm also a bit confused as to what Phoenix must have told you."

"Well, allow me to clear things up." Luca gritted his teeth and pointed at Phoenix.

"I'd rather you not." Chase stood. "You see, every minute I hear you disrespecting Trace is another minute I'm adding on to the time I get my hands around Phoenix's neck and personally introduce him to Jesus Christ, when he will surely receive his just reward—an eternity in Hell. So allow me to clear things up with you. If you touch my girlfriend, I will kill you. I won't stop in my pursuit to pull your beating heart out of your damn chest and feel its last beat through my clenched fist as your blood drips from my fingertips. I suggest, Mr. Nicolosi, that you get your information straight before you come to our country, our city, and our family. I'm warning you: Don't push us too far, because we sure as hell *will* push back."

The hair fell from Luca's fingers onto the table. In an instant, Phoenix was pulled out of his seat and slammed against the wall, a gun held to his neck.

"What else are you lying about?" Luca pushed the gun further into Phoenix's neck. "Hmm? Is your only goal to destroy the family standing in the way of your ultimate power? Wake up, child. You are not a man, you are a vessel that I am using in order to make sure our business dealings are not discovered by either of our governments. Allow your jealousy to make you weak and I will show you the true meaning of pain." He released Phoenix and let him fall to the floor. In an instant he was giving orders to the other two men in the room.

One of Luca's men stepped forward, producing a thick envelope. Inside were pictures.

Of Chase and Tracey.

I almost lost it right there.

Chase had put his life on the line for both of us, and now I knew there was no going back. It had to be real. I had to help them make it real because if they knew we'd lied...

We were all going to die.

"This." Luca pointed at the first picture. "Is this what you're talking about?"

Chase was on top of Tracey, pinning her to the ground. I stared at the picture and prayed I was keeping my expression bored when my heart was breaking inside my chest. I knew what they were doing; I knew it was part of their KI class training session. But still.

We'd been spied on for the past week; that much was certain. I was suddenly thankful that Chase had been the one with Trace the whole time. Chase had used his security detail as a brilliant excuse for their relationship.

"To be fair," Faust said next to Luca, "they could be sharing her."

This time Tex spoke. "No offense, Faust, but men in our family don't have problems catching women. Unlike some people..."

Faust's nostrils flared but he said nothing.

"This." Luca pointed to the pictures. "This is true? The Alfero heir and you; you are together?"

Chase rolled his eyes. "Why else would I be on top of her in class. I'm trying to get as close to her as possible even when the professors are looking."

My heart slammed against my chest. I knew it was a lie, but damn if it didn't feel like truth.

"If you are lying..."—Luca sighed—"things will not end well for you."

"We don't lie. We aren't rats. Now, tell us how we can help you. The way I see it"—I leaned forward on the table and folded my hands—"is the quicker we work together, the quicker you row, row, row your boats back across the Atlantic."

"Straight to the point. No threats, just questions?" Luca nodded. "I like that."

"I'm a likeable guy." I flashed him a toothy grin and licked my lips, pausing for effect. "We have kept order for a very long time. My proposition is this. Allow us the rest of the fall semester to continue to dive into the De Lange family, without interruption. Hand over Phoenix, allow us to do our jobs, and in the end, if we cannot find a solution, we hand over Mr. Alfero and you leave. All of you."

"Time. You want time."

"And Phoenix. Don't forget him." I nodded to Phoenix. "We have some unfinished business. I don't suppose Faust told you about the rape allegations to Chase's girlfriend."

"I did not think it necessary," Faust interrupted.

"Not necessary?" Luca threw his head back and laughed. "Do you ever feel, Mr. Abandonato, that you are the only one who is not an idiot?"

I grinned and leaned back in my chair. "All the damn time."

"Me too." In an instant, Luca had his gun pointed at Faust and pulled the trigger seven times. Faust fell to the ground. The men around him pulled his lifeless body into the corner.

"Now." Luca reached his hand across the table. "I believe we have a deal."

Chapter Eight

Chase

I'd lost my damn mind. But I panicked. I didn't know what else to do. I didn't see any other way out of our predicament. And I knew, I knew it was possible they'd been watching us. The photos would prove my story. Now I just had to make sure my cousin wasn't going to shoot me and throw my body into Lake Michigan.

We walked silently to the car. I started it and headed back toward Nixon's house. Nobody said a word. All I could focus on was the faint music of AWOLNATION in the background and Nixon's heavy breathing—which meant he was pissed.

Great.

"So," Tex finally said ten minutes later, "that was a rush."

I smirked and then heard Nixon chuckle next to me. Soon all of us were wiping tears from our eyes because we were laughing so hard.

"It's like living on a bad TV show." I chanced it and looked at Nixon. He was still smiling, but the smile wasn't reaching his eyes. Stressed. He was stressed.

Nixon sighed. "It's so much worse than that. I, uh"—he licked his lips and reached out to touch my shoulder—"I owe you, man. I wasn't thinking clearly—I couldn't think. When he pulled out a lock of Trace's hair, I just—"

"We all panicked," I interrupted him. "I was just hoping you would catch on to what I was doing."

"Took me a few minutes because I blacked out at first with visions of strangling you." Nixon moved his hand from my shoulder and hit my chest.

"Ouch," I huffed.

"Thank you," Nixon said. "Both of you. For protecting her. For helping me redeem my family's name."

"Well…guess we get to torture it out of Phoenix and the rest of their family," Tex said from the backseat. "Our mission just turned a hell of a lot bloodier."

I pulled into Nixon's driveway and waved at one of our men standing outside the door.

I turned off the car and faced Nixon.

"Don't hold back," he whispered. "When you interrogate, don't hold back. Pull fingernails off, rip skin, use hammers; get as graphic and scary as you can. Because if we don't figure this shit out soon—"

Trace's grandfather was going to die. But it was so much more than that. When someone was killed—it never stopped with the boss. No; the Family normally took out the entire line. The Sicilians did a cleansing, and Trace would be included in that. She would be cleansed, just like her grandfather. And a new leader would be appointed.

One we had no control over.

Nixon sighed. "Phoenix has to know something we don't. There was a moment..." He shook his head. "I don't know, a moment when he seemed genuinely scared."

"Um." Tex raised his hand. "Who wouldn't be scared? That was Luca Nicolosi. Rumor has it that he and his brother are still at odds from some sort of drama that happened over twenty years ago. Last time they saw each other they were both in the hospital for months."

I looked at Nixon. He pressed his lips together and pulled the car to a stop.

"Tex," he said without turning around, "give me and Chase a few minutes, okay?"

Tex reached for the door and paused. "You guys gonna kill each other?"

"No," we said in unison.

"Because if you are—"

"Tex," Nixon growled. "Go."

"Fine, fine." The car door slammed and again we were blanketed in silence. Shit.

Nixon pulled out his favorite antique gun and began playing with it. Hell, all I knew was that if his finger slipped it would be no accident. I leaned back in my seat and waited for him to say something. I tried to look unaffected—but Nixon only pulled out that gun when he was feeling sentimental about the person's death. Great.

He unloaded the gun and played with one of the bullets, weighing it in the palm of his hand before loading that one single bullet back into the chamber. With his other hand he pulled back on the hammer and aimed the gun at my head. Well, shit.

"Just because you're blood doesn't mean I would hesitate to pull this trigger," Nixon said, calm as a freaking sunny day. "My love for

Tracey trumps my love for you—always. While I appreciate what you did tonight, I can't seem to get over this sinking feeling that you've been just waiting for an opportunity this whole time, and I've been blind as sin while you swept in."

I swallowed. "I guess you'll just have to trust me."

Nixon laughed. With the gun still pointed at my neck he leaned in. "That's the damn problem. I trust you more than anyone."

"Why is that a problem, then?"

Shaking his head, Nixon pulled the gun from my neck and put the safety back on. "It's a problem because you're my family. You've been to hell and back with me. If I lose you—" Nixon cursed. "You're like a brother to me, Chase. Being betrayed by you? Well, I can't imagine a worse fate, other than being betrayed by Trace. So how do you think it makes me feel, to put the two most important people in my life together? She loves you. I know she loves you. I know you love her. And I'm forcing you together...I can't control what happens and in the end, if I'm betrayed...Shit, Chase, I don't know if I could actually survive it. Do you get what I'm saying?"

"Yeah," I croaked. "You're scared as hell."

"Got that right." Nixon laughed. "But I guess if I wasn't scared shitless, she wouldn't be worth it, right?"

"She is." I swallowed and paused. "Worth it, I mean."

"It would be a hell of a lot easier if she wasn't."

"You'll have to tell her tonight."

Nixon exhaled and rubbed his eyes. "I know."

"And then—"

"I said I know," Nixon snapped. "Just, give me tonight, give us tonight and I'll see about putting her in her own room next to yours, all right?"

"For appearance's sake," I said out loud, more to convince myself than anything.

"Yes, just in case Luca decides he wants to have a family dinner with us and we have to invite the devil into our promised land."

"Right."

The car fell silent again. I didn't know what to say; I mean, what are you supposed to say? If I'd been hanging by a thread yesterday, then you can damn well assume I was hanging by thin air at this point. I would never betray Nixon—never. In that moment I decided—I would rather die than hurt my family, and I'd rather die than hurt Trace. This meant only one thing: Even if it killed me, I could no longer put myself in a position where I was lusting over Trace. Yes, we had to make it look real, but I needed to be mindless about it, just like I was mindless about killing...Right now, both of these things were my job. My heart screamed in outrage, as if the idea of ignoring its pulsating rhythmic chant of Trace's name was a cardinal sin. But I knew it wasn't. No, the great sin would be to give in to myself—and if that happened Nixon wouldn't have to kill me, I'd put the bullet in my own frantic heart. It wouldn't be worth it. There would be no justification for my actions, just a very dark future in the seventh circle of Hell.

Chapter Nine

Nixon

I slammed the car door and jogged inside the house. Pino, one of our men, was waiting outside the door.

"Any action tonight?" I asked.

Pino laughed. "No sir, not if you count several of the men begging the young ladies to turn off the *Godfather* action."

"*The Godfather?*" I repeated. "I thought they were watching chick flicks."

Pino sighed. "Yes well, Trace and Monroe thought it would entertain us more to watch a movie about our lives."

I chuckled. "*Our* lives?"

"Yes." He rolled his eyes.

"I'm trying to figure out if I like the idea of Marlon Brando playing me." I patted him on the back. "Make a call to Uncle Tony, would ya? We have some business to take care of tomorrow night and I'll need his help."

"Right away, sir." Pino pulled out his phone and opened the door for me.

I stepped inside and was immediately hit with the smell of chocolate-chip cookies. Without thinking I walked into the kitchen, eager for food. With all the stress of the evening I'd forgotten to eat.

Trace had on one of my ma's old aprons. TI's newest song was playing from her iPhone; she was singing super loud and off-key as she spooned up cookie dough and placed it on the sheet.

"Tasty." I winked.

Blushing, she stopped dancing.

"Nope, you have to pretend like I'm not here. Go ahead, shake your ass. I'm sure somewhere on that little bucket list of yours is singing off-key in the kitchen while your boyfriend watches. Only, my bucket list includes you in nothing but the apron; but hey, I'm not picky."

"Very funny." Trace turned up the music and twirled around then walked up to me and pulled me into her arms. "I was worried for you."

"Don't worry." I kissed her mouth. She tasted like chocolate chips and suddenly I forgot about everything—about Luca, Chase. It was only Tracey and the faint taste of chocolate-chip cookies on her tongue.

Without breaking our kiss I lifted her into my arms and walked down the hall. My father had been a paranoid freak, so all the bedrooms were on the first level in case of a need for an easy escape.

I kicked open my bedroom door and slammed it closed behind me. If this was our last night for a while, I wanted to savor it; I wanted to savor her.

Trace moaned into my mouth as I continued to suck the chocolate from her tongue. Damn, I would miss her taste.

She pulled back and took off the apron, then wrapped her arms around my neck and attacked me—really, there was no other word for it.

Hot. That was the first word that came to mind when Trace's lips pressed against mine. *Urgent*, that would be the second word as her tongue ran along my lower lip, causing me to curse aloud—just before I jerked her against my body and slammed her against the bedroom door. And then—nothing. Words left me. It was an out-of-body experience kissing Trace. It scared the hell out of me, that one touch could devastate not only my body but my soul—it scared me to my core and I hated that in her arms I was unable to show strength, only total weakness.

Maybe that was the third word. *Weakness.* When I lifted her into my arms and felt her body pressed tightly against mine—when her soft moans drove me insane, causing my hands to tug her shirt from her body—I realized one thing.

Weakness meant death, especially now.

And it was only a matter of time before they discovered mine... only a matter of time before everyone found out that she wasn't Chase's, but mine. Time was of the essence and I only had a limited amount of it.

Desperation, the final word that echoed into my conscience as I urged her to wrap her legs around my waist and promised myself I would protect her at all costs, even if it meant my own life. I'd already lost my heart. Losing my life? I pulled back and looked into her big brown eyes. Hell yeah, it would be worth it.

"Nixon?" Trace's breath tickled the side of my neck as she leaned in to rest her head against my chest.

"Yeah?"

"Tell me it's going to be okay."

Sighing, I kissed her soft cheek. "I'd rather show you..."

A knock sounded at the door. With a curse, I dropped Trace onto the bed and stomped over to the door. Who the hell had the nerve to interrupt me?

I pulled it open. A grinning Chase stood on the other side. My idiot cousin knew better than to barge in when I was alone with Trace and he sure as hell knew I was alone with her. Hadn't we decided that I needed to have tonight with her? He was going to get her for months! I wanted one night.

"What?" I groaned. "What could you possibly need?"

Chase sidestepped me. "Good question." He cleared his throat. "I have an answer for that."

"I'm listening." I clenched my fist and watched as Trace leaned in toward Chase, her thigh almost touching his. I was going to totally lose my shit if any part of her body touched his. Holy crap, it was going to be a very long fall semester.

I needed a damn sedative. Shit; now I was taking Tex's advice? Something was very wrong with that picture.

"Mo is totally sneaking in Tex every single night!"

I rolled my eyes. "That was the news? That she's been sneaking in her boyfriend every night? She's an adult. She can—" The wheels turned faster in my head. What the hell, that was my twin sister!

"Wait for it," Chase whispered.

Trace laughed.

"Wait for it some more."

I cursed, but there was no use. Images of my twin sister with one of the Elect—my friend and business partner—coursed through my head. Was he touching her? Oh God, was she naked? Did they . . . "I'll kill him with my bare hands!"

"Ah, there it is." Chase clapped loudly. "Well done. You controlled your anger a whole second longer than last time."

"Last time?" Trace asked.

"When he found out you and I—"

I held up my hand. I seriously did NOT need Chase to repeat to me that he and Trace had shared a bed several times when he was assigned to protect her.

Trace frowned. "When we what?"

Chase shook his head. "Nothing."

"What; you could tell me but you'd have to kill me?"

"No." Chase chuckled. "I could tell you but then he'd have to kill me."

"Solid point." Trace sighed and leaned back on the bed. "So what are you going to do, Nixon? Run into her bedroom guns blazing and shoot at Tex's feet like Grandpa did to you?"

"Best day ever," Chase sang.

"Why are you here again?" I asked.

"Mo. Tex. Sweaty, earth-shattering—"

I didn't let him finish. Instead I ran out of the room in search of Mo and Tex.

Chapter Ten

Chase

I sighed happily and lay back on the bed.

"You dirty little liar!" Trace hit me across the face with a pillow. Smirking, I leaned up on my elbow and winked. "I wasn't lying! Besides, it's a huge security issue if we have Tex sneaking in and out all the time. He should probably just stay here, especially now." Ah, words left unsaid. I moved a bit away from her and licked my lips.

"What's wrong?" She sighed and scooted closer to me. "You seem upset."

"Nothing. Just thinking."

"About what?"

"Oh, you know." I reached out and played with a bit of the comforter. "Guns, blood, revenge, typical boy stuff."

"Boy stuff my ass—what's going on, Chase?"

"Nothing," I lied and forced a smile. "I'll let Nixon talk to you about all the gory and fun details. For right now, just be happy. You're safe."

"I may be safe, but I still have to go to school tomorrow."

"Yeah," I snorted. "And I have to go to that stupid Women's

Rights class. Hell, I should bring my gun. Seriously, those girls get crazy in that class."

"Admit it; you had fun yesterday." She pushed my arm. "Admit it now or I'm telling Nixon that you cried during *The Notebook*."

"They died holding hands, Trace!" Holy shit! Was the girl seriously going to let that hang over my head forever? At least it made the pain in my heart dissipate, if only for a second.

"Who died?" Mo said from the doorway.

"The old couple," Trace clarified.

"You killed an elderly couple?" Tex asked as he peeked into the room. The sad part was that he actually looked intrigued.

"Weird. I thought you'd be on the opposite end of Nixon's gun right about now." I got up from my seat on the bed and clapped. "Well done. You've managed to thwart—"

"Tex!" Nixon's booming voice echoed through the hall.

Monroe's eyes widened as she stepped into the room and stood behind me. Right, like Nixon wasn't already two seconds away from killing me.

"Tex." Nixon growled as he grabbed Tex by the shirt and pulled him into the room, slamming the door behind him. "Okay, new rules. Everyone listen up."

Wasn't he going to talk to Trace first?

"Security is going to have to be tight over the next few weeks. Tex and Chase know what's going on, but please don't ask them details. They won't tell you and you'll just get your feelings hurt when they deny you information. So please, do us all a favor and just go about your lives. Go to school, eat three square meals, smile at your professors, and let us do what we do best."

Mo swallowed and looked down at the ground. "It's that bad, isn't it?"

Trace's eyes widened slightly before she went to Nixon's side and leaned on him. His gaze flickered to mine as he wrapped his arm around Trace and pulled her close. "Yes, it's bad, but it's nothing we haven't handled before. Because security will no longer let Tex sneak in, he's going to have to stay here. No way am I allowing either of you to sneak out and have your dirty little rendezvous."

"They aren't dirty!" Mo defended, while Tex chuckled and held up his hand for a high five. The dude was playing with fire. Seriously.

"Whatever." Nixon pinched the bridge of his nose and left Tex hanging. "Just...keep it PG under my roof, all right?"

"Fine." Monroe breezed past him. "Come on, Tex. Let's go be PG."

"PG means parental guidance," Tex pointed out. "That mean you want to come guide us, Nixon? Or are you good?"

"Ass." Nixon rolled his eyes. "Just be..."—he waved at them—"careful."

I winced at Nixon's helpless face.

Things didn't get weird until the door slammed and it was just me, Trace, and Nixon. The tension was so thick I started to sweat. I looked at Nixon and then back at Tracey. I could tell she was trying to figure out what the hell was going on. But I didn't want to be the person to drop that bomb on her. No, that needed to come from Nixon and only Nixon.

"So." I shoved my hands in my pockets. "I'll just be down the hall if you need me."

Nixon nodded while Trace came up and kissed my cheek. Out of the corner of my eye I saw Nixon briefly close his eyes and mumble a curse word. Yeah well, it wasn't going to be easy for either of us, but it was necessary. So he needed to keep his shit together. What was I thinking? I needed to do that just as much if not more.

Chapter Eleven

Nixon

Sit down," I said softly.

"Still ordering me around?" Trace jutted out her hip and glared.

Smiling, I played with my lip ring and laughed. "Sorry, farm girl. Can you please, sit down."

"Why, I thought you'd never ask." Trace winked and sat on the bed.

I moved to stand in front of her and reached for her hands. "I'm not sure what I should tell you or what I should keep from you."

"Do I get a vote?"

"Absolutely not."

"Why?"

"Because if it was up to you you'd know every gory detail. You'd want to know names, numbers, details—everything. And the more you know, the more danger you're in."

Her eyes fluttered closed for a few brief seconds before she looked at me through her thick dark lashes. "It's something really bad, otherwise you wouldn't be looking at me like that."

How I could be that transparent with her but totally aloof with assassins was beyond my realm of understanding. "And just how am I looking at you?"

"Like you're never going to see me again. You're looking at me like you did when we were kids and I told you I was going to save you. Your eyes were so sad; it was like you knew what I was saying I wouldn't be able to follow through with, but you hugged me anyway."

And maybe that was the problem. I trusted myself, and to an extent I trusted Chase, but Tracey? I wouldn't blame her if she left me. I wouldn't blame her if she chose someone who could protect her better than I could. Because the truth of the matter was, my life would never be safe. Our existence together would never be a for-sure thing. Death was my daily reality; it was my burden, not hers and not Chase's.

Maybe if I was a stronger man, I'd leave her and suffer alone. Maybe if I was the type of guy who put others first—I would walk away from her.

But she was my weakness. I'd make it two steps before turning around and begging on my knees for her to take me back. Which meant I had to trust in us, I had to trust in her.

"Trace, we can't be seen together right now."

She jerked her hands away from mine and glared. "Oh no you don't, Nixon Anthony Abandonato!"

Wasn't expecting that. I laughed without really thinking, and then she slapped me across the face. It stung like hell. "What was that for?"

"You aren't leaving me!"

"Did I say I was?" Although my cheek was throbbing I couldn't help but keep laughing at her response. And this was why I would never walk away. Who would walk away from such a little pistol?

"Oh." Trace tugged her lower lip between her teeth and sheepishly looked up at my cheek. "You should probably put some ice on that." I winced as she touched my cheek.

Covering her hand with mine, I winked. "Yeah, well, I've had worse. Promise."

Her eyes welled with tears, but to her credit she kept them all in. If anything I fell in love with her a little bit more. Her strength was so damn sexy, I couldn't even put into words what she did to me.

I kissed her softly and sighed against her still chocolate-tasting mouth. "Sweetheart, Chase was...well, today he was gifted with a stroke of brilliance. The head of the Nicolosi family talked with us this evening, and he had Phoenix with him."

I quickly explained to her what had happened, leaving out all the violence, guns, and threats. So basically I censored everything and then dropped the bomb. "You and Chase need to pretend to be together. People will be watching you, they'll be following you."

Tracey swallowed and licked her lips. "And you'll what? Pretend you hate me again?"

"Hell no!" I snapped, grabbing her ass and lifting her until her body was firmly pressed against mine midair. "I'll just be the friend. Basically, Chase and I are switching parts. He gets to play the boyfriend, I get to play the jackass."

That earned an eye roll and a laugh from her. I dropped her to the ground and kissed her nose. "If they find out how much you mean to me, they'll use that against our family and against your grandfather."

She was silent for a moment. Her hands traced circles around the tattoo peeking out from underneath my white t-shirt. The writing was in Sicilian, but it said, "Every Saint has a past, every sinner has a future." I had always wondered which I was. The saint or the sinner?

It was Trace's favorite tattoo, even though I had several down my left arm and a few on my stomach and back. Her favorite had always been that one, on the left side of my chest. She said it gave her comfort. I guess she was using it for comfort right now.

"Okay," she whispered, "I'll do it."

I was waiting to feel relieved, but all I felt was tense. My muscles literally tightened underneath her touch the minute the word "okay" had fallen from her perfectly pouted lips.

"I'm going to apologize in advance, though." Tracey sniffed as a tear ran down her cheek.

"Why are you apologizing?"

Her eyes met mine. "Because I'm going to break your heart."

Chapter Twelve

Nixon

Break? It was already broken! Horrified, I watched her look down at the ground, her shoulders slumped in defeat.

"Nixon." She placed her hands against my chest. "I need you to do me a favor."

"Anything." My voice was hoarse with emotion.

"Trust me. Trust in us. No matter what I say, no matter what I do—and I'll do some terrible things—know that I love you. No matter what."

"Kind of sounds like the speech I gave you a few weeks ago." I sighed.

"Sucks, huh?" She laughed a bit and leaned her head on my chest where her hands had just been. "Regardless of what I do, you have to know, I love you, Nixon. I choose you and only you. I'm going to break your heart every day I hold his hand instead of yours. It's going to kill me to laugh at his jokes knowing you're dying just a little bit inside. And if he kisses me—I'll kiss him back, Nixon. I'm going to break your heart—because you've given me no other option."

"I know." Damn if I wasn't ready to burst into tears myself. I knew it would be hard—not this hard. "Just do me a favor, Trace?"

"Anything."

"Think of me…"—I smirked—"not him. When you're kissing him, do me a favor and just keep your eyes closed so you can imagine it isn't my best friend and yours. And I swear to all that is holy that if he puts his tongue in your mouth I will cut it the hell off."

Tracey laughed against my chest. "You've got yourself a deal, Godfather."

"Heard about that…Wanted to give some of the men some entertainment?"

"It was more of a history lesson for me." I tensed as she kept talking. "Mo said that the writers of the movies had to actually talk to real mafia members in order to keep it realistic. They even had to ask permission to make the movie. Crazy, right?"

Nope, not crazy at all. It was a world people rarely got to see, and if they did they either went blind afterward or wished that God would strike them dead. Living in a constant state of fear wasn't living—it was hell on earth.

"Don't pollute your mind with Hollywood's version of our reality, okay, Trace?" I kissed her head. "Now, let's go get some of those cookies before Chase eats them all."

She pulled back from me and linked her arm through mine. "Nixon." She stopped walking and looked up at me. "Tell me there's a happy ending."

"Trace, I—"

"Lie," Tracey ordered. "Lie if you have to. I just need to hear you say it."

"Trace." I twirled a piece of her hair around my fingers. "For us? There will always be a happy ending. Always."

She squared her shoulders and gave me one silent nod before dragging me out of the room. Hell if I didn't feel like the world was literally resting on my shoulders—*her* world, to be exact.

Chapter Thirteen

Phoenix

The room was cold and dark. Hell, I had every crevice, every plane of the wall memorized. Ironic that the very room I used to play in when I was a kid had been turned into my own personal chamber of Hell.

I deserved it.

All of it.

I was too selfish to kill myself, although the thought had crossed my mind more times than I'd ever admit to anyone, let alone Nixon.

My eyes adjusted to the darkness and focused on the door. I knew it was only a matter of time before Nixon came bursting through, guns blazing. At least I was dealing with Nixon instead of Chase. *There* was a melodrama I didn't want to deal with—two guys both in love with the same girl—and lucky me, I was the object of both of their hatred.

I would hate me, too. I did hate me. I hated what I was, I hated what I did, I hated what I represented; but most of all, I hated that the legacy I would leave behind as a De Lange was that of an attempted rapist and a rat.

I would hang. And I would deserve every damn second the noose tightened around my neck. Some things can't be undone—or unseen—and my eyes, they'd seen and experienced it all. My dad had made sure of that. He'd wanted to expose me to the darkness of our family—I prayed for the first time in years, the day they sent Mil away. She was only my stepsister but I would have done anything to save her—anything to protect her from the ugliness that my father was a part of. Because I knew it was only a matter of time before she was brought into his circle. I'd only been sixteen when it happened to me, and I could still see the blood on my hands.

"What do you mean?" I asked. "You want me to…"—I swallowed back the tears—"hurt her."

"It won't hurt." My dad chuckled. "I imagine she'll like it."

I licked my lips and glanced back at the door. It was hard to see because the lights kept flickering on and off—as if they couldn't decide whether or not to shine light on the hell I was experiencing, or darken—allowing me to forget what was right in front of me.

My dad slapped the girl across the face. She had two faint bruises on her right cheek and a bloody lip. Her blond hair was matted to her head, and I could see cuts and scrapes all over her body, as if someone had used her as his personal sharpening tool.

"Do what needs to be done, son." My dad slapped my back. "It's easier this way. This way, you won't feel, do you understand?"

I shook my head as the girl's eyes pleaded with mine. I wanted to shout, to cry, to do anything. Instead I just stood there as my dad explained again.

"Money, son. We need it, our family needs it. Sometimes we have to do bad things in order to get to the good."

I nodded my agreement and stuffed my hands in my pockets to keep from choking the life from his body.

"So, we sell the girls." Dad shrugged. "Truly, it is not as bad as it looks. They are sold to very wealthy men who are willing to pay immensely for someone so—young."

"Young?" I nearly whispered.

"Underage," he clarified. "Lucky for you, this particular girl doesn't need to be…pure, if you get my meaning. The sooner you remedy the situation the better you'll feel about everything. After all, it's just sex."

Just sex? I'd never had sex. I was the only one of my friends who hadn't. They thought it was because I was waiting—never would they guess it was because I envisioned it as rape. I could never see it as any different, because my entire life I'd watched my dad rape my mom over and over again, and now, he was asking me to do the same thing.

I wiped a stray tear and looked away. "Can't we just get someone else to do it?"

The slap came so fast I didn't have time to duck. It stung like hell as I fell against the concrete next to the very girl I was trying to save.

"You want in the business? You want to be boss someday?" Dad threw a knife onto the floor. The clatter may as well have been a bomb going off for as loud as it was. "You either do this"—he nodded down toward the knife—"or I'll kill her. The blood will be on your hands and you'll get to tell our client exactly why we were not able to deliver as promised. Think of your mother, your sister, and make your choice." He

looked down at his watch and scowled. "I'll be back in twenty minutes."

The minute the door shut, I let a few more tears escape before looking at the girl shivering next to me.

"I'm—" I croaked and closed my eyes.

"Do it." Her voice was barely above a whisper. "Just make it fast, please just make it fast."

"I can't…"

She grabbed my hand. The nameless girl that was getting sold into slavery grabbed my hand to comfort me. "If you don't we'll all die anyway."

I nodded and numbly worked the buttons on my shirt, pulling it off, and following with my jeans.

The minute I touched her, the light that had once been in her eyes, the very last shred of dignity that had remained in her possession—disappeared. All I saw was black, all I felt was evil, and Dad was right. Because when everything was over—I felt nothing.

Headlights shone through the tiny window above the door. My hands gripped the chair and I waited, but nobody came to the door.

Exhaling in relief, I tried to focus on something, anything, to make the memories of my childhood go away. But in the end, I knew nothing would work. I had no soul. And people who had no souls? They didn't—couldn't—feel anything but darkness, and that's what I was—Lucifer himself.

Chapter Fourteen

Chase

It's staring at me." I sipped my coffee and handed Trace back her phone. "I don't like it when things stare."

Trace rolled her eyes. "It's a cow, Chase. What do you expect it to do? Talk to you through the phone?"

"Moo. Aren't cows supposed to moo? It looks weird just standing there eating."

"You were the one who said you wanted to see what my home was like."

I laughed. "'Home' as in 'house.' I didn't think you'd give me a half hour speech on farm life and how to breed cattle. Thanks for the pictures and video, by the way. I'd always wanted to know why farmers stuck their hands up the cows' asses—"

Trace took my coffee out of my hands and took a sip. "Don't be a prude."

Laughing, I jerked my coffee away from her. "Honey, that's the first time I've ever been accused of such."

"My mistake." Tracey snatched the coffee back. "Chase, don't be such a whore."

"Better." I stole my coffee back. "Now stop taking my coffee. It's eight a.m. and I'm still not fully ready to face the day, especially that professor in your Women's Studies class. Seriously, the chick needs to get laid. I think she hates men."

"To be fair"—Trace tried to grab my coffee but I held it over my head so she'd have to get a ladder to grab it—"she"—Trace jumped—"only hates you"—she jumped again—"because you called her fat."

"Not true." I yawned and kept the coffee in the air. "I asked when her baby was due."

With a huff Trace gave up and put her hands on her hips. "Right, and she wasn't pregnant, so basically it's the same thing."

I shrugged. "My mistake." Trace was still eying my coffee. "Fine, we'll go get you some coffee, but remember you can't be late to any more classes."

I checked my watch. "Okay, we have exactly fifteen minutes to go across campus, buy you coffee, and head up to the Social Sciences building."

"We'll be fine!" Trace grabbed my hand. "Let's go."

We ran across campus and stood in line at the coffee shop. Luckily, there was only one person in front of us.

But as my own personal luck would have it, the person standing in front of us just happened to be Luca.

What the hell was he doing on campus? And how would he have any idea we were even heading to get coffee? Was he truly watching us that carefully?

I gripped Trace's hand hard within mine.

She looked up at me. "Chase, seriously. Get over the cow thing."

I laughed and went into action. "I'll get over it, if you get under me."

Her mouth dropped open. I tilted my head to the left. She didn't need any more information. In an instant her arms wrapped around my neck and she leaned into me, her mouth inches from mine. "Hmm, how about we skip class then?"

"Nice." I was seriously sweating. Everything felt awkward and off-limits. If I just went with instinct I knew it would make Tracey uncomfortable and I only had seconds to decide what the hell I was going to do. Luca turned just as I leaned in and pressed my lips against Trace's.

I was counting on her reaction to be timid—and it was.

Mine, however, was like unleashing a starving tiger from its cage. I thrust my tongue into her mouth and tasted her, like really tasted her. Shit, I was going to go to Hell for enjoying this so damn much. With my body as tight as a drum, I opened her mouth with my tongue and continued to take what wasn't mine to take. She put her hand on my chest, almost as if she was pushing me away, but I shook my head as I deepened the kiss and slid her hand down my abs to the loop in the front of my jeans.

A throat cleared. Slowly, I pulled away from Tracey and looked up into Luca's amused face.

"Chase." He nodded. "And you must be?" He was looking at Trace with more curiosity than anything. Shit, did he know we'd played him?

"Oh, um," Trace giggled. "Sorry we got carried away, I'm Chase's girlfriend, Tracey."

"Lovely." Luca took her outstretched hand and kissed it. "What a beautiful couple. A pleasure, Miss Tracey. Chase, we'll be in touch."

I nodded as he walked off with his coffee, saw that a few of his men were with him.

I faintly heard Trace order a drip and then she directed me out of the coffee shop toward the Social Sciences building. I pretended everything was fine on the inside, but it wasn't.

I was far from fine.

I was ripped to shreds on the inside.

Because until a few minutes ago, I'd had no idea what I'd been missing. And now...now I did.

And suddenly betraying everyone I loved was back on the table. Because Tracey—she held a part of me I couldn't take back, and it scared the hell out of me.

Chapter Fifteen

Nixon

I reached into my shoulder bag and felt around for my gun. I knew I was seriously going to lose my mind if I was checking my gun every five seconds of the day, but I couldn't help it. I was worried about everything.

Damn, if my ma could see me now.

I went to my one and only Tuesday class and tried to look scary. No way was I in any shape to talk to students or my professor with the whole Trace and Chase situation hanging over my head. Holy shit, their names even rhymed. How the hell had I missed that?

I groaned aloud.

"Mr. Abandonato, something you'd like to share with the rest of the class?" Mr. Smith asked.

Hell. No. "Sorry, headache."

He grimaced but said nothing. Probably a good idea since I was literally two minutes away from losing my shit.

Class ended five minutes later. I made my way toward the opposite end of campus—toward the *Space*.

I called it the *Space* because calling it anything else just seemed weird. We used the building for special things; having it on campus was reserved for special purposes.

And I had a hell of a purpose today.

Ruin Phoenix's life and gain my sanity back. Easy, right?

I burst through the door only to find Phoenix glaring at me from a metal chair. His hands were cuffed behind him and a gag was in his mouth.

I pulled the gun from my bag and tucked it into my pants.

"How was your sleep, sunshine?"

Phoenix's eyes were dripping with hatred, but he didn't make a sound.

Sighing, I went over to the *cupboard of death*, as Tex liked to call it, and pulled out my tools.

Phoenix started jerking against the chair, but I continued to pull out the medical instruments. I wasn't really going to do anything to him—not yet. The unfortunate part was that I'd been trying to clean up the family business—apart from the Sicilian influence.

The mafia was alive and well in Sicily, but here? Here we'd been keeping the peace, flying under the radar. As long as we didn't red flag our business dealings, we were left relatively alone.

It had all started with Trace's parents' murders and I hoped to God it would end there. I knew there wasn't an out; there would always be people trying to get my family. Greed would always exist. But it was order that I was counting on. The Sicilians had a certain way of doing things, a respectful way to keep order within the families.

They were here because if for some reason things went south, they didn't want it traced back to them.

Too much money was at stake. And Phoenix knew that, so I may not torture him, not now, but I knew that was where it was headed. I hated that I would have my ex-best friend's blood on my hands almost as much as I hated myself for wanting to kill him every damn second of the day.

I pulled out the concrete mixture and poured water into it.

Phoenix's eyes widened but he said nothing.

It was a fast-setting concrete. I mixed it for a few minutes then pushed the bucket over to where Phoenix sat.

"So." I bit down on my bottom lip and crossed my arms. "I want you to look at this. I mean, really look at it."

Phoenix's eyes flickered to the concrete-filled bucket.

"Now." I pushed the bucket closer to him. "This is your future. Do you see it? Look really hard. Your future is in this bucket. Know that if you double-cross me I won't hesitate. Your feet will be so heavy from the concrete surrounding them that when I drop you into Lake Michigan you won't even have time to suck in one final gasp of air. Nobody will find you. Nobody will care. So it's your choice."

Phoenix closed his eyes.

I pulled the gag from his mouth so he could talk. "Now, say thank you."

"What?" His voice was hoarse.

"For giving you a choice. Say thank you. And tell me everything you know. Or else…I'm placing your feet into the concrete bucket and praying for your damned soul."

Phoenix seemed to actually think about it, which proved his idiocy right then and there. If he had to think about whether he'd rather live than die? That meant his shit was deep and he didn't see a way out of it except death on both ends.

"Damn." I pulled up a metal chair and took a seat across from him. "That bad, huh? Who's got you, Phoenix?"

"It's…" He cursed. "It's complicated."

"Families always are."

There was a pregnant pause while he continued to stare at the bucket. "I'm imagining it."

"What?"

"Which death would be quicker."

"I won't shoot you." I laughed. "Sorry, but the minute you tried to rape Tracey was the minute you lost all rights to a quick death."

"I know," Phoenix snapped. "I'm just—"

"Thinking." I pulled out my brass knuckles and slid them onto my right hand. "Allow me to help with your decision."

The knuckles dug into the flesh on the right side of his jaw as I pulled back from the punch.

Phoenix swore, but otherwise did nothing.

"Say thank you." I swore.

"Thank you." Blood dripped from Phoenix's face onto his white shirt.

"Thank you, what?" I cupped my ear.

"Sir. Thank you, sir."

"For?"

"Being gracious and giving me a choice."

"Better." I took off the knuckles and wiped them on my jeans. "Now, what would you like to tell me?"

He smirked and leaned back in his chair. "You're all going to die—and you don't even know the worst part."

"Oh, it gets worse?" I laughed bitterly. "Tell me. Now."

"A shitstorm's coming your way and you have no idea. Neither does the Nicolosi family. Everyone thinks this is about some old beef, some jealousy between the Alfero and Abandonato families? Hell no. It's not about jealousy. It's about blood. It's about the wrong blood leading; it's about the secret your family's been keeping—is still keeping. And the best part?" He leaned forward, a shit-eating grin on his face. "I'll take it all the way to the bottom of Lake Michigan. Hell, I may not get a last breath, but I'll die with a smile on my face knowing that you never even knew who your real father was."

I don't remember how many times I hit him before he passed out. Blood dripped from both my hands and I still wanted more. What the hell kind of mind game was Phoenix playing?

I quickly dialed Uncle Tony's number and told him to meet me. We needed to move faster than I thought—I needed all the information, the leads that we'd collected over the years, the evidence. I wanted and needed it all.

Something told me we were running out of time faster than I could possibly imagine, and I knew Phoenix held the key. The only question? Who was holding the information over his head?

Chapter Sixteen

Nixon

Are you sure this is all you have?" I asked for the third time. Tony had given me a USB drive with all the information that we'd collected over the years, including pictures of the De Lange family's comings and goings, and active accounts.

Shit, they were worse off than I thought.

And that was the problem.

As far as I could tell they weren't receiving any payments from any outside source. Nobody seemed to be bribing them. No wire transfers; nothing.

Tony snorted. "Nixon, you're not only my boss but my nephew. Why would I of all people keep vital information from you?" He lit his cigar and walked over to the large bay window in my kitchen.

Hell. He was lying to me; the son of a bitch was lying. I could always tell when someone wasn't being honest. Not that I liked to brag, but whenever people lie they tend to give more information than necessary. They do this in order to convince you that because they have details, they're innocent.

If Tony was telling the truth, he would have shrugged and said "yup."

He didn't even deny it. No, instead he turned the tables and said, "Why would I of all people keep information from you?"

Guilt dripped off every word.

Why indeed?

I pretended to scroll through the bank accounts on the computer. It was all information I'd seen before. Things that didn't really matter and wouldn't help our case one bit.

What motive would Tony have to hide something from me? What would he have to gain? He was loaded. All of our business dealings were managed by different companies. I oversaw all operations.

The man was worth close to a billion dollars. Granted, that was a drop in the bucket compared to my own fortune, but still.

It couldn't be money. He had money.

"Well." Tony puffed on his cigar and faced me. "I think I'm going to head home. You'll tell me if anything comes up?"

Here went nothing.

"Nah." I leaned back in my chair. "I don't think it's necessary you know all the gory details. Just do what I pay you to do."

Tony's nostrils flared; his eyes remained cool and distant. "And what's that?"

I smiled. "Your damn job. Manage the transactions coming in and out of the banks, make sure every member of the family gets paid by the end of the month. You know, that sort of thing." I looked back at my computer, dismissing his presence.

"Now, listen here, Nixon, you may be—"

"We're done now." My eyes flickered to his. "If you'll excuse me, I have a mess to clean up."

He seemed to struggle with what he wanted to say. Instead he nodded. "Yes sir." And stormed out of the room.

"Angelo," I called behind me.

"Yes sir."

"Tail him. I want to know what he eats for breakfast, lunch, and dinner. I want to know what toothpaste he uses at night, what whiskey he prefers, all of it. I want you to know him so damn well that if I placed his skin on your body, people wouldn't be able to tell the difference. Anything suspicious, you call me. And Angelo?"

"Sir."

"Nobody, and I mean nobody, will know of this. If you get caught—"

"I understand, sir." Angelo nodded once and left the room.

I groaned and put my head in my hands. Things weren't looking up. I wondered if Trace had had a better day than I did. Actually, I didn't hope; I knew she had to. After all, what could be worse than threatening to kill your ex-best friend and finding out your uncle was a possible rat?

*   *   *

Chase walked into the house looking like he was about five seconds away from holding a gun to his own head.

"Dude." I threw a can of beer in his direction. "Who died?"

He caught the beer midair and set it on the table, then took a seat. "No one. That I know of, at least. Well, let me rephrase. I didn't kill anyone. Why, did you?"

"Not yet." I shook my head and then burst out laughing.

"What's so funny?"

"Us." I took a seat next to him and sighed. "Who asks that when they come home at night?"

"Damn shame we're not kidding."

"Damn shame," I agreed and touched my beer to his. "So, what has you looking so pissed off? Trace get mud on the boots you get her or something?"

"Nah." He cleared his throat. "Nothing like that. I just hate going to her classes. They suck, by the way, and I was a freshman three years ago, thank you very much. Plus, I swear every single one of her professors wants to murder me."

"Well." I took another sip. "You did sleep with two out of four of the women professors. Pretty sure that's reason enough for a grudge."

Chase snorted. "They should thank me, not hold it against me. I gave them the time of their lives!"

"So you say." I chuckled. "They, however, explain the situation a bit differently."

"You asked?" Chase's eyes widened.

"Chase, you can't seduce an older woman and then call her a cougar to her face, especially if you're the one that sweet-talked her into bed in the first place."

"Not my fault!" Chase held up his hands. "Can we please change the subject?"

"Fine."

"Do you…" Chase swore. "Do you think that maybe Tex should help out a bit, too, with Trace, I mean?"

"You do realize you're making it sound like she's our love child, in need of a babysitter during the day?"

Chase didn't laugh. What the hell was stuck up his ass?

"Dude." I nudged him. "Snap out of it. What's wrong?"

"I—" He closed his eyes and shook his head. "I'm just really—"

"Nixon!" Trace burst into the room and threw her arms around my neck, then sat on my lap. "I missed you." Her lips found mine and my concern for Chase went out the window.

He cleared his throat a few times before Trace pulled away from me. "So he told you, then?"

"I was about to." Chase's voice cracked.

"Tell me?" I asked, looking between the two of them.

"Luca." Trace sighed. "That scary-looking Nicolosi guy? He followed us today."

"What the hell!" Still holding on to Trace, I reached over and smacked Chase in the shoulder. "Is that what crawled up your ass and died? You can't just keep that from me, man. I need to know these things. Why didn't you text me?"

"I wasn't thinking." Chase swallowed and looked away. "I'm sorry. I guess I was in such shock that I didn't know what to do, but don't worry, Tracey was safe. We were fine."

"Fine?" Trace snorted. "Nixon." She turned in my lap and touched her forehead to mine. "Chase has been acting like a complete lunatic all day. I think he's defective."

"I'm not defective!" Chase yelled.

"And he's not a toy..." I defended, smirking.

"Plaything." Tracey nodded. "Definitely a plaything, but what I'm saying is, he's been so damn depressed all day that I can't handle being around him."

"Right here. I'm sitting right here." Chase sighed.

"Please?" Tracey kissed my mouth, licking part of my lip ring and then nibbling my lower lip. Her lips trailed to my ear where she whispered, "Something is very wrong."

I nodded and pulled her face away from mine, being sure to kiss her nose as I looked into her eyes. "Go change into some comfortable clothes for dinner, okay? I'll be up in a minute."

"Okay."

Once Trace was out of earshot, I reached over and grabbed Chase by the arm, dragging him with me all the way into my father's old study. I closed the doors behind me.

"What the hell happened?"

Chase wouldn't meet my eyes. He shoved his hands into the front pockets of his jeans and stared at the ground.

"Chase?"

"I kissed her."

"You have exactly five seconds before I shoot you in the face. Explain why you kissed her. Now."

"Luca, he was standing in line in front of us, and I panicked. I kissed her, she kissed me—not very well so you've got that going for you—and then I introduced her to Luca and we went to class. That's all that happened."

"Was there tongue?"

Chase's head snapped up. "What?"

"You heard me. Was there tongue?"

"It, uh…" He waved his hand in the air. "It happened so damn fast, Nixon. Yeah, probably, I don't know. I'm not sure. All I can say is I'm sorry. It was the only thing I could think to do. I was afraid Trace would be pissed, but she understood."

"So you're upset because ... ?"

"Well, I like living, thank you very much." Chase smirked. Was everyone going to lie to me today? Could I trust no one but myself?

"And?"

"Nothing." He forced a smile. "It just ate me up all day, that's all. It felt wrong, it feels wrong; you know what I mean?"

My eyes narrowed. That part, at least, seemed genuine. "Yeah, I know what you mean. I hate it more than I could ever say, but Chase, remember, this isn't to torture you."

He snorted. I continued. "It's to keep her safe."

"I know that. Don't you think I know that?" Anger filled Chase's eyes as his mask of guilt slipped off, and in its place ... something I hated to see. It was as if a knife was being thrust into my back and there was no way for me to pull it out.

Betrayal.

He wanted to betray me.

And there was nothing I could do except pray that when the time came ... he wouldn't.

Chapter Seventeen

Phoenix

I woke up with blood pooling around my head. I tried to maneuver my chair so I could at least sit comfortably but I knew it would take strength I didn't have—and honestly, what did it matter anyway? If I died lying down or sitting in a chair or getting thrown into the lake?

My throat felt tight. The minute I'd seen Nixon coming into the room I knew the truth: He'd never forgive me. It would be better for me to die with the knowledge that I had—than put him in any more pain or danger. I refused to be the cause of even more turmoil than I'd already heaped upon him and his family.

If I'd had a heart to break, staring at my ex-best friend and the look of betrayal on his face would have done it—shattered it into billions of pieces and burned it on contact with the air. I could never fully explain to him the depth of my humiliation—of the horror I'd experienced when I was with Trace.

They thought I'd tried to hurt her because I was a monster—and that was true. I was sick; they just weren't aware of how sick. I'd always hidden it the best I could. The first time I blacked out during an episode, my dad had called in the best doctors.

"He's not remembering things! Is my son stupid?" His tone was on edge; after all he'd just spent thousands of dollars he didn't have in order to get me seen by the world's best shrink.

"Sometimes"—the doctor gave me a sad smile—"when people experience trauma, or continue to experience it, the senses completely shut off. It's as if the body performs on auto-pilot. It looks like he's aware of what he's doing and in a way he is—and he's powerless to stop it. After the episode, he doesn't recall details, only that something bad happened, and the cycle repeats."

Dad slammed his fist onto the desk. "So? He's dumb? He's crazy? What do we do?"

"None of the above." The doctor had way more patience than I would have had. "Hypnotherapy might be advised, if you're willing to have—"

"Out of the question," Dad interrupted. "How do I know you aren't just trying to brainwash him? How do I know—"

"Mr. De Lange." The doctor licked her lips. "Your son needs help. You can't just keep ignoring the problem, it will get worse. It's almost as if…" Her voice died off.

"What?" I said numbly. "As if what?"

"As if your rage is so deep, so unforgiving, that even if you loved someone beyond measure—even if you were willing to die for someone… If they set you off, you'd kill them and you'd feel nothing."

Well, that felt good to hear. Not only was I crazy but I was about five seconds away from killing those I loved.

"We're done here." Dad crossed his arms and glared while the doctor grabbed her briefcase as well as the thick manila envelope he'd given her, and walked out of our house.

"Doctors don't know everything. The way I see it," Dad snorted, "is you'll be the best mafia boss in the history of the family."

"How do you figure?" My voice dripped with sarcasm.

Dad's grin was evil as he leaned in and patted me on the back. "You'd kill your own blood to get ahead and not even blink. Apparently, you're more useful than I thought."

I froze in my chair. I wanted to run, I wanted to scream but again, I felt nothing. It was as if all the darkness inside kept swallowing up the guilt and shame I should have been feeling. If anything, I was in a constant state of loss.

"So this girl." Dad licked his lips. "The one who eats lunch with you."

My head snapped up. Of course he'd know about Trace. After all, he was the dean of Eagle Elite. And it was for that very reason that Nixon was protecting her. He knew a pretty girl like Trace would appeal to my father's tastes. Not that my father would ever cross Nixon, but still.

"How old is she?"

"Old," I replied fast. "Eighteen, too old for you."

He moved to slap me but I caught his wrist in my hand and flipped him so fast against the table that I heard his arm crack. Good, let him feel pain.

"You should probably take the doctor's advice." I kept twisting. "After all, I'm about five minutes away from losing

my shit. Who knows what I'll do. Remember, you said I'd
kill my own family—don't test me." I released his arm and
stomped off.

My head pounded with the memory—it seemed like an eternity
ago. I'd walked away from my dad that day feeling more empowered
than I had in a long time. I'd actually fought him; I'd threatened him.

A smile curved across my lips—hell yeah, that was the day I'd
become invincible, and lost my moral compass.

I'd seen Trace the next day at school and noticed something
was different. Nixon's eyes were lingering on her, as well as Chase's,
but when she looked at me? Nothing. It was as if she could sense my
darkness. Which pissed me off. She didn't know me! Maybe that's
why I did it, why I tried to scare her away. If I couldn't have her—
the one girl that for the first time in my life made me want to smile—
then I didn't want anyone else to have her, either.

And that's when I'd felt a snap.

The girl I'd raped. That same girl. She hadn't been wanted by
the client after all—just like Trace wouldn't be wanted by Nixon or
Chase if I did something to prevent it. If they could see that she wasn't
deserving. Matters were made infinitely worse when it was her fault
I was excommunicated from Nixon's inner circle. After the hell I'd
been through—every sacrifice I'd made—and in the end I had nothing, all because of her. The hatred that I felt for her in that moment
was stronger than anything I'd ever felt toward my dad. I wanted her
to suffer because she'd stolen my family from me. I'd never loved my
dad, but Nixon? Chase? Tex? We'd been blood brothers until that
bitch had stepped in. I lost it—all of it.

Bile rose in my throat as I puked up blood. For the first time in seven years, I cried like a baby; the only sound in that hollow room was my own screams and whimpers. The terror on her face, her soft pleadings, and my hands, my bare hands ripping at her clothes. My teeth chattered as the memory hit me with a force so strong that I was gasping for breath. I did that. Not my dad. Me.

If I could just go back and fix things I would—and that's why I did what I did. Because I couldn't go back in time. That's why I was lying in that chair. I sucked in a deep breath—they'd never know the full truth—I couldn't let them, but I knew exactly how I could redeem the darkness my life represented.

After all—in every redemption story a sacrifice needs to be made. Maybe the sacrifice needed to be me.

Chapter Eighteen

Chase

I felt like shit. All day I alternated between wanting to shoot Nixon and wanting to shoot myself. To say my day sucked would be like saying the Sicilians were only mildly intimidating.

FYI, they were terrifying. Many a man shit their pants in their presence and I was living in my own personal hell.

How did I get so lucky?

I knew I shouldn't have told Nixon, but I also knew I couldn't lie to him even if I wanted to. He knew me too damn well and he could always smell a rat or liar hundreds of feet away. Which left me with blatant honesty.

I could read him as well as he could read me.

I was basically an exposed wire when it came to him.

And I knew he knew.

In that brief encounter in the study, it was as if all his fears were realized. He wasn't stupid; he knew I was affected, but he still entrusted *her* to me.

So what did that say about the type of guy I was? Or the type of trust Nixon had in me?

Nixon left me alone in the study while he went to go see how the rest of Trace's day was going. I had exactly five minutes to get my shit together and then I needed to do something, and that something was make dinner. I needed a distraction, one that didn't start with "T" and end with a "y."

I took a few deep breaths and strolled into the kitchen. Finding an apron, I wrapped it around my waist and poured myself a large glass of wine. I would get through this, I would make it through and I'd be fine. I'd just have to screw a lot of girls and possibly be drunk the entire time to do it. Right. No big deal.

A large gulp of wine worked wonders as I began chopping up the vegetables for my pasta *ncasciata*. I'd just finished arranging the eggplant and getting the peas ready when Tex walked into the kitchen with Mo.

"Aw shit." Tex poured himself a glass of wine. "Your damn dog die, Chase?"

"He doesn't have a dog." Mo reached for Tex's wine.

He pulled the wine away from her. "Get your own wine, and it's an expression, Mo."

She rolled her eyes and slapped me hard on the back. "What's up, cousin? You only cook when you're either trying to impress someone or ready to commit murder."

"Yeah." Nixon waltzed into the kitchen, Trace in tow. "That's only partially true. Remember last summer when he baked for three months straight?"

"Why?" Trace came up alongside me and examined the eggplant, a confused look on her face.

I took the eggplant from her grubby hands and put it back into the bowl. "It was an experiment of sorts." God, she smelled good.

"Experiment?" Mo choked on her laugh. "Is that what you're calling it now?"

Tex chuckled behind me. "Chase replaced sex with cooking."

Tracey burst out laughing. "And he lasted three months?" Seriously? Even Trace thought I was that bad of a player? Really? Well, there went my self-esteem, not that it was dangerously high or anything in the first place. After all, I'd stuck my tongue down her throat and pondered suicide all within the same amount of time it took for her to not only forget our heated exchange but kiss my cousin directly in front of me. Where the hell was a gun when I needed one?

"Oh look, dinner's almost ready! Who wants to help with the pasta?" I clapped my hands loudly and tried to distract everyone in the room but they just kept talking.

"Three days," Nixon snorted. "He lasted three days, but he didn't want anyone to know about his epic failure, so he cooked dinner every night for three months."

"That is..." Tex took a sip of his wine and grinned. I rolled my eyes and waited for him to continue. "Until we told him we already knew he'd failed but had wanted badass dinners. He bought our silence with food."

"Bastards." I threw a towel at Tex's face. "I slaved for days on end for you two!"

"And we appreciate it, Betty Crocker, we really do." Nixon smirked in my direction. The only reason I was able to smile back was because I knew he was just trying to make things normal for everyone.

We'd sit. We'd eat. And I'd pretend that I wasn't in irreversible love with his girlfriend. No. Big. Deal.

"Need help with the pasta?" Trace grabbed my glass of wine and took a sip. It was decided. God hated me. Her lips were everywhere on my glass and now I had to drink after her? *You've got to be shitting me.*

In true Sicilian fashion I had made the noodles from scratch, which would take anyone who didn't know what the hell they were doing a long time. "Pasta." I pointed at my handiwork. "It's almost done, why don't you go relax? Drink some wine, put your feet up, do your homework."

Trace groaned. "Did you just tell me to do my homework?"

"No?" I took a step away from her. The perfume she was wearing was literally killing me and I could only hold my breath for so long. And I was sure that if she touched me I would probably explode with frustration, or just scream and have to be institutionalized. Wonder if the mafia had connections in the loony bin.

"Look, you do have a lot of homework. Maybe Nixon can help you?"

"Help me?" she repeated, and then tilted her head to the side. Before I could back up any farther she reached up and felt my forehead. "Are you sick?"

"No." I swatted her hand away. "I'm just...cooking."

Oh God kill me now.

"Cooking?"

"Are you going to repeat everything I say?"

"Depends." She shrugged. "You gonna stop acting like an ass?"

I grinned. "Nope."

Trace swatted the back of my head. "There he is. Welcome back, asshole; don't scare me like that. You're making me nervous with all this baking and ordering me to be responsible and do my homework. You're not my brother, you know."

The huge gulp of wine I had just taken spewed out of my mouth and onto the stove.

The room fell silent, and then Nixon clapped. "Well done, you've finally shocked the hell out of him, Trace."

I wiped my face and threw the wine-stained towel at Nixon's head. "Whatever. Wash up, children, dinner's almost ready."

"Yes ma!" they all yelled as they went to set the table, leaving me alone in the kitchen yet again.

I leaned over the sink and told myself to keep the contents of my stomach inside, not out.

Brother? A freaking brother? Was she insane? Yeah, pretty sure I would never, ever think of her as family. She wasn't family. She was—shit. She was everything.

Chapter Nineteen

Nixon

Well, that was awkward. Points go to Chase for not completely losing his shit while Tracey touched his forehead and then proceeded to tell him not to be an ass. If it hadn't been my girlfriend he was crushing on—I may have found it funny.

But it wasn't.

So instead, to rein in my anger I was clenching my fork and trying my damnedest not to bend it in half while we all sat around the table like a happy little family.

"So." Mo dipped her bread in the olive oil in the middle of the table and stuffed it into her mouth. "Any updates, Nixon?"

I shrugged and poured myself another glass of wine. "Nothing helpful. I've been looking through all the accounts from the De Lange family. The same as always. We're working on a hunch. We know my father didn't kill anyone, but that's it. We don't know anything else, and now that Trace's grandpa isn't here it's not like he can even help us. I mean, he'd die before we could even gain access to what we'd need."

Trace dropped her fork onto the plate. "My grandfather?"

"Yeah." I rubbed her back. "Trace, I'm sorry, it's just, he's the only one involved in this who wasn't still watching cartoons and playing with toy soldiers when everything took place."

She grimaced. "I wish I could be more help. I feel like everyone's risking so much for me and I'm not even doing anything to make it better. If anything it's worse."

"Whatever." Mo thrust her fork into the air. "Boots, things sucked before you came around. Nixon never smiled and I'm pretty sure if you hadn't have shown up Chase would have gotten one of his professors preggo."

"Thanks, Mo." Chase flipped her off.

"Whatever." Mo rolled her eyes. "This is our family. This is life, take it or leave it. If it wasn't you it would be something else, so for right now we just need to focus on..." Her eyes darted to mine. In fact, everyone's did. Right. No pressure.

"The past," I said slowly. "We need to focus on the past."

"Trace..." Tex leaned in and grabbed a piece of bread. "Do you remember anything about that night—?"

"Tex," Chase snapped. "Leave her alone."

Staying true to my ability to be a complete ass, I said, "I agree with Tex. Sorry, Trace, but we need to know. I know you were six, but do you recall anything at all? Any words your grandfather said to your grandmother? Anything in Sicilian?"

Trace looked down at her plate. "Guys, I wish I could help you but there isn't anything—"

She jolted out of her chair and ran out of the room.

"Well done," Chase snapped. "Cause her to have a nervous breakdown why don't you?" He threw his napkin onto his plate and stood just as Trace ran back into the room.

"This!" She held a small book in her hand. "My grandma kept this with her all the time. She even slept with it at night. Before she died, she said she wanted me to tell their story. How her and my grandfather met, but...the thing is...although my grandfather gave it to me, he never gave me the key."

"We don't need a key." I held out my hand.

Trace placed the small leather case onto my palm. It was secured with a pretty legit lock, but it was also really old. I pulled at the lock a few times.

Tex chuckled and said in a terrible impersonation of my voice, "We don't need a key."

I flipped him off and tried again.

"Idiots." Mo sighed. "All of you." She held out her hand. "Give me the book."

"Pardon?"

"Give me the book."

"What? You looking for a mirror? Mo, just let the guys take care of this one, okay?"

Trace slapped the back of my head so hard I could have sworn my teeth went numb. "Asshole, hand her the book."

Cursing, I dropped it into Mo's hands.

Tex chuckled. "Trace totally just proved her true heritage right there. I swear if I had a dollar for every time my ma smacked the back of my head—"

Mo did the honors that time, making Tex almost spill his wine as he caught himself against the table.

Tracey followed Mo to the breakfast bar, where Mo dug through her purse. She pulled out something small, and then fit it into the lock.

Three seconds later she was dangling the leather book in front of my face. "You were saying?"

"Girls rule, boys drool?" I offered sarcastically as I snatched the book from Mo and turned to the first page.

" 'Secrets are hidden in our past—they define our future. This, my love, is our story. In these pages you will find all you need to know. All there is to know. Always my love—Grams.' "

"Well." I turned the page. "That wasn't cryptic."

Everyone was silent as I turned to the next page and read aloud. " 'I saw him across the room—' "

Tex groaned.

Laughing, I continued. " 'I shouldn't have looked, but I couldn't help myself. He wasn't mine to stare at, yet I was still staring. And I knew...I would have him and damn your grandfather to hell. Damn him for keeping it from me, and damn him for buying my silence. I would be with this man, I would get back at the Alferos in the name of my family's honor—They destroyed what I had, and because of them, I refuse to keep my silence any longer.' "

I swallowed and closed the book. "Shit."

"Maybe this isn't the best thing to be reading..." Trace tried to grab the book but I snatched it away.

"We'll read every damn page. Together, okay? But we need to know what she knew, Trace. I know we're grasping at straws, but unless Phoenix talks or someone confesses, it's all we have."

Her gaze flickered to Tex's, Mo's, and finally Chase's. He nodded at me and then placed his hand on Trace's. "Nixon's right."

"Okay." She squeezed his hand and then turned to me. "But we read it together, agreed?"

"Agreed."

The book may as well have been a guest of honor. It sat on the table the rest of dinner earning curious stares from everyone, Trace included.

Finally, once we were done eating, I grabbed the book and nodded toward the wine. "Might as well make it a party."

"Thank God," Mo whispered. "I'm not sure I can make it through dirty laundry without wine and I know Trace is gonna need it. It's her grandmother, after all."

Trace smiled but didn't laugh. We walked into the living room and sat down, each of us with a glass of wine.

"Who wants to read it?"

"I vote Chase." This from Mo. "He always got straight A's in reading class and I've always wondered why the teachers found his voice so alluring…"

"I was seven." Chase glared.

"He started so young." Tex put a hand over his heart. "Now read, bitch. I have a seven a.m. lab to look forward to."

"Right away." Chase saluted and picked up where I'd left off. "'I followed him with every intention of propositioning him. I wanted to feel desire. Perhaps, the De Lange right-hand man could give it to me?'" Chase choked and closed his eyes. "Yeah, feeling like a perv right about now."

"Read!" everyone yelled in unison.

Chase cleared his throat and kept reading, "'He went outside. He lit his cigar in the shadows, and then I saw another person walk up. They exchanged pleasantries about the weather, and then he was handed an envelope. I remember thinking it was so strange, to be handed an envelope and not examine what was inside first? It meant they trusted one another. I had no way of knowing that the next day he would be dead. Nor that it meant my own husband would be blamed. My shame was exposed for all to see, for I had to tell everyone what I'd seen and why I saw it. I did not think he would ever forgive me. But he did and that's why I'm writing this story. To explain forgiveness to you, Trace. So you understand, that when you read the final chapter of this story, it does not mean the end for your family or for his. It is okay for you to love him.'"

Shaking, Chase set down the book and laughed awkwardly. "Um, any chance your grandma was psychic or something?"

Trace's mouth was still hanging open. "Um, no, no chance. What the hell?"

"Alzheimer's?" Chase pleaded, ignoring Trace's question.

"No."

"High? Was she high a lot?"

"Chase!" I smacked him. "Seriously?"

"How else would she know?" Chase pointed at the book. "How else would she know about you—"

"That's just the thing," Mo piped in. "How do we know it's Nixon she's talking about? And not Tex? Chase? Any guy?"

"Good point." I licked my lips and watched as Chase's eyes lit up. Oh, hell no. "But"—I cleared my throat—"chances are, she's just saying 'him' as an example, right? I mean, who knows." Chase handed the book back to Trace.

"Right," Trace whispered and held the journal close to her body. "I think we should all... go to bed. Maybe reading that first entry will help me remember?"

Tex yawned. "Fine, but if I dream of your grandma having sex, I'm coming into your room and firing a gun into the ceiling."

"You do realize that the bathroom is directly above her bedroom?"

Tex shrugged. "So pray I don't hit the toilet tank."

"Gross." Trace rolled her eyes while Mo hit him again and waved good night to everyone.

Leaving me, Trace, and Chase awkwardly looking at one another. Whoever said threesomes were a good idea was clearly deranged.

"I, um...I'll just be in the room." Chase brushed by me and jogged down the hall.

Tracey's eyebrows furrowed as she watched him run away like a scared deer. "Is he okay?"

I put my arm around her shoulder. "Of course. Why do you ask?"

"He's not himself." Her eyes met mine. "I mean, he's acting like he hates me one minute, then the next it's like he's going to break down and cry. Chase never cries."

"Chase never cries." I tilted her chin toward my face. "He's fine, I think the pressure's just getting to him. After all, he's trying to still pass his senior-year classes, protect you, and not have a nervous breakdown all before he turns twenty-two."

"But why aren't you acting that way?" Her face appeared so dejected. I couldn't tell her the truth—that Chase was acting that way because he was a man in a tough spot. And she was only making it tougher. I wasn't sure if I should just tell her in order to get her to lay off for a while, or just let things play out.

Her lips curved into a smile. "Something's on your mind."

"You." I kissed her nose. "You're always on my mind."

"Good." She hugged me and inhaled against my t-shirt. "Can we be together tonight?"

With a heavy sigh I shook my head. "Trace, I wish we could. I know our security is the shit, the house is on lockdown, we have men everywhere, but it's a huge risk. If something happened and you were in my room and someone happened to see it was me and not Chase? Yeah, I'm not willing to take that chance."

"Then why don't I just stay in my own room?"

I tucked her hair behind her ear. "Because, I don't trust any of my men as much as I trust Chase. He would take a bullet for you without blinking." Which both aggravated me and made me relieved. He'd do anything for her—I was counting on that loyalty to keep her safe from death—but from him? Jury was still out. At this point I didn't trust anyone. I just knew that if Chase was taking care of the love of my life, at least I could sleep at night knowing she wasn't in danger.

"But—"

I pressed my finger to her lips. "I love you. And I promise, this weekend, I'll find a way for us to be together. Would you like that?"

"Yes!" She pointed her finger in my face. "But it better be a date. A real date, with real food, and fun and—"

"Stop trying to tell me how to be a man. Pretty sure I rock at the date stuff."

She rolled her eyes. "Right, because last time we didn't get chased by men with guns."

I shrugged. "First date bad luck. Nothing more."

Her laughter was like balm to my damaged heart. "Fine, I trust you."

"Do you?" I grasped her hand within mine. "Trust me?"

"With everything."

"Your safety?"

"Yes," she breathed.

"Your life?"

"Of course."

"Your heart?" I whispered across her lips.

"You tell me, Nixon." She dipped her fingers into my hair and pulled my head down to hers. Her mouth met mine in a frenzy. "You're the one holding it."

I sighed in relief and kissed her hard on the mouth, pushing her farther into the hall where we were hidden from any windows and blanketed in shadows.

"You sure you can't stay with me?" She panted, reaching under my shirt and running her hands down my bare back.

"Believe me," I growled, nipping at her lips, "if I stayed with you, the freaking President of the United States would know something was up. When I'm with you, Trace. That first time. It won't be a damn secret. It won't be something we have to hide from the world. It's going to be life-altering, and you will be mine over and over and over again until the only word on your lips is my name. Got it?"

Her breathing picked up as she nodded and said in a hoarse voice, "Yes."

"Good." I exhaled. "Now I need to go take a cold shower."

"Need company?" She winked and swatted my ass before walking off toward her room.

"Tease," I called and went in search of some very, very cold water.

Chapter Twenty

Chase

I knew the instant she came into the room. It took exactly three seconds for her perfume to float from her body and into my personal hell.

I was lying underneath a giant white down comforter and trying to breathe in the smell of the laundry detergent.

"Chase?" she whispered.

Shit. I squeezed my eyes tightly closed and answered, "What?"

"I'm sorry."

"Huh?"

The light was off so I couldn't see her, but I knew she was close. Soon her cold feet were touching my legs as she got out of her bed and lay down next to me in mine. Thankfully, the comforter was creating a really nice boundary between her and my body. Otherwise... well, I would have probably died.

"For whatever I did to make you mad." Her hand reached out to pat my arm. "I'm sorry."

"Trace..." I groaned, "you didn't do anything." And that was the problem, wasn't it? My pride was hurt a bit; that much was sure. But, part of me, a small part—or maybe a large part—thought we had something. A connection that she and Nixon didn't have. What we'd shared over the past few months had been unique, different. I felt it and she didn't. She shouldn't be apologizing for being the strong one.

"Come here." Suddenly I wasn't so concerned with losing control. I was her friend, she'd put me in that zone, and the last thing she needed was for me to be an ass about her not loving me when her grandfather was stuck in hiding and her almost-rapist was chained to a chair on the grounds threatening to kill everyone. "I'm the one who should be sorry." I kissed her head and sighed when she wrapped her arm around my chest and tucked her head under my arm.

"What are you sorry for?"

Oh so many, many things. "Not being who you need me to be."

"You mean like earlier when you were being a jackass in your stupid Betty Crocker apron?"

Chuckling, I squeezed her closer. "Hey, don't hate on the apron. And yes, like earlier today. I guess…well I guess I'm just not used to all your hormones."

"What?" Her voice bordered on murderous.

I laughed. "Trace, I'm just used to a lot more violence and killing, and here you show up with a cow keychain, a fetish for every damn squirrel on campus and the ability to make me laugh my ass off, regardless of if you mean to or not. You're just…"

Amazing, she was amazing.

"Perfect, and your light kind of makes my darkness seem a lot more lonely."

"But you're with me twenty-four-seven?"

Yes, just another problem. "Right, but you aren't mine. Get it? It's like getting a present for Christmas only to find out someone's going to take it away on New Year's."

"What kind of present am I?" Trace laughed. "Come on, you can tell me."

"A bike." I shook with laughter. "Because I would ride you so hard that you'd—"

Her fist knocked the wind out of my stomach pretty effectively, ruining the arousal I'd had going for me about fifteen minutes ago.

We lay there in complete silence for a while, and then she said in a sleepy voice, "Don't leave me again, Chase. Please."

"I won't," I vowed. "I swear."

*   *   *

The next day didn't suck so bad. First of all, it was Tuesday so it was lab day for Trace, meaning I got to sit and watch her learn how not to do chemistry. The girl really needed to decide on a major soon. Those Gen Eds were going to be the death of one or both of us.

"You can't mix those." I reached out and took the beaker away from her and set it near the Bunsen burner that, luckily, wasn't currently on. Shit, at the rate she was going she was going to burn down the entire school.

With a sigh, she slumped onto her stool. "It's official. I hate chemistry."

Winking, I sat down next to her. "I got an A in this class."

"You slept with Dr. Stevens?" she gasped. "Chase Winter, shut up; you'll stop at nothing for a good grade, won't you?"

Scowling, I looked toward the front of the class, where a very old Dr. Stevens was writing on the Smart Board. "She's eighty."

"Players don't discriminate." Trace held up her hands in mock surrender.

"I earned the A; I didn't—do sexual acts for it. You seriously need to stop believing everything Tex says."

"Funny, that's what he says about you."

Things had been super easy with us all day. As long as I didn't touch her or think about the kiss, I was fine and I didn't want to jump headfirst out the window. I just hoped that Luca and the rest of his men weren't going to jump out of the bushes or question my relationship with her. We were hanging out enough to make it look real. At least I hoped we were.

The door to the classroom opened.

And in walked Luca. Shit, that only meant one thing. He'd gone above Nixon's head—directly to the school board. No way would Nixon let him in this place on a regular basis. Lucky for Luca, Nixon couldn't say a word against him without causing questions.

"Class!" Dr. Stevens whistled. "Today we have a special treat for all of you! Luca Nicolosi is a world-renowned researcher in the chemistry field. He will be here for the next month visiting family and has agreed to teach my Chemistry 101 class for the duration of the month. I, uh…" Her smile was forced. "As it is, I haven't taken a vacation in quite some time. It was perfect timing. Truly. Wonderful timing."

Shit. She was lying, trying to convince herself of the idea; that much was clear. I kept an indifferent smirk on my face as Dr. Stevens continued to fire off all of Luca's wonderful attributes.

Luca was brilliant. I should have seen that one coming but my focus had been on Trace, not on the Sicilian who snaked his way into our own private university.

When she was done, Luca spoke. "I'm honored to be here at Eagle Elite and have heard glowing reports of its student body. I'll be more than happy to share my knowledge with anyone willing to pursue a career in the interesting field of chemistry."

"Thank you, Mr. Nicolosi." Dr. Stevens cleared her throat. "Class will be dismissed a bit early today."

The room erupted into cheers as students gathered their things and headed toward the door. Trace reached for my hand. I squeezed it and put her bag on my other shoulder.

Luca watched us the entire way to the door. "Chase, Tracey, I look forward to seeing you in lab Thursday."

"That's if Tracey makes it that long," I joked and nudged her a bit. "Chemistry isn't her strong suit, almost burned down the classroom today, huh, babe?"

"Sorry." Trace nuzzled my neck and sighed. "Thanks for rescuing me."

"Well." Luca cleared his throat. "How very convenient that a senior such as yourself, Mr. Winter, was able to enroll in a freshman class."

"Damn convenient." I winked and kissed Trace's hand. "See ya Thursday."

I could feel Trace's hand shaking in mine even as we left the room. "He's still watching," she whispered.

We walked farther down the hall. "Now?" I asked, as we paused in the middle of the hall pretending to look in her bag.

"Yes."

"Damn." I grabbed her by the shoulders and slammed her against the wall—not hard, but hard enough to gain attention from passing students.

My lips were on hers in seconds. The only difference between last time and now—the girl was kissing me back as if her life depended on it.

Which in this instance, it did.

Her tongue touched mine, my body responded as if I'd just gotten electrocuted. I knew I had seconds, maybe a minute. I savored her taste. I plundered and pushed, and tasted, and sucked. I moaned when her hands tugged my hair. I about died when she bit down on my lip, and almost cried when she pulled away.

"He's not looking anymore," a male voice said behind me. Paralyzed, I watched as Trace's eyes welled with tears. And I knew, before I even turned around, that the voice belonged to Nixon and he'd seen every damn thing.

Chapter Twenty-One

Nixon

The shitty part was that I couldn't react. Chase hadn't answered my last text and I knew Trace's schedule like the back of my hand.

To say my heart was shattering into a million pieces would be a gross understatement. I'd never felt such pain as when I saw the fear in Trace's eyes as she clenched Chase's hand and walked down the hall. I watched Luca watch them and I knew it was bad. So bad, in fact, that if Chase didn't do something soon, to prove we weren't playing him . . . Well, things wouldn't be good.

He slammed her against the wall.

My girlfriend.

He took her hand, *my* hand, and pressed it high above her head, while he used his other hand to dive into her thick luscious hair. His mouth was on hers.

Her mouth was on his.

Tongue. Oh hell yeah, I saw tongue. Her tongue, to be exact, so I couldn't really get pissed at Chase. Shit, I knew what that tongue was capable of. It would bring any male to his knees. Which was why it surprised me to see Chase being so rough with her.

Not tender. And maybe that was the problem. An issue I'd have to talk to them about. He was aggressive; she tried to fight him back in the aggression. They weren't a team about what they were doing. Anyone with two eyes could see they looked like horny teenagers. But in love? No. Not at all.

I was both relieved and terrified.

And in that moment realized I had to talk, with both of them, but mainly with Trace. Damn if I didn't need to do what I'd promised I'd never do.

But if I was protecting her? If I was saving her life by driving her into another man's arms? Would that redeem me in the end? Or just damn us all to hell?

"He's not looking anymore." I smiled sadly at Trace as her eyes flickered to the ground. I could tell she was about two seconds away from bursting into tears. Chase looked like he'd just gotten a hit of heroin, his color was so high.

"Both of you. Bat Cave, now." I grinned for show, gave Chase a hard slap on the back and nodded to Trace.

Ten minutes later and we were all sitting in silence.

"That was…"—I whistled—"the worst acting I have ever seen in my entire life."

"What?" they yelled in unison.

"Yeah." I nodded. "As in, you guys couldn't even star in a porno, it was that bad. You guys are all…just wrong."

"Wrong?" Chase stood and began pacing. "I did the best I could—"

"I know what you were doing and I appreciate it. You guys do a really good job of acting like teenagers who've never had sex before."

Trace blushed while Chase just looked offended.

"He's a brilliant man." I ran my hands through my hair and looked between the both of them. "If he hasn't already figured it out, he will and soon."

"So what do you want us to do?" Trace whimpered. "I told you I'm a terrible actress—"

"Stop lying," I said calmly. "Trace, you love him. It's okay that you love him, I'm not stupid, you know."

"What?" A few tears fell down her face. "What are you talking about?"

"I don't want to lose you. At the rate you're going, you guys are going to get us all killed by not giving us the time we need to dig deeper. Everything is on you making this relationship sell. Okay?"

"But—" Trace's lower lip trembled. "We are trying!"

"No." I shook my head. "Who bought you boots, Trace?"

"What does that have to do with anything going on?" Chase yelled.

"Trace," I repeated. "Who bought you the damn boots?"

"Chase did," she whispered.

"Who saved you from ridicule at the welcome back party when I called you out in front of the entire student body?"

She closed her eyes as a single tear ran down her cheek. "Chase."

"Who protected you from Phoenix?"

Trace said nothing.

"Who never left your damn side when I listened to your grandfather's orders and pushed you away?"

And again with silence.

I had to get it out. I had to do it. There was no other way. "So as far as I'm concerned, it's always been Chase. It's never been me, Trace.

All along it's been him, and only him. From here on out, I'm the other guy, I'm the asshole who embarrassed you in front of your peers, the guy that threatened to destroy you. I am nothing, and Chase? He's your savior."

I walked out of the room and didn't look back. I couldn't. I knew if I did I would either fall to my knees and apologize for being so harsh, or cry for the first time since I was twelve.

I'd just singlehandedly given the love of my life to my best friend—on a silver platter, with a shiny bow attached.

And I didn't care if I died, but if Trace died? Because of me? Because of my pride and inability to get over myself? I would pray for death. So if it meant I had to give up the only thing that I was living for? It would be worth it. If she was safe. It would be worth it. I repeated that to myself for the rest of the night, and when Trace came home and said nothing over dinner. I said it again, and again, and when I opened that bottle of whiskey and sat in my room, I said it again.

Until I passed out.

*   *   *

I woke up with a killer hangover. My fault. Grumbling, I took a shower and went downstairs to get some breakfast before I went over to the Space to see if Phoenix would change his tune.

"Hey." Trace was sitting at the table eating some toast.

"Hey." I waved. Idiot. She was sitting right in front of me.

Her eyes didn't leave mine. I was frozen in place and could literally hear every beat of my heart in the silence.

"You're wrong, you know." She stood and walked toward me. "About a lot of things—everything, actually. And you're an ass."

"I—"

"I'm talking, you're listening." She smirked and grabbed the front of my shirt and pushed me toward the pantry. She slammed me against the door, pretty forcefully, I might add, and then opened it and shoved me in. I mean, I could fight her but I was too damn turned on and curious to do anything except stare at her.

"I. Want. You." She took off her shirt. What the hell? "Only you." Her jeans were next.

The pantry immediately became my number one favorite spot in the house.

Facing me in nothing but her scandalous white lacy underwear, she whispered in my ear. "This. What you see? What's in front of you, it's not just about me wanting you. I want all of you. I want to be vulnerable with you, exposed. But you have to let me...maybe the reason I don't want to open up that part of myself to Chase is because he isn't you, Nixon. He doesn't have this." She placed my hand on her bare skin right above her breast. Shit, I was slowly dying inside. Did she even realize what the hell she was doing to me?

"He doesn't have our history, our past, our drama. I love him, you're right. I love him so damn much that I can't imagine life without him. But he and I—we aren't this. So tell me, Nixon. Tell me if you want me to forget. I'll forget what we have, if that's really what you want. If you want me to jump into his arms without looking back, I will. But know I'll hate you forever for giving me up."

"I'm not," I interrupted her. "You can't give up something you never had."

She slapped me hard across the face. "You promised, Nixon. You promised me."

I kissed her hard on the mouth, clenching her wrists in my hands as I pinned her against the door. "You're right," I growled and pulled away. "And I'm sorry for hurting us, for hurting you, but Trace...next time you trap me in a closet, in nothing but your underwear. I will take advantage of you. I'll screw you until you forget your own name. Don't play with fire, and don't mess with me. I'm still terrible for you; he's better, and I stand by what I did. Now move out of the way before I truly lose control and steal your virginity next to the damn Cheerios."

She crossed her arms over her chest and glared as I sidestepped her and walked out of the pantry and directly into Tex.

"Whoa!" Tex looked at my face and then lower. His smile widened. "Taking care of business in the pantry or Mrs. Butterworth just make you horny?"

"Shut up."

"It's cool! She's naked, I get it!" Tex called after me, while I raced back up the stairs, grabbed my phone and keys, and then ran out of the house. Away from Trace, away from everything.

Chapter Twenty-Two

Chase

So you wanna talk about it?" I slid the cup of coffee across the table in the commons and waited for Trace to say something.

Wednesdays were always early days for Trace and her classes, but by the looks of it she got less sleep than me. She'd screamed his name last night. I pretended not to care, even when my heart threatened to break into a million pieces.

"No." She took my peace offering and grimaced. Her dark hair was pulled back into a tight ponytail. Her Eagle Elite white collared shirt was untucked from her skirt and she looked like she'd been crying.

"That's fine." I leaned back in my chair and watched people as they walked by, each of them staring at us as if me and Trace had some sort of disease. It had been like that ever since she'd enrolled this fall. People stared. I flipped them off, and oftentimes threatened their lives.

I glanced back at Trace and couldn't take it anymore.

"Fine," I grumbled. "I'm going to give you the damn speech."

"Huh?" Her head snapped up. "What speech?"

"The speech." I cleared my throat and reached across the table, engulfing her hand in mine. "Tracey, you're perfect."

"Chase?" She tried to pull her hand away but I gripped it harder.

"Choose me. Pick me," I whispered. "I'm better for you...plus Nixon's...too tall."

"He's too tall?"

"And buff. Do you really want a guy that looks that scary?" I shook my head. "Not gonna happen. So choose me. Be with me. Let me love you, let me protect you, let me honor you. Let me screw your brains out."

"Ass." She cracked a smile.

At least she smiled. I cleared my throat and released her hand. Walking over to her side of the table, I pulled her to her feet and tilted her chin toward me.

"I'll keep you safe."

"I'm not worried about my safety."

"I'll kiss you better."

"Again, not worried about kisses."

I sighed and with a shrug leaned in until our lips were inches from touching. Such sweet, painful agony. "Here's the thing..."—my bottom lip grazed hers—"Kisses are exactly what you should be worried about."

"Why?" She exhaled. Her top lip trembled as air escaped through her mouth.

"All it takes is one kiss. One kiss can save you. One kiss can ruin you for life. And my kisses? They better ruin you, Trace. Because if they don't, then I'm clearly not doing a good enough job, and let's be honest—I can't really act to save my life, so my kisses are exactly what you should be worried about." I trailed my finger over her lips.

"Because my kisses are real—they mean a hell of a lot more than yours, and from here on out—I'm not holding back."

I kissed her.

Not hard.

It probably didn't even look like a kiss. Our lips touched for the briefest of moments, but in that short connection of our mouths meeting, of exchanging the same air, I made a choice.

To share my soul with her. To be her everything—even if it meant I was going to get nothing in return—because I'd been given permission to do so—I decided I was going to steal her. No longer was it betrayal—it was survival.

Trace covered her mouth with a shaking hand and closed her eyes. "We should probably go to class."

Her cheeks were stained with a pretty blush. I nodded and grabbed her hand. I didn't ask for permission, I didn't need it. As far as I was concerned, she was mine to protect, mine to save, and mine to take. I was making it real—because to me it was.

"Chase, I—" Trace released my hand and then examined her own, as if it had somehow sprouted a face since coming into contact with my person. "I, um..."

"Spit it out, Trace, or we're going to be late," I joked.

"I don't know." She sighed. "I don't know if I can do this."

Without thinking, I tugged her arm and walked toward one of the large oak trees.

"I'm not him." I trapped her body with mine, noting how every time our bodies came into contact she literally trembled against me. "Look at me."

Her eyes flickered open. Torn. She was torn, and she needed to be sure.

"You can do this," I whispered hoarsely. "Because you love Nixon. Right?"

She looked away. Was that uncertainty speaking or just my own lame hope that she felt the exact same tug in the pit of her stomach that I did? Maybe it was ridiculous to wish for another person to feel as horrible as you did—but it's what I wanted. I was sick for her, and I wanted her to feel the same way for me.

"Right," she finally answered with a sigh. "But Chase...I feel like I'm betraying both of you. When I'm with him, I think of you. I wonder how you are, I worry about you, I love you—you know that. And when I'm with you...it hurts, it hurts so damn bad because it's like I'm taking a knife to his heart every time it's your touch instead of his."

"Well damn." I chuckled to myself. I mean, really, what else was I supposed to do? Cry?

"What?" She pushed against my chest. "This is serious. Why are you laughing?"

I shrugged. "It was a nice speech."

"Thanks but—"

"I'm gonna beat it, so watch out." I silenced her with my lips. She tasted like mint and coffee. Tenderly, I coaxed her mouth open with my tongue. Her mouth was like velvet—every single damn part of my body was hit with adrenaline—so hard in fact that I braced my hand against the tree, allowing my body to push against hers.

"Don't fight it," I mumbled across her lips. "For once, just stop thinking, and don't fight it, Trace. It's just you and me. There is no mafia, nobody's out to kill us, and we aren't putting on a show. We're making out, behind a tree, at college, like normal college students do." I gripped her hands and helped her wrap her arms around my neck and I pushed her a bit harder against the tree. The feel of her body pressed against mine almost made me pass out. I groaned as she began playing with my hair and then her tongue was in my mouth.

In my mouth.

Her hands. In my hair.

Her body against mine.

We broke apart. Her eyes weren't condemning, she didn't freak out. Instead, they softened as she laughed. "That was a damn good speech."

Grinning, I pulled her into my embrace and kissed her forehead. "And people say I'm all action, no talk."

"Um, no." Trace laughed against my chest. "People say you get too much action. There's a difference, Chase."

"Details." I sighed and kissed her forehead again. It was like I couldn't stop myself. It felt so real, so right.

"Thanks." She sighed. "For saying all those things, for being so… great. I swear I'm probably the last person you want to have to be with for all of this."

My smile faded. "What do you mean?"

"Admit it." She punched me in the arm. "I'm going to kill your game for the rest of the year if people think we're together."

I tripped as I backed away from her. Was she shitting me? She thought I was seriously just saying those things to say them?

"No wonder girls fall all over themselves for you, Chase Winter. You kiss like a god and you make girls forget you're a player."

Shit. Well played, Trace. Well played. There went that damn friend-zone shield she was so fond of.

"Class?" She gripped my hand first this time.

"Um, sure, yeah. Let's go to class." And pray I didn't pass out from exhaustion and lust before we got there.

Chapter Twenty-Three

Nixon

I was still reeling from my encounter with Trace and Mrs. Butterworth that morning. Damn, I'd never look at syrup the same again.

Unfortunate that Tex would probably never let me live it down, either. The bastard. I walked across campus to the Space and unlocked the door to the warehouse.

Blood was caked on Phoenix's face from our last meeting. You'd think his expression would be less smug, but if anything it got worse. I pulled up a chair and sighed.

"So…" I popped my knuckles. "Sleep well?"

"Like a baby."

"You ready to talk yet?"

"No."

"Thought so." My knees cracked as I got to my feet and slowly walked away from Phoenix. I reached into my back pocket and pulled out my knife. The light from the one window caught the edge of it, making it shimmer in the otherwise dark room. "What is your life worth to you?"

"Nothing. Either way I'm dead."

I nodded. "What if I tell you I'll put you into hiding? I'd do it, you know. Not because I'm particularly fond of you, but because I need to know what the hell is going on and you seem to be the only one stupid enough to rat people out to save your own damn hide."

"True." Phoenix smirked. "But this is bigger than you, Nixon. It's bigger than us."

"What's that supposed to mean?" I slammed the knife down onto the table.

"It's not even about us. It's about them; it's about him and what he did. Shit, you don't even know what I know. Believe me, if you did, you wouldn't trust Chase as far as you could throw him."

"Chase?" I shook my head. "What the hell does Chase have to do with anything?"

"He has everything to do with it. Every damn thing goes back to your family. The Abandonatos. How many people do you think... died to protect the secret? Hmm? Your father took it to his grave; your mother, bless her heart, never got a chance to tell you the truth; and now the one person who knows..."—he chuckled and winked—"won't tell a soul."

"How do I know what you're saying is even true? And why the hell would someone be stupid enough to tell you?"

"I wasn't told. I overheard."

"From?"

"Nope." Phoenix laughed. "Does it kill you that I know something you don't? That your family's dirty little laundry is going to die right along with me? Maybe that's a good thing. We don't want to mess with the way the family does things."

"I'll kill them all," I said softly. "Every last one of your family members. I'll kill them."

"Do it. I dare you."

"You shouldn't encourage me. I'm teetering on the edge of insanity right now."

Phoenix shrugged. "First, the Nicolosi family would find out you've been offing my family members. Second, it's almost impossible to find all of them, unless you plan on hacking our accounts and seeing where we send payments in order to buy silence. You see, in our family, money talks...probably because it's scarce."

I grinned and stuffed the knife back in my pocket. "Thanks, Phoenix. Great doing business with you."

His smile fell.

"I'll send Tex over to throw a bucket of water onto your face so you can clean up a bit. Wouldn't want any of those cuts getting infected."

"I could die and you'd probably smile while performing my eulogy." Phoenix spat.

I paused, my back to him as I sighed. "You're wrong. You were one of my best friends. When my dad beat me, you told me not to cry. When I told you I wanted to kill him, you said you'd get me a gun. When Trace was taken from me, you told me she'd come back. And now? Now all I see is my *ex*-best friend." I turned around and faced him. "You look like the Phoenix I grew up with, you sound like him; hell, you've always walked around like the world owed you something. I just don't know how the hell we got from there to here. I never wanted this. I would have never chosen this for either of us."

Phoenix closed his eyes, and when he opened them it was almost as if there was a chasm between us. His choices, my loyalty to Trace, our past demons—there may as well have been a lifetime of separation from the door to the chair.

"I didn't want it. But I was given no choice. He took it from me the minute I found out the truth."

My heartbeat picked up. "Who? Who told you?"

"I know I'm an ass." Phoenix licked his dry lips and broke eye contact. "And I know what I did to Trace was unforgiveable. Jealousy's a bitch and all that, but honestly, the only way I can atone for my many sins is to keep you the hell away from him, away from the truth. I'm taking it to my grave not because death sounds like a really fun idea, but because the second I tell you anything, I damn you and the rest of your family along with me. He'll stop at nothing."

"But—"

"Just say thank you." Phoenix laughed bitterly. "For saving your sorry life."

I swallowed. "That's just the thing. It was never supposed to be at your expense."

"Better mine than yours," Phoenix growled. "Leave me alone, Nixon. Go home to your perfect life, your beautiful girlfriend and loads of money. Go home, and if you come back, you better be prepared to shoot me in the head."

I closed my eyes. I couldn't look at him when I promised... "I'll discuss it with the rest of the Elect."

"Not good enough!" Phoenix shouted, his voice hoarse with emotion. "When we made our little club, we promised. If any of us got into deep shit, if any of us were putting someone else in danger, we'd shoot them. Do me the favor. Drown me, for all I care. But shoot me before they get the information because I don't know if I'm strong enough, man. I don't know if I'm selfless enough. Damn, I know I'm not selfless enough to crack even though I know I'll still die. So, when you come back, bring your gun and some prayer beads."

"All right." I slammed the door before I could go back on my word.

We'd made that contract, the Elect contract, when we were teenagers. We knew the family business, saw lots of our uncles and friends die for information or die because they were rats.

We knew what happened to them when they were tortured.

One night, Phoenix had walked in. Blood caked his fifteen-year-old hands.

"I killed him."

"What?" I grabbed some old clothes from the floor. "What do you mean, you killed him?"

"Uncle John." Phoenix sniffled. "I killed him. Dad said it was time to break me."

"Break you?" I repeated. "As in—"

"Time to learn the business." Shaking, Phoenix fell to his knees in front of me, tears streaming down his pale face. "I didn't want to hurt him, but Dad said we had to silence him for what he did."

"What did he do?"

Phoenix shook his head. "I don't know." He wiped his sleeve across his nose and sniffed, "It must have been really bad, though."

"I'm sorry, Phoenix. What can I do?" I put my arm awkwardly around his shoulders and sighed.

"What if that's us?" he whispered. "That could be us. What if I trust the wrong person and get killed? What if I do something to piss my dad off, or worse, your dad?"

I cringed, because I'd thought of that exact same thing over and over again until I could no longer sleep at night.

"I don't want to die that way, Nixon."

"What do you mean—?"

"They beat him!" Phoenix's lower lip quivered. "They beat him in front of my aunt and then…I beat him because they told me to and she…" He began to hyperventilate. "She told me it was okay. She handed me the gun and—"

"It's okay." I patted his shoulder. "You don't have to talk about it."

"It's not like TV, Nixon. It's not." He began rocking back and forth. "There's so much blood and it's quiet, Nixon. It's so damn quiet when someone dies. It's just like, all of a sudden, their eyes have no life and there's blood, and people started talking about the game last night as if someone didn't just die."

He looked up at me. "Promise me something…"

Tex walked into the room with Chase; both of them looked from Phoenix to me then back to Phoenix.

"Anything." I knelt down on the ground and faced him.

"We make a pact. The four of us." Phoenix looked up, his eyes glassy from crying. "If any of us get into deep shit, regardless of if it's our fault or not, we do the person the favor of killing them. I don't want to die a rat. I don't want to die like that, Nixon."

I glanced at Chase. He nodded once and pulled out his knife, slicing open his palm and then handing the blade to Tex.

"We promise," I said, slicing my own hand and shaking each one of their bloody hands before wiping my own blood onto my jeans. "A quick death."

"In the head," Tex agreed.

"It's done."

Phoenix nodded and rose to his feet.

I'd made him a promise. Funny thing was, I had totally forgotten about the promise and now that Phoenix had reminded me, I knew I couldn't go back, not on a blood oath, no matter how old I was when I made it.

I sent a quick text to Chase.

BATCAVE

He replied right away.

OMW

The only good part about my day was that I was going to see Trace again, but technically that could be defined as bad, considering I'd pushed her almost-naked form away from me this morning.

Shit, she'd looked good.

Damn.

Hell.

There weren't enough curse words in the world to describe how irritated I was with my decision to push her into Chase's arms. But really, what choice did I have?

I needed her alive more than I needed my next breath. Even if it meant she would never be mine. I needed her to be okay.

I went into the Elect hangout and rummaged around in the fridge for a sandwich.

Giggling interrupted my hunt. What the hell?

Whispers and then more giggling.

I shut the fridge and walked over to the spare bedroom and opened the door.

"Tex?"

Tex tumbled out of the bed, using the sheet to cover his body. I rolled my eyes and was briefly traumatized over the fact I was about to see my sister naked, when...my eyes saw blond hair, not brown.

"Son of a bitch," I yelled and lunged for Tex. His eyes widened briefly before he backed up.

"Wait!" He put his hands up. "I can explain."

"Make it fast." I clenched my teeth and leaned in. "Because I'm about five seconds away from murdering you!"

"Mo knows!" Tex held up his one hand in front of himself. "We broke up! Okay?"

"So if I call her right now, and ask her if you guys are dating, she'll say no?"

"No." Tex cursed. "Because we decided this family had enough drama going on, without us adding to it."

"I still don't believe you." I crossed my arms. "You've been sneaking in and kissing and—"

"Wow, you really don't know your sister as good as you think you do."

"I have a gun," I pointed out. "Don't piss me off."

"Go away!" Tex yelled at the girl in the bed. She grabbed her clothes and scurried out of the room as fast as her bare legs could take her. Tex sat on the bed and cursed. "She's scared shitless, man."

"Who is?"

"Mo!" Tex yelled. "See? This is what I mean! Everyone's so damn worried about Trace and her grandfather and Luca, but shit, Nixon! Your sister just lost her father a few months ago. You're all she has and you aren't making it better by acting like you're five seconds away from losing it whenever we're all together."

"I don't know what you mean—"

"Shut the hell up," Tex snorted. "I've known you since we were three and were forced to play in the same sandbox. You're freaking out over Trace and I bet you aren't sleeping, not with Chase in the same room as she is."

Damn him for knowing that.

"Everything's under control," I snapped.

"It's not!" Tex sighed. "Shit, I'm like one day away from stealing pot from one of my dad's men just so I can get high and pretend I don't have something stuck up my ass."

"Good plan." I sat on the bed and faced him.

"Clearly, I haven't thought it through," Tex grumbled. "The point is, I stay with Mo every night because she has nightmares. She's scared, Nixon. We all are. It's not just about you and Trace. It's about all of us. Someone's leaking information and until we find out who betrayed whom and who's talking... we're all on the chopping block."

"He's right," Chase said from the doorway. Trace was standing behind him, a confused look on her face.

"He's naked." Trace pointed at Tex as he covered himself with a sheet and cursed.

"Shit, man." Chase chuckled. "Didn't know you'd be desperate enough to switch teams since you can't have a girlfriend anymore."

"Shut up," Tex and I said in unison.

Still laughing, Chase nodded to Tex. "I take it you and Mo aren't an item anymore?"

"Who says 'item'?" Trace nudged him from behind and rolled her eyes. "And no, they aren't an item, weirdo. They're on a much-needed break."

"Thanks," Tex interjected. "I knew Mo would tell you."

"I know all." Trace sighed.

I shoved my hands in my pockets and looked at all the expectant faces. Even though Trace wasn't technically part of the Elect, anything that happened with Phoenix directly affected her.

I walked to the door and shut it, cloaking all of us in silence as I ran my fingers through my hair and cursed. "Phoenix wants me to kill him."

"Do it," Chase snorted. "No, actually, allow me."

"That sly son of a bitch," Tex snorted. "He's calling up the oath we made that night, isn't he?"

"Yup." I bit down on my lip ring and glanced quickly at Trace. It was impossible to read her expression, but if I was a betting man, I'd say she was pissed.

"We made that damn oath when we were fifteen." Chase moved to stand in front of me. "No way in hell am I being that kind to him, not after what he did."

"We"—I enunciated my words carefully—"made an oath. Regardless of age, we keep our promises. He wants us to return tomorrow. He's going to die either way."

"What?" Trace pushed Chase out of the way and approached me. Was it my fault that the minute she stepped within arm's length it took every ounce of willpower I had not to pull her into my arms and kiss her senseless? Damn, I missed her touch. I missed just being by her. It was killing me slowly from the inside out. "Why would he die either way?"

"Someone has something over him," I answered honestly. "The way he tells it, he found out some information he should have never known and because of the knowledge he has, he'll die either way. He's afraid that if it gets into the wrong hands it won't end well for any of us."

"Well, great." Trace put her hands on her hips. "So what do we do?"

Shit. I hated bringing her into my world, into my darkness. "We do what he asks. We kill him."

"Tomorrow," Tex agreed. "After our afternoon classes?"

Trace sighed. "You guys talk about death like it's a doctor's appointment or something."

"Death always is," I mumbled. "An appointment, I mean. We all have our time. Sometimes it's not up to us to schedule it, sometimes we miss it, and other times..."

"Someone carries it out for you," Chase finished.

Our gazes met.

Shit, as if I didn't have enough stress in my life, he was looking almost...happy. There would be only one reason he was happy. Trace.

I looked between the two of them. Trace leaned her head on Chase's shoulder and I had to look away. If I continued to stay focused on them then I wouldn't be helping my family. I'd be useless.

"I need to go look over the accounts again for the De Langes. I still feel like I'm missing something." I scratched my head and bit down on my lip. "I'll see you guys back at the house tonight."

I walked out of the room as fast as I could.

"Nixon," Trace called from behind me. So close.

"What's up?" I turned around and tried to smile, tried to look happy and indifferent when really my heart was slamming so hard against my chest that I was afraid she could hear it.

"Thank you…" She swallowed.

"For what?"

"For stopping at nothing to protect me." She laughed awkwardly and looked behind her. "But mainly, for loving me." Her eyes welled with tears. "So damn much."

I closed my eyes for a brief minute before opening them. Only this time I saw Chase come up behind her and wrap his arm around her shoulders.

"I have to go." I nodded to Chase and winked at Tracey before I walked briskly out of the room. Forcing myself not to cut off Chase's hand as my mind replayed images of it touching her soft shoulder.

Chapter Twenty-Four

Phoenix

Damn, I hated the silence, almost as much as I hated my own reflection. It was the eyes that did it. I knew mine looked like hers used to, like they should be full of life, but instead of light—utter darkness.

I was going to die. But at least they'd be safe; at least I wouldn't go to Hell wishing I would have done something to redeem what happened. If I died, the secrets died with me, meaning they would never know the truth. But in the end, if I told them it would be like putting giant targets on all their backs.

Better it be me than them.

The pact we'd made so long ago suddenly seemed like the best option. I'd take a bullet in the head at the hands of my three brothers over getting beat within an inch of my life by him any day.

I just hoped they'd be good on their promise. I was banking on it; otherwise there was going to be a hell of a lot of blood and it wasn't going to be just mine.

A cold chill wracked my body. I couldn't huddle to gain warmth, I couldn't move to the corner of the room to protect myself from the draft, and in that moment I realized that's what my life was. I'd been tied to a chair of my father's own choosing, but I'd been the one to lift my hands up in surrender. And with my surrender I gave everything, hoping to protect those I loved—and to protect myself.

I laughed—really there wasn't anything else I could do. I was freaking freezing my ass off in that stupid room because Nixon had, most likely on purpose, left the air-conditioning on full, and all my brain did was replay memories and choices over and over again, making my stomach recoil with disgust.

I imagined Hell was a lot like what I was currently experiencing. I thought of Mil, my stepsister. When things went to shit, I knew she'd be okay. I'd sent her everything she needed to know—I'd trusted her above all else and in return she'd promised she'd stay in hiding. Damn, I was lucky the girl had balls of steel—because she was the only one in the entire freaking universe that knew the truth about me, about Nixon, about Trace's parents—and I hoped to God in the end—once the bullet was lodged in my head—she'd find a way to save our families before it was too late.

Chapter Twenty-Five

Nixon

I made it as far as my Range Rover before I felt my control snap. I punched the driver's seat five times as hard as I could with my fist...it didn't help. I needed a baseball bat, or something; everything was so messed up and I didn't know how much longer I could handle being around her—around them—before I blew my own cover.

"Remind me to never piss you off," a voice said from behind me.

I turned to see a woman about my age with chestnut hair and bright blue eyes. She was wearing an Eagle Elite uniform but I'd never seen her before in my life. "Can I help you?" I asked, trying my best not to sound scary.

"Depends." She put on a pair of black sunglasses and walked over to me. She was tall for a chick, probably around five-ten.

"On?" I leaned against the SUV.

"On you, I guess." She reached into her red leather purse and pulled out a small flash drive. "Take it."

"Why?" I paused before taking the drive into my hand and shoving it into my pocket. "What does it have on it that I need? The answers to my final at the end of the semester?"

"Well, you're right about part of that." She sighed. "You'll find some answers, but they won't be what you expect."

"Oh yeah, and why's that?"

The girl sucked in a breath and then fell against me. I caught her around the waist, and my hands came into contact with blood. Lots of blood.

Mind going into overdrive, I quickly lifted her into my arms and put her in the backseat of the SUV. She'd been hit in the back, but I couldn't tell exactly where and I wasn't taking any chances.

I quickly dialed Uncle Tony's number as I drove to the nearest hospital.

He answered on the first ring.

"Yes, Nixon?"

"Minor problem. Some random girl just gave me—"

"Gave you what, Nixon? I don't have time to hear about your extracurricular activities."

Remembering the way he'd acted earlier, I lied. "She said she had information to give me...but she was shot before she could say anything. I have her with me right now. I'm on my way to the hospital—"

"No, Nixon. We'll take care of it."

"She could die," I ground out through clenched teeth. "I'm not letting one of our own take care of her. She needs a hospital, not some cousin who used to be a surgeon back when he was still able to see straight without a bottle of liquor."

"I said"—Uncle Tony cleared his throat—"we'll take care of it. We can't have any loose ends. We have no idea who she is, and we cannot alert any of the cops. Gunshot wounds are basically like waving a red flag in their eyes. They'll investigate and they'll stop at nothing to get to us."

"I know that," I yelled. "Don't you think I know that? But what if—"

"Nixon." His irritation shone through the way he said my name, as if it was a curse word rather than an identifier. "For once in your life, just listen to someone who's older and has more experience than you."

"Fine," I snapped. "I'm on my way."

I hung up the phone and turned toward the bank. Most of the family would be there working, meaning that by now Tony would have told them what was going on and how they needed to prepare.

"Don't," a raspy voice said behind me. "Don't take me to him."

I ignored her plea. Hating myself the entire time.

"He'll kill me."

"You're dead either way," I said as softly as I could.

"I can help you."

"You almost died just trying to help me. Correct me if I'm wrong, but if that's the type of help you're offering, I think I'll pass."

"Fine." Her voice was getting weaker. "Just tell him I'm sorry I failed."

"Who? Tell who?" I pulled up to a stoplight and turned around.

She smiled sadly. "Tell Phoenix I failed."

"Phoenix? How the hell do you know Phoenix?"

"I thought you didn't want my help." She grimaced and reached behind her. "Thank God. I think the bullet just grazed me."

Biting on my lip for a second, I thought of what I needed to do. Damn if the web wasn't getting more tangled. With a curse, I pulled off to the side of the road and turned around. I pulled out my gun and pointed it at her head. "If you're dead either way it shouldn't matter, right? Now, you have exactly five seconds to plead your case, or I shoot you here. And I promise you, what I have planned is kinder than where I'm taking you to."

"I know who killed Tracey's parents."

I pulled back my gun and stared at her. "Fine. Who killed them then?"

"Your father."

I pointed the gun back at her head again, this time with the intention of shooting her, except she shook her head and looked almost . . . sorry for me. Which was weird because she was the one who was going to die.

"Not the father you've always known, Nixon. Your real father."

Well, shit.

I pulled the gun back and shot her in the foot. I needed more blood in order to prove my case.

She screamed in pain and fell back against the seat. "What the hell was that for?"

"If you're lying"—I shrugged—"you know I'll be good on my promise to end your life. If you're telling the truth, I officially have to lie for you and put you into hiding. Now, take off your clothes."

"What?" She began to shake. Great; now she was going into shock.

"Don't make me repeat myself. Take off your damn clothes." I put my gun away and held out my hands so she could hand over her clothing.

Fumbling with her shirt, she pulled it off over her head and followed suit with the rest of her clothes, until she was lying there in nothing but her bra and underwear.

"ID?" I held out my hand.

Closing her eyes she thrust her purse forward. "You really are a bastard, aren't you?"

"Aw, people been talking about me, sweetheart?"

She shivered and then cringed. "People say you're the devil."

"I'm much worse." I fumbled through her purse and pulled out her ID and nearly passed out when I read the last name. "Emiliana De Lange?"

"Pleased to meet you…"

"But that would mean…" *Shit.* "You're Phoenix's stepsister."

"Ah yes, the redheaded stepchild the family doesn't like to talk about. Yes, that would be me. Now can we please hurry before I pass out? I'm really close and as much as I'm enjoying being naked in your backseat, we have to go."

"Phoenix isn't going to like this."

"Phoenix can go to hell. I'm saving his sorry ass!" Emiliana yelled.

With a curse, I got out of the car and grabbed the bloody clothes. I put them in the trunk with her ID and then pulled out a blanket so she could wrap herself in it.

I hopped back in the SUV and made a beeline for my house, dialing Uncle Tony on the way.

"Where the hell are you?" he yelled.

"Lake Michigan. She didn't make it. I did what I had to do."

"Any ID on her?"

"Nope, but she did say something about someone wanting to kill her. Any ideas?"

Tony sighed. "How am I supposed to know? This business is delicate. Did you burn the clothes?"

"On my way to do just that. She's sinking so fast, I doubt they'll find her. I'll let you know if I have trouble cleaning up."

"All right, Nixon."

"Bye."

I hung up the phone and slammed the steering wheel with the palm of my hand.

"Thanks." Her voice was getting weaker. I really needed to pull the bullet out of her foot. Well, first things first. We had another person to hide. But first, I was going to find out what she knew. Apparently, I was a bastard. Great. Add that fun fact to my list of damning qualities.

If the father I'd hated my entire life wasn't my real father, then that begged the question, who was? Because right now...it also meant...I wasn't the boss.

I never had been. I'd just been allowed to play the part—why?

Chapter Twenty-Six

Chase

Nixon needs us." I grabbed Trace's shoulder bag and pushed her toward the car. "Like, right now."

His text had seemed frantic. Some of the words were even misspelled.

We drove in silence out of the school lot. We hadn't spoken that much since the kiss or since our encounter at headquarters. Damn, I just wish I knew what she was thinking.

I reached across the console and grabbed her hand.

She squeezed back and didn't let go.

Not when we drove into Nixon's driveway.

And not even when we walked to his door.

She was trying.

And I loved her even more for it.

"Honey, I'm home!" I announced when we walked in the door. Nixon was covered in blood and drinking straight-up scotch. What the hell?

Next to him were some bloody clothes, a purse, and—my eyes fell to a girl. A nearly naked girl lying on the floor. She was bandaged up.

"Who the hell is this?" I pointed at her.

She turned to face me, her eyes wide with horror. In an instant she had pulled Nixon's gun from the table and pointed it at my face.

I already had my gun pointed at her.

Nixon smirked.

Trace released my hand and stepped away.

"Chase, meet Emiliana De—"

"I know who the bitch is!" I yelled.

"Chase." She smirked. "Just relax, you need to let the past be the past." Her chestnut hair hung in waves over her bandaged but otherwise naked back. I had to look away before I did something else stupid.

Memories came flooding back to me. Shit. It had been so long ago. I didn't think I'd ever see her again—no one did.

"No." I laughed bitterly, bringing my gun back up to aim it at her. "What I need is to put a bullet through your head."

Nixon burst into laughter. "Chase, sit down, have a drink. You too, Trace. Let's drink to our misfortune." He looked wasted already.

"Have you lost your mind?" I stood in front of Trace, blocking her from seeing both of the insane people in the room. "She's Phoenix's stepsister, and why in the hell is she nearly naked?"

"I know." Nixon winced as he took another sip of scotch. "Tell me, Chase. How was your sixteenth birthday party in Vegas?"

"Son of a bitch." I shook the gun in the air. "Seriously, Mil? You told him?"

She grinned. "Let it go, Chase. It was one time, and I didn't even tell anyone…"

"Until now," I grumbled, setting the gun on the table. In a moment of pure stupidity I had slept with Phoenix's sister. I blamed

Vegas. I didn't know at the time, but she was fourteen. Meaning it was like two kids going at it. Everything that could go wrong went totally, and I mean totally, wrong. It was so damn embarrassing that I made her promise not to tell anyone. Which had worked out just fine until her mom found out and sent her to reform school shortly after.

It didn't help matters that Phoenix had walked in on us. I earned a black eye and bloody lip. We ended up in a fistfight while Mil was taken away in a car, never to be seen again. Phoenix and I swore we'd take it to our graves. Guess the secret was out.

With a wink she set her gun on the table and took a seat.

"Who's the whore?" Tex asked as he charged into the room, gun raised.

"What is with you people and guns?" Trace waved her hands in the air. "Put it down, Tex."

He glared.

Mo followed close behind and took in the scene. "We going shooting or something?"

"Or something." Nixon nodded. "Let's just say 'or something.' Unless Chase really wants to shoot Phoenix's stepsister."

"I *knew* you looked familiar!" Tex slapped his leg and let out a laugh. "What happens in Vegas stays in Vegas, eh, Chase?"

I groaned into my hands and briefly contemplated turning the gun on myself if it meant I would be able to escape past memories, regrets, and embarrassments.

Mo giggled behind him. Oh great. "Does everyone know? Seriously?"

"I didn't." Nixon held up his right hand. "Swear. I didn't know anything until she told me and I'm pretty sure it was the painkillers talking."

"I plead the Fifth on why y'all have drugs in the house." Trace groaned, plugging her ears.

Rolling my eyes, I pulled her fingers out of her ears and looked at Nixon. "It's three in the afternoon. Why the hell are you drinking?"

He shrugged as he took another sip, eying Trace the entire time. What the hell was he planning?

"I need to know you guys will protect Emiliana." He set the glass down and folded his hands. "Regardless of what happens to me, promise you'll protect her."

Trace snorted. "Um, you do realize Chase was just holding a gun to her head five seconds ago."

"Oh that." Nixon grinned. "He misfires all the time, doubt he would have met his mark, huh, Chase."

I gripped the table so hard I'm surprised it didn't crumble beneath my bare hands. "Seriously? What the hell is wrong with you?"

"So many things." Nixon took another sip, and his eyes glazed over as he looked out the window. "Just promise me."

"Fine." Tex put his hands out between us. "We'll protect her. We'll figure something out."

Something was up. Nixon wasn't acting like himself, he was acting like . . . shit, I don't know, like the world was ending, like we were somehow losing, like he was going to die or something.

"Is that all?" I asked. "All you needed from us."

"Yup." He took another swallow of scotch. "She'll be staying with us for a while."

"Okay." Trace sounded confused. She looked between me and Nixon.

"Perfect." Nixon pushed away from the table. "I, uh, have to go see about something. Trace, can I talk to you for a minute?"

"Sure." She eyed me before looking back to Nixon.

"My room," he said. "Alone."

I'd be lying if I said I wanted her to go. I had no idea what the hell was going on but for the first time in my life, I didn't trust Nixon to not do something stupid. He had that look in his eyes, the same look he'd had when he was a kid watching his dad beat his ma.

Reluctantly, I watched Trace follow Nixon down the hall and close the door.

"Bet you wish you were a fly on that wall," Tex mumbled.

"Shut up, Tex." I grabbed Nixon's empty glass and the bottle of scotch and poured myself a healthy dose.

Chapter Twenty-Seven

Chase

I eyed the scotch on the table and poured myself a healthy dose of liquid and tossed back the contents, all before taking a seat next to Mil's spot on the floor.

"So." She tried her best to cover herself with the blanket but failed miserably. I hated myself that I was actually staring. But I was a guy; who would—*could*—blame me? I couldn't decide if I was more embarrassed of the past we shared or the fact that everyone else in the room most likely knew about my feelings for Trace, too, and pitied me while I sat on the floor with the girl I'd lost my virginity to. "You look good."

"I'd say the same"—I cursed and pulled the blanket around her—"but you look like hell."

She shrugged and pulled the blanket higher, exposing her foot. "Did you get hurt?"

She took the drink from my hand and motioned for me to pour her more scotch. After she took a sip she sighed. "Nixon shot me."

"In the foot?"

"Yup."

"Why?"

"To prove a point, the jackass."

I tried to hide my smile. "He may be an ass but at least he's protecting you. Why is he protecting you, by the way? And why are you here? Aren't you supposed to be at some boarding school in Florida?"

"Not when I'm needed here." Her eyes drooped as did her hand. I reached for the glass and set it on the floor.

"Mil," I urged, trying to use a nice voice considering I'd just had a gun aimed at her face. "What's wrong?"

"You have any regrets, Chase?"

Um, seriously? I looked back down the hall. *Regrets*. Nice, I freaking hated that word. It seemed to define everything that was happening in my life lately.

I regretted that I loved Tracey.

I wished I didn't.

But I did.

I regretted that I'd do anything to have her.

And I regretted that in the end, it was Nixon in that bedroom and not me. So I answered, "Sure, I think everyone does."

"I have lots."

"Am I one of them?" I joked.

She laughed. I'd forgotten how pretty her laugh was. It was what attracted me to her in the first place. She'd always laughed like she didn't give a rat's ass if people heard her. She'd throw her head back and put her entire body into it; her entire face lit up like a Christmas tree and I was drawn into her web. Scary that some fourteen-year-old girls are born to look more like they're twenty-two.

"Nah." She looked up with her bright blue eyes and shrugged. "You weren't a regret."

"A mistake?"

"Yeah, I'll drink to that." She laughed again. For some reason it made me feel better, like if I focused on my past, my future wouldn't look so bleak. "I hated you for a long time, Chase Winter."

"Hated, as in past tense?"

"Oops, I slipped. I meant 'hate.'"

"Noted."

"You seduced me."

"I was sixteen and it was hardly a seduction, Mil. You knew exactly what you were doing."

"Clearly, you didn't."

"Very funny."

She licked her lips. "I don't regret you, Chase, so stop feeling sorry for yourself. And if you look down that hall one more time I'm going to smack you."

"I'm that obvious?"

She shook her head. "You're pathetic. Sure you don't want me to shoot you and put you out of your misery?"

"Ask me later." I took another drink of scotch and winced.

"I regret not being there for him," Mil said in a quiet voice. "I regret that when he needed me most, I didn't believe him. Not until it was too late."

"It's never too late, Mil." I put my arm around her. "I promise, there's always a chance." I had to believe the words I was saying, because if I was wrong then that meant my future was just as bleak as hers. Wow, we really were pathetic.

"You talking about Phoenix?" I asked after a few minutes of silence.

"He's my stepbrother." She yawned. "And I think I'm too late. I don't know if Nixon can fix it."

"Fix what?" My hair stood on end. What did she know that I didn't? "Mil?" I shook her a bit. "If Nixon can fix what?"

"Do you think we go to heaven?" She'd changed the subject again. Clearly the drugs really were kicking in.

"Mil?"

"Nixon said yes." Her eyes fluttered open and then closed. "If he can't fix it, I hope he does."

"Does what?" I whispered.

"Go to heaven." And then she slumped against me.

With a curse, I rose to my feet and picked her up into my arms. I wasn't sure where Nixon was keeping her, but I knew she'd have one hell of a headache if she slept on the floor like that. So I walked her into the room next to mine and laid her down on the bed.

It really was a shame I was in love with someone else.

Because I needed some female companionship.

Not that Mil would offer.

Shit, how lucky was I? The one girl I loved didn't even know it and sure as hell didn't love me back like that, and the only other one I could trust with my secrets and lifestyle wanted to shoot me in the face.

I backed out of the room and walked slowly by Nixon's.

It was the silence that did it for me.

It killed me inside.

And then I heard Trace laugh.

And I felt like I had been killed all over again. How many times can a guy experience death before he's ready to allow it to consume him? I went in search of more scotch and promised myself I'd try harder with Trace. I'd make her want me. I'd make her choose me.

In the end, I was better for her. She just didn't see it because all she could see was Nixon, but if I could change that…If he could just…stay out of the picture like he'd promised. We'd have a chance. In the end, hurting her, in order to gain her? It seemed like it was worth it. I knew being away from Nixon was difficult for her—but I couldn't give a damn if he stayed away forever. Because he was stealing my reason for living. And when she was gone, I wouldn't feel so much like living anymore.

Chapter Twenty-Eight

Nixon

Emiliana's information felt like it had left a burning gaping hole in the back of my brain.

Not my father, not his son. Not who I thought I was. Talk about a major identity crisis. It didn't help that Angelo had nothing on Uncle Tony. Nothing sketchy. The man was squeaky clean. He went golfing in the afternoons, drank brandy at night, made sure to check in with his many businesses and went to bed at eleven every damn night.

Something wasn't adding up and I knew that I couldn't figure it out on my own. I needed help and a plan, one that would potentially hurt me more than anyone. But it was hopeless. Knowing what I did—my future was hopeless. And if I didn't do something soon— Trace's would be, too.

It was harder than I thought it would be. Damn, I wanted to wake up from this nightmare. But no matter how hard I shook my head, how many drinks I had, my reality was the same.

I was going to go for broke.

I had one trick, and one trick only; and after hearing everything Emiliana had to say, I knew—my real father? He'd stop at nothing to gain control of the family, and now it was time to flush him out.

"I need your grandmother's diary," I told Trace.

"What?" Trace smiled. "I thought we were going to all read it together."

"That was before."

"Before?" Her eyebrows arched in question. "Before what?"

"Before now." I shrugged. "May I please have it? I promise I'll return it as soon as I can."

"Why do you need it?"

"I can't tell you that."

"How long will you have it?"

"I can't tell you that, either."

"Nixon." She said my name like an expletive. "What the hell is going on?"

Oh nothing...just lots and lots of lying, death, love, tragedy. Forget TV. This was way worse.

"The diary has some information in it, a few missing pieces that I need to put together."

"So it's like a puzzle piece." She chewed her lower lip and walked over to my bed. I caught a whiff of her sweet perfume as she sat on the end and folded her arms across her chest.

"Kind of." I shrugged.

"Okay." She didn't look at me. "You can have the diary—"

"Thank you." I exhaled in relief.

"But." She looked up at me. "I want something in return."

"Didn't know we were negotiating." I chuckled. "What do you want?"

"I want you to hold me."

Stunned, I stared at her. "I'm sorry, what?"

Trace stood and grabbed my hands. "Call it paranoia, but...I feel like something's wrong. You aren't acting like your bossy self."

I looked away but she grabbed my chin and forced me to look at her. "It's bad, isn't it?"

Unable to lie, I nodded my head. "Yeah, Trace. It's bad."

"And my grandmother's journal will help you?"

"It helps my case, yes. I promise I'll bring it back—and put it where I'll always be. By your heart."

She shuddered. "And if it doesn't help your case? What happens?"

I'd ruin everything if I told her the truth. It had to happen exactly as I'd imagined it in my head, but damn if I didn't feel the walls closing in as I watched her watch me. I'd always wondered what it would be like, to say good-bye to someone you loved, knowing good and well that you'd never be able to feel the warmth of their skin on yours ever again.

I didn't want this for us. I *still* don't want it for us, but to save her—well, I'd go to the ends of the earth if it meant protecting her— if it meant fighting this battle for her. She could point a gun at my head and I'd still do it. I'd still fight as long as I had energy to do so... After all, if something doesn't cost you absolutely everything—did you ever truly love it in the first place?

She would cost me everything I had.

And that very fact put a smile on my face. Was she worth it?

I gave her a sad smile. Hell yeah, she would always be worth it.

"Trace." I cupped her face. "I need you to listen to me."

"Nixon, you're scaring me."

"Don't be afraid." I kissed her forehead. "I need you to trust me, okay?"

"Okay."

"I love you."

"Nixon, I—"

"I'm not finished." I pressed my finger against her lips. "I would die before I let anything happen to you, but—"

"But?"

I smiled. "But, sometimes in life, things don't end how we want them to. Sometimes, what we want to happen and what has to happen are two very different things."

"Nixon." Her lips pressed against mine, softly, and then more urgently as she grabbed me. "Please don't leave me, please. I don't think I can take it if you do. I don't know what I'll do if you leave."

"Who says I'm leaving?"

"Your eyes," she whispered. "You're saying good-bye. Damn it, Why are you saying good-bye?"

I sighed, touching my forehead to hers. "Sweetheart, I'm only going away for a while, okay? Remember that. If you remember nothing else, remember that. I'm going away. But I'll always be here." I pressed my hand to her chest. "And when the time is right..." I kissed her lips and then grazed them with my fingers. "I'll be right here, kissing you, loving you, being with you and only you."

"Swear it." Trace wrapped her arms around my neck. "Swear it or I swear I'll hunt you down myself."

Laughing, I kissed her nose. "I swear it.

"Good-bye." Emotion clogged the back of my throat.

"Bye." She closed her eyes and kissed me hard on the mouth.

"Good-bye, good-bye, good-bye," I repeated over and over again as I lifted her shirt over her head and helped her pull off mine.

We didn't speak.

I wasn't sure I could say anything. I was afraid to ruin the magical moment that we were currently living in.

She knew.

I knew.

And we needed each other more than anything else in the world.

Just this once...after all...every man on death row gets one final wish, right?

I tugged her down onto the bed and hovered over her. Trace reached up and trailed her hands over her favorite tattoo. I closed my eyes. Her touch was almost like a burn, so powerful, so perfect.

Kissing her neck was my perfection, my last meal, my last drink, my last everything. I wanted to memorize the exact moment my lips touched her neck, the exact minute she screamed out my name.

The second she found her pleasure.

Her lips found mine again as our tongues twisted together, fighting, coaxing, tasting.

More clothes were discarded and then it was pure skin. Hot, soft skin pressed against all of me.

"Are you sure?" I whispered.

A tear streamed down her face as she nodded. "Yes."

Maybe I shouldn't have been that selfish. To take the one thing I knew she had to offer another man. But I *wanted* it. I wanted her and if I couldn't have her forever, I at least wanted a part of her that would be no one else's.

I wanted to hate Chase in that moment.

I wanted to hate him for being able to touch her in places I wouldn't be able to. I despised that it would be his lips that kissed the part of her hips where her long legs met the rest of her body, where her soft curves invited and begged a man's touch. Promising him nights of pleasure.

"I love you." I gripped the headboard and looked down at her. "I love you so damn much."

"I love you, too." She arched beneath me and pulled me down to her.

*   *   *

We stayed in my room the rest of the night. I knew Chase assumed what was going on and was probably either drunk or just really pissed off.

At two a.m. I needed to go. I grabbed my stuff and the journal Trace had given me permission to use.

One final kiss on her shoulder, and I was out the door. I got into my car and started it.

Did I have the balls to do this?

No.

But my heart left me no other choice.

I sighed as the smell of Trace floated around me. I shouldn't have done it. I should have allowed her to freely give her heart to someone else, because if things went badly, she'd forever hate me for stealing that one thing that some other man should have gotten.

A battle raged inside of me. I felt guilty and thankful at the same time. I didn't want to be that guy. The one that pressured a girl into sleeping with him by saying lame crap like, "If this is our last night together…blah blah blah." No, hell no. It was so much more than that. It was my own selfish need to know that for the rest of her life, she would remember me. I had this paralyzing need to mark her as mine—even though I knew in the end the odds weren't in favor of us—but of them.

Girls always remembered things like that.

Their first kiss.

Their first time.

Only usually, good girls, girls like sweet innocent Trace, gave that first time to their husbands, and only them.

I wondered if she'd be thankful or upset.

I couldn't find it in my heart to regret what I'd done, because I truly was hanging on to every ounce of love Trace gave me, to get through the night. To do what I had to do.

It was my death row.

My last sentence.

I prayed.

Maybe God truly was that forgiving, that after all the sin I'd committed in my life for my family, in the name of blood—he'd still be gracious enough to protect her while I knew I couldn't.

The drive was short. As those drives typically are, the one time you want to dally, and all the lights are green and there's no traffic.

Campus security was high as per my instructions. I unlocked the Space and let myself in. I couldn't kill him, but there was something else I could do.

Chapter Twenty-Nine

Phoenix

The door handle turned. So this was it. I was going to die. I wish I could say I wasn't terrified. Would it hurt? Would I even feel pain and fear? Or would it be over so fast that I'd just feel nothing but my body finally resting? Nixon walked into the light. He had a garbage bag in one hand and his gun in the other.

"Phoenix." Nixon said my name slowly, purposefully. Aw shit, he'd come alone. Which meant I was going to get a hell of a lot more than a bullet to the head. Visions of knives, bloody knuckles, and syringes came to mind.

"Nixon." I couldn't help the shaking in my voice. I knew what was coming, I wasn't totally fearless.

"I'm giving you one last chance to tell me the truth."

"Never was really good with the whole honesty thing." I smirked. "I think I'll take my chances with death."

"Damn it!" Nixon kicked the table next to me and then with a curse threw it over onto its side, causing dust to explode into the air. "Why is it," he said, voice strained, "that out of all the shit we've been through—now's the time you've decided to develop a conscience?"

I shrugged, trying to act indifferent.

Nixon gripped my shirt and pulled me to my feet then slapped me so hard across the face I felt it all the way down to my toenails. The sting throbbed as he pushed me backward, making the chair that was attached to me twist my arms in such a way that I'm surprised nothing broke.

I'd seen Nixon pissed and I'd seen him calm as hell when he was interrogating, but this side of Nixon? It was nothing short of desperation.

"I can't," he finally whispered under his breath. "I'm sorry, Phoenix. I know I promised you, but I can't."

With a final shake of his head he walked over to the exposed bathroom in the corner and began grabbing towels. He ran water into a large bucket. Seconds later he was dumping the bucket over my face, and for a second I thought he was going to waterlog me. It took me a few minutes to realize what he was actually doing—cleaning me up.

We in the family had always been strong Catholics, but never in my life had I ever understood the absolute humility of washing of a sinner's feet—until Nixon began cleaning the wounds on my face.

Words wouldn't form on my lips as he continued to clean my cuts. He moved to my hands next, wiping the mixture of dirt and blood. He didn't say anything and I still wasn't able to talk without losing my shit, so I sat.

Funny, when you've hit rock bottom, you never imagine someone may throw you a rope. But that's what he was doing. Nixon looked into my watery pit of despair, and rather than killing me inside it, he offered a life raft, one I didn't deserve.

"So." Nixon dipped the washcloth into the bucket and wiped my cheek one last time. "Someone will be here tomorrow to…"—he shrugged—"see you."

"The guys," I answered, finding my voice.

Nixon didn't answer. He untied my hands and pulled fresh clothes out of the trash bag, tossing them at my face. "Put these on, then sit back down."

My hands shook as I slowly peeled the bloody clothes off my body. My movements felt slow and awkward; my wrists hurt like hell after being bound. When my dirty clothes were off, I took a seat on the metal chair and slowly pulled the fresh-smelling hooded sweatshirt over my head. The jeans were another matter entirely. I winced as pain shot through my hands at having to pull the rough material over my exhausted and mangled body. What should have taken me seconds took at least ten minutes, but I hadn't felt that clean in days.

Nixon pulled a granola bar out of his pocket and handed it to me. What the hell was up his sleeve? Either he was fattening me up before death or he really was a freaking saint. Damn him.

I basically swallowed the granola bar whole and waited for Nixon to grab his gun again. Instead he cuffed me back to the chair and walked toward the door.

"Is that it?" I called. "You're just going to leave?"

His hand was on the doorknob. Without looking back he answered, "You were one of my best friends, Phoenix."

"What's your point?"

"Every friend deserves to die with a little dignity, wouldn't you agree?" He turned, meeting my gaze.

"Not me."

He smirked. "Well then, thank your lucky stars I'm not the one making calls on Judgment Day. Try to get some sleep. You've got a long week ahead of you."

"I look forward to our bloody meeting tomorrow," I called back.

Nixon's face fell. With a nod he opened the door and left. Confused as hell, I could only sit and wonder why.

Chapter Thirty

Nixon

I pulled up to the building and made it three steps before I heard the sound of footsteps lightly tapping against pavement. It took less than a few seconds for his men to grab me by the arms and drag me the rest of the way to the large wooden door.

"What do you want?" a man in a thick accent demanded.

"He's here for me," a crisp voice said from the doorway.

I looked up into Luca's eyes. "That I am."

"Do you have what we discussed?"

"Right here." I pulled out the journal. "Let's talk inside."

He nodded and we walked into a small kitchen.

Luca poured me a large glass of wine. "You work faster than I expected."

"I had help." I sighed and pointed at the journal. "I'll keep your secret if you keep mine." It sounded like a taunt, when it was more like a plea.

"And what do I have to gain in this little exchange?"

I took a large gulp of wine. "You've been trying to cover it up for too long, Luca. At least admit that much."

"It has become...trying."

"She should know you're her great uncle."

"Trace does not need to know these things. It is best to keep them...private."

"Like how you fell in love with her grandmother? Things like that?"

Luca slammed his fist onto the table. "That woman should have left well enough alone! To write about it in a diary is beyond my comprehension."

"Wasn't as if she could tell anyone." I sighed. "But, you have the diary, you have something you need...and I still have a problem."

"The killers? You haven't found them?" Luca paced in front of me. "I thought that you were coming to celebrate! Finally, we can put the past behind us, yes?"

"Soon." I drummed my fingertips on the countertop. "I have discovered some information about my parentage."

"And?" Luca took a seat. "Why does this concern me?"

"Because my real father killed Trace's parents."

"I see. And who is he?"

I played with the stem of my wineglass. "You wouldn't believe me even if I told you. I need more proof than someone just telling me. I need to catch him."

Luca nodded and took a tentative sip of his own wine. "You mean to catch the fly."

"I mean to make such a damn good web that everyone within forty square miles will know he's a rat, but it's complicated."

"Our business always is."

"Right."

Luca pulled out a cigar and sniffed it. "Let us speak plainly. What can I do for you, Nixon?"

My heart hammered in my chest as I looked into his eyes and said, "I need you to kill me."

Chapter Thirty-One

Chase

I watched him leave and did nothing. I wasn't sure if I had a right to be pissed; after all, technically they were dating, right? Or were they? Even I was confused at this point and all I really wanted to do was drown myself in a bottle of something.

She was in his bedroom.

Sleeping.

And I knew I had to go get her and bring her into her own room. How could he be so careless? What if Luca would have come by? It was strange that Nixon would just leave her in the bedroom without telling anyone. What if they had eyes on the house? Or worse yet, what if they had someone on the inside watching the whole damn time? Shit.

I walked into the room and lifted Trace into my arms. I covered her as best I could and set her carefully onto her own bed, then lay down next to her.

Well. Nobody ever said life was fair and by the looks of it, I'd been dealt a pretty shitty blow.

Nixon had slept with her and then left.

Nixon didn't do things like that. *I* did things like that. The feeling in the pit of my stomach didn't dissipate.

Trace moaned next to me. She moaned his name, not mine, and the knife went deeper into my heart.

"Sleep, Trace. It's okay, you're safe." I tucked the blanket around her body and sighed when she turned to me and wrapped her arms around my stomach, thinking I was him. And for the first time in my life, I wished I was.

*   *   *

I awoke to a loud banging on my door. The clock on the desk said seven a.m. Who the hell would be waking us up this early? And how did they get in? Tex knew not to pound on my door that early and Nixon—well, I guess he could be pissed.

Sighing, I swung my feet from the bed to the floor to stand when the door burst open.

"Dad?" I rubbed my eyes. "What the hell are you doing here?" Normally my dad was good about texting or calling before he stopped by, so as not to get shot on the spot. We never took any chances—even with family. Which meant only one thing. Something was wrong. Maybe Nixon let him in? I shook my head to clear all the thoughts swarming around.

His eyes fell to Trace and then back to me. She was starting to wake up, but no way was I letting my dad see that she was barely wearing any clothes. I pushed her down and covered her further with the blanket. "Nixon?"

"No." I swallowed the emotion in my throat. "It's Chase.

"Dad, can't you see I'm a little busy?" Irritated, I glared at him and then pointed back at Trace.

"*This* could not wait." His eyes looked tired. Bags hung beneath his lashes and the lines around his mouth seemed more pronounced. He'd always been a good-looking man, but right now he just looked old.

"What is it?"

He kept looking at Trace. Why the hell was he looking at her? She was covered in blankets, for crying out loud! I sighed. "I don't have all day."

"It's Nixon."

I could feel air in the room tense around me. It was one of those moments where it literally felt like time stood still. I watched my dad flinch as I looked down at Trace and then back up into his eyes. *Please God, I didn't mean it. Please let him be okay.* I finally found my voice and asked with a croak, "What about him?"

"He's dead."

Chapter Thirty-Two

Chase

How we treat the dead says an awful lot about how we live. For the strong and able to serve the helpless dead..." I choked on the word "dead," and my hands shook as I continued reading, "to honor the frail remains..." My eyes fell to Trace, her body was slumped against Tex, her eyes hollow, as if her soul had gone to the afterlife right along with Nixon. "...Reaches deep inside us to something basic to humanity—Paul Gregory Alms."

Early afternoon light danced around the Holy Name Cathedral, almost as if mocking the darkness around everyone. There was standing room only. In the two days it took for us to plan the funeral, never once did it occur to me that it would be such a public affair. Families traveled from Sicily to offer their condolences. And people I hadn't seen in years were coming up to me and shaking my hand, as if that made it better. A damn handshake? To bring back my best friend? Hell no.

Mo had wanted me to give the eulogy. I didn't deserve the honor—hell, I didn't even deserve to be in the same room as Nixon's casket. I'd tried to go through the motions, making decisions for Mo, but I was dying inside right along with her.

"Nixon was my best friend." I licked my lips. "He was one of the good ones. The type of guy you never wanted to piss off but, at the same time, wanted on your team. Everything he did was for others. 'Selfish' was never a word in his vocabulary. I think, if we take anything away from his unnecessary death, it's that he lived life to the fullest, but he lived it for others." My eyes locked with Trace's. Tears poured in rapid succession down her cheeks. "He lived for those he loved, he died protecting what was most precious to him. And for that, he earns a place in heaven, because when it came down to the very end, he was willing to sacrifice everything for family—for blood. I don't know how long I'll be on this earth, but my prayer is that I go out just like that—fighting for the only true thing in our existence."

I folded the paper and stuffed it back into my pocket. Taking the steps two at a time, I made my way to Trace's side and sat. She gripped my hand so hard I winced. I hadn't left her side since we received the news a few days ago, and I sure as hell wasn't going to leave her side now.

The rest of the funeral was depressing as hell. I watched as the priest said a final prayer about not understanding the ways of God, but it was seriously falling on deaf ears.

It was like his mouth was moving but I couldn't understand the words coming out of it. I tried to stay strong on the outside. I put my arm around Trace and held her close. She was shaking in my arms. I wanted to fix it.

I was so damn pissed at Nixon. How could he go and die on us? With every fiber of my being, I wanted to jump into that damning hole and open the casket. I wanted to shake him, I wanted to hear him yell at me and tell me to do my damn job.

But he was dead.

And I was alive.

Holding his girlfriend.

Mo was inconsolable. She leaned against Tex and refused to even look at the casket. She hadn't eaten all morning and kept saying that if Nixon had died she would have felt it—apparently it was a twin thing. When one was in danger the other felt the loss.

It took us two hours to convince her he was gone. Even then, she refused to believe us and began screaming his name up and down the halls.

Trace locked herself in the room.

Between the two of them, I was ready to lose my damn mind, not to mention the fact that I'd just lost my cousin and best friend. I was a wreck, ruined, and I wasn't quite sure I'd ever be the same again.

Apparently Luca had lied to all of us. Nixon had gone over to plead our case, and offered himself up like a lamb to the slaughter.

Mafia lesson number one, don't do the noble thing. You'll just end up dead. Nixon wasn't stupid. He'd known it was a suicide mission, but he went anyway, leaving me to pick up the pieces.

According to my dad, he'd confessed to his own father murdering Trace's parents and said he sought punishment for all wrongdoings. Luca had said a life for a life, and he'd meant it. He meant to make an example out of Nixon—out of all of us.

One bullet to the head. That was all it took. The sick bastard even did it from behind. Nixon had to know it was coming, though. Anyone with a brain would have. And he'd just stood there…he stood there and did nothing. He took the fall.

The morning of Nixon's death my dad received a package with a picture of Nixon's dead body. The ring he used to wear—Nixon's family ring—was enclosed.

I was in such denial that I didn't believe it, not until my dad showed me the picture.

When the priest finally stopped talking, we all got up from our seats and slowly followed the crowd outside. The procession to the gravesite was so long that the police had to direct traffic. Trace and I rode in silence the entire way. I didn't know what to say to make it better—nothing would make it better and that was the problem. A piece of her was missing, buried in the cold, wet ground, and I was left trying to fix a heart that was broken in half.

*   *   *

Later that evening when we finally returned from the funeral, I ran to the bathroom and lost everything I'd eaten that day. I'd never been so violently ill in my entire life. I was in the bathroom for an hour before Tex finally came in to tell me that Trace needed me.

I found her in the corner of the room rocking back and forth. She was staring at the damn picture. Who had been so careless as to leave it on the counter in the first place?

Guys always have this insane need to fix things. I wanted to pick up her heart and hold it in my hands. I wanted to revive her, but how do you revive someone when your own heart is breaking at the same time?

"Trace?" I knelt down in front of her and pried the picture from her hands. She wasn't crying, which freaked me out. Shouldn't she be crying? I mean, I had even cried.

"I don't understand," she whispered.

I pulled her onto my lap and held her. "I'd be lying if I said I did, Trace. I have no idea what the hell he was thinking."

Seriously. What. The. Hell. Was. He. Thinking.

He took her virginity. At least I'm assuming he did, and then he went and got himself killed? Knowing full well that going to see Luca made that a huge possibility.

For once in my life I was so ridiculously pissed at him. Angry that the one guy who'd been a selfless monk for the past few years had done something that rash and stupid.

Which just proved again how desperate he'd been for any piece of Trace to take with him into the afterlife. And if I was completely honest with myself, I would have probably done that and more. And I wouldn't have regretted a damn thing. Not that I could tell her that.

"What do we do now?" Her voice was so quiet. Shit, she was freaking me out.

"I don't know," I answered truthfully. "Go to school, pretend like we aren't dying a little bit every minute he's not with us. We live, we move on, and we make him proud." Geez, I sounded more together than I felt.

She nodded and then a tear slipped down her cheek, followed by more. Her arms went tight around my neck as she sobbed. "Don't leave me, please don't leave me. I can't—Chase, I can't do it. Please, please, please!"

Her teeth began to chatter as she clung to me for dear life.

I held her so tight it was hard to breathe. "Never, Trace. You hear me? I'm never leaving you. Got it?" I gripped her as hard as I could and crushed my mouth to her cheek. It was impossible for me to show her how important she was to me—how keeping her safe and happy was my number one priority.

"Say it again. P-please say it again."

I pried her arms from my body and cupped her face with my hands. "I swear to you. I will never leave your side."

"Okay." She exhaled a shaky breath. "Okay."

I have no idea how long we stayed like that, but it was long enough for my legs to fall asleep and for Trace to stop hiccupping.

"Chase?" Tex knocked on the door and let himself in. "We need to take care of something."

"All right." I helped Trace up and led her to the door. "Go hang out with Mo. I'll come get you in a bit, okay?"

I could tell the last thing she wanted me to do was leave; her eyes begged me to stay, but this was the job. Death or no death, we had a job to finish. Finally, she nodded and walked off like a zombie down the hall.

"Hell," Tex muttered under his breath. "I don't know how she's able to even function at this point."

"Shock," I muttered. "Not the choice I would have made, Tex."

"Me either." His brow furrowed. "But since he's gone, we need a new boss. There's some confusion on who's next in line so while the men discuss and meet, we need to go take care of one final loose end."

"What loose end?"

Tex cursed. "Phoenix."

"I hate this family. I hate what they've made of us. We're too young for this shit." I scratched the back of my head and walked to the kitchen counter to grab my gun. I checked to make sure it was loaded and put on the safety.

"I'm going with you," Mil piped up from behind us.

"No." I stuffed the gun in the back of my pants and pulled my shirt over the gun to cover it.

"Yes." She slammed her hand on the countertop. "He's my stepbrother. He's...he's family. Just let me go with you, please?"

"So you can save his sorry ass?" Tex spat.

"So I can save yours, you prick." Mil pushed against Tex's chest and then turned to glare at me. "Family sticks together, and I'm the only sure thing you guys got right now."

"How do you figure?" I snorted.

Grinning, she pulled out a note from her back pocket and handed it to me. It was in Nixon's handwriting. Holy shit.

"Because," she said with a sigh, "he left instructions."

I almost didn't want to open the letter. Shaking, I handed it to Tex and told my stomach to stop heaving, otherwise I would pass out from lack of food and dehydration.

"What's it say?" I asked as Tex opened it. His grin grew as he continued to read, until finally he started laughing. I couldn't tell if it was hysterical laughter—you know, the kind of laughter people get when they're about to lose it—or if he really just thought the letter was funny. He wiped at his eyes. And handed me the letter.

"See for yourself, but Mil's coming with us."

I snatched the paper out of his hands and scanned it.

"'She's a smart bitch. Protect her at all costs. Where you go, she goes. She'll help you put Phoenix into hiding. It's the only way. I'm sorry—for everything. Nixon.'"

I laughed, but mine was more bitter, more painful. If I listened really carefully I could almost hear Nixon's voice in the room, and that sucked. He didn't deserve any of this.

His entire life had been spent protecting others and in the end, when it was our turn to protect him, when he needed us most—we'd failed.

"Let's go." Tex grabbed the keys. I followed him with my head down. I didn't feel like I could meet anyone's eyes and not want to shoot myself. Was it just last week that I was contemplating betraying Nixon just because I was in love with what wasn't mine?

Yeah.

It should have been me. I should have taken the fall, because in the end, Nixon had more to lose and I had nothing. What a freakishly depressing thought.

Chapter Thirty-Three

Chase

You'd think I would have calmed down a bit by the time we reached the Space, where Phoenix was being held.

I hadn't.

I wanted to shoot something—anything.

If a squirrel were to cross paths with me, it wouldn't end well for it. Hell, if a spider looked at me funny I was going to end it with a bullet.

"Wow, nice setup." This from Mil as we let her into the room and flipped on the lights.

Phoenix was sitting in the chair as if he'd been waiting for us.

He looked good. Why the hell would he look so good? Hadn't Nixon been torturing him? And why did his clothes look clean? And why in the hell was he smiling at me?

Before I could process the ramifications of my actions, I stalked toward him and punched him so hard across the jaw that he fell over in his chair.

"Shit," Tex grumbled behind me. "We're supposed to help him, not give him a concussion."

Mil walked up beside me. "He probably deserved it."

"And more." I reached down and yanked up Phoenix's chair, setting it to rights with him still in it. Grunting from how heavy it was, I was already beginning to sweat when his eyes met mine, with a burning question.

"You're either still pissed about me and Trace, or you have rage problems."

"I'd bet on both." Mil smiled at Phoenix. "Hey, brother."

"Mil." His eyes narrowed. "You look old."

"Thanks. You look like hell." She reached down and squeezed his chin between her fingers, examining his face. When she was done she jerked her hand away, pulled a gun out of her back pocket and shot at his feet.

"What the hell, Mil!" Phoenix yelled.

"Just checking to see how your reflexes are." She winked.

Tex chuckled next to me. "Is it wrong to be turned on right now?"

I rolled my eyes.

"So." Phoenix licked his lips. "Who's gonna do the honors? And where the hell is Nixon?"

"Nixon isn't your concern." Voice hoarse, I cleared my throat. "Not anymore, at least. And although I'd love to do the honors and shoot you in the head multiple times, this one over here"—I pointed to Mil—"apparently has information that can save you. Only, by my count she has about ten seconds to spill it before I kill both of you." I turned to Mil. "So. Talk."

Mil rolled her eyes. "Chase. Always so dramatic."

Phoenix exhaled and looked at Mil. "Nothing you know can save me."

"Watch and learn, big brother, watch and learn." She pulled out her cell phone and dialed and then said, "We're ready."

Within seconds a knock came at the door. What the hell? Nixon always had cameras locked on the place. Any time anyone as much as breathed near the building it would send us a text alert. The electricity was still on, so why weren't the cameras working? Or the alarm system? Did Mil know about the security?

"What the hell?" I grabbed her arm. "If you've double-crossed us, I will kill you, no hesitation."

She jerked free. "Nixon said to trust me, so you either listen to him or you betray your word."

Shit. Did she have to use the word "betray"?

I nodded and crossed my arms as she went to the door and opened it.

Nothing could have prepared me for what I was about to see.

Frank Alfero walked in with Luca in tow.

"Are you freaking kidding me?" I yelled, about one minute away from charging the man responsible for my cousin's death.

"Mr. Winter, please control the level of your voice." Frank patted me on the back and approached Phoenix. "You will still pay for what you did, for what you tried with Trace."

"I know," he whispered.

"You will help us...hunt."

Phoenix's head snapped up. "What are we hunting?"

"A rat." This from Luca.

I couldn't look at him. If I did, I would shoot him and that would just make everything worse. Why the hell was he even still here? It pissed me off that in our world, killing was as normal as eating breakfast. I was supposed to be calm. It was how everything worked. I knew the rules, but damn if I wasn't itching to end Luca's life. He'd taken my mom and now my cousin. But what hurt the most was that he'd ruined Trace's life. I would never forgive him for that.

Maybe he sensed my irritation or just felt the anger I had toward him. He turned to face me. "A life for a life, Mr. Winter. You are lucky that your friend took the fall for the lies told."

"You son of a bitch!" I charged him but Tex wrapped his arms around me as my muscles flexed in protest, and held me back.

Luca laughed. "Is that how you treat someone who is helping you? Name-calling and empty threats will get you nowhere, Mr. Winter. We work together or we leave you to pick up the pieces of your broken family."

"Together." Frank was already taking the cuffs off of Phoenix's wrists. "We work together, and expose what should have been exposed long ago."

Luca's eyes saddened. He approached Mr. Alfero and put his arm around his shoulder. "For what it is worth, I am sorry."

"So was she," Frank mumbled. "So was she."

"Holy shit!" Tex dropped his gun to the floor with a loud clatter. "Holy shit!"

"What?" I hit him. "What's wrong with you?"

"You guys are..." He pointed at Mr. Alfero and Luca. "You guys are—"

"Brothers," Phoenix grumbled. "They're brothers."

I looked at the two of them. How had I not seen the resemblance before? It was uncanny. Obviously Frank was older by a good fifteen years, and they both had the dark hair, though Frank's was sprinkled with gray. They had the same blue eyes, nose, chin. Really, it was strange to see.

"But..." My mind was unable to work that fast. "Phoenix, how did you know that?"

"Phoenix made his money as an excellent spy. Didn't you, son?" Luca spat. "Going through Trace's things, reading the personal journals. Then, in an instant of trying to discover everyone's dirty little secrets, you saw something. Something you were not supposed to see. And that's the problem with spying. Eventually you will be caught."

Wordless, Phoenix hung his head.

"And your father paid the price with his very life."

Phoenix shook his head. "It wasn't supposed to go that far. I thought I was helping. I thought that if I exposed him, or at least caused unrest with the families that day, it would buy me time, that they would see that there were so many lies and it was never about my family. And...I was scared, all right? We owed money to him, and my father wasn't doing anything about it and then when I discovered we weren't to blame I freaked. I wanted him out of the equation. He was ruining everything."

"What do you mean? This isn't about your family?" I asked.

"No." Phoenix looked like he was shaking. "It's about yours."

"Well, shit." Tex rubbed the back of his neck. "So what do we do now?"

"We'll be in touch," Frank said.

Phoenix winced as Frank slapped him hard on the back. "The less you know, the better it will be for everyone."

Mil stood silently in the corner. Nothing was adding up.

"So, what do we do?" I pleaded. "There has to be a way we can help."

"Kiss your girlfriend." Luca winked. "Pretend everything is fantastic, because I promise you, in a few days, we'll be nothing but a horrible dream."

"People don't die in dreams."

Frank hung his head and muttered a prayer. Luca grabbed his gun and held it to Phoenix's side.

"'Til we meet again." Luca nodded and stood on the other side of Phoenix as he and Frank walked him out of the room.

"Mil?" Tex asked. "Any other fun secrets you aren't telling us about?"

She shrugged and then shook her head.

I pulled out my gun and pushed her against the cement wall. She winced in pain and closed her eyes as I pushed her hair back with my gun. "Talk."

"Not much for talking," she said through clenched teeth.

"Let me refresh your memory," I seethed. "My best friend dies a day after he meets you and now you're letting your stepbrother run off with the guy who killed him? Who just so happens to be holding Trace's grandfather captive like a damn prisoner."

I pressed the gun further into her neck, causing her throat to convulse against the metal. "Nixon said to protect me at all costs," she said.

"And that"—I released her with a jerk and tucked my gun in the back of my jeans—"is the only reason you're still breathing. If I suspect anything, if you sneak out to meet someone, if you suddenly disappear," I swore, "Mil, I will hunt you down, I will torture you until you beg me to kill you and you know what I'll say?"

"What?" She rubbed her throat, tears pooled in her eyes.

"No." I smirked. "I'll say hell no and I'll just keep torturing. I'm protecting you as a promise to my very dead best friend—don't make me regret it."

"Anything else?" she croaked, a smug smile tugging the corners of her mouth. Damn, I wanted to strangle her.

"No."

"Then let's go home." She pushed past me, shoving my body to the side as if she had enough strength to take me down. I watched her the entire walk to the car, I watched and waited for a misstep. Nothing added up—she had to be the answer.

Chapter Thirty-Four

Chase

When we got home, I was torn between searching for Trace and just letting her be alone for a while. I mean, I couldn't even look at myself in the mirror. *Guilty, guilty, guilty,* my conscience screamed at me.

I should have done something.

But no, I was too stuck in my own drama and jealousy.

And now my best friend was dead.

And the love of my life's heart was broken. Damn, I wasn't even sure if she knew where the pieces had fallen, and the worst part was, I still wanted to find every damn one and fix it—fix everything. But you can't fix what refuses your help, and right now it seemed all Trace wanted to do was suffer.

"Chase?" Trace was walking toward me in the hallway. She looked how I felt—like shit.

"Yeah?" I put my gun on the table and met her halfway. "Have you eaten anything?"

She shrugged. Her eyes were sunken and her hair looked somewhat matted to her head. It looked like she hadn't showered or done anything outside of staring at the wall since I'd been gone.

"Trace, you need to eat."

She was like a ghost. If she shrugged one more time I was going to lose my shit. Instead, she did nothing. There was no expression on her face, just emptiness.

Did I get it? Hell yeah, I got it. I was hurting, too, but she was precious; she'd been everything to Nixon. What kind of person would that make me if I let her go down that road? If I let her sulk? This was about tough love—shit, she was going to hate me—but she needed to snap out of it and take care of herself. There was mourning and there was burying your soul with the one you'd lost.

She was doing the latter.

And damn if I was going to let her do it.

I grabbed her hand and dragged her down the hall.

"Chase." She pulled against me. "What are you doing? Chase!"

Good, let her be pissed.

I dragged her into the bathroom and slammed the door. In one swift movement I had the water on in the shower. The bathroom was massive; the rain shower was one you could walk into without having to step over anything. It was the best therapy I could think of, other than getting her drunk, and I was pretty sure that would just make her suicidal.

"Get in." I pointed to the shower. "Or so help me God I will strip you naked and toss you in there myself."

She met my eyes. A slow-burning fire radiated from them, and then extinguished as she shrugged one last time.

"That's it." I grabbed her by the elbow and dragged her, literally, into the shower, both of us with our clothes on.

Once we were under the water, I held her there. Hot water

ran down our faces. She tried to jerk free from my grip but I held her there. Pissed at her for not fighting—for not being strong like I needed her to be.

"Snap the hell out of it, Trace."

Her nostrils flared, but at least she didn't shrug.

She tried to jerk away from me again but I held her firm. She started kicking at my shins. I ignored the slices of pain radiating through my bones and yelled, "Who are you?"

"What?" She squirmed under my touch.

"Who. Are. You?"

"An Alfero," she whispered.

"What do Alferos do?"

She said nothing.

I shook her a bit. "Damn it, Trace! What do Alferos do?"

"We fight!" she yelled and tried to push at my chest. "But I can't. My heart, it's broken. It's so damn broken, I feel like I can't breathe." She hiccupped and struggled against me.

"Then breathe in me." I released her and took off my soaked black t-shirt. "Breathe in my atmosphere because then at least I know you're breathing. At least then I can hear you inhale and exhale. Trace, I can't fix what's been broken, and I'm not trying to take his place. God knows I can't, no matter how badly I wish I could."

She slumped against me and wrapped her arms around my neck, clinging onto me so tightly that I could feel her heat through her clothing.

"I'm sorry." She sighed. "I'll eat."

"And what else?" I pried her away from me. "What else are you going to do?"

"Fight."

"And why are you going to fight, Trace?" I whispered.

She took a deep breath. Water fell across her full lips. "Because that's what he would have wanted."

"Damn right." I grabbed her hand and kissed it.

She gasped and then, somehow, I don't even know how it happened, we were kissing. No—we weren't kissing—I was devouring her.

Was it wrong to be thankful? To be so damn lost in another person that even though what they were offering were their broken and used pieces—you still grasped at them for dear life and wished that somehow if you loved them enough, those pieces would magically fuse back together?

"I'm not him, Trace," I said against her lips.

"I know." She sighed into my mouth. "I know."

Our lips broke apart. Both of us stepped away from each other. Damn if it didn't feel like a part of me was dying right along with Nixon.

She looked down.

Our relationship was going to be complicated; that much was sure. But I wasn't letting her go—it would take an act of God for me to let her go.

"Take off your clothes." I sighed.

"What? No! Then I'd be naked!"

I tried to hold in the laughter, tried and failed.

She swatted me with her hand and then joined in. Tears streamed down her face; I wasn't sure if they were from amusement or just exhaustion.

"Kinda the point, Trace. I promise I can control my urges. Now take off your clothes, we'll shower on different sides, I'll be turned around the entire time. Even though, I have always imagined what you'd look like naked…"

"Ass." She lifted her shirt over her head.

"Always." I winked. "I'll always be an ass for you."

"How sweet." She stepped out of the workout shorts she was wearing and stripped herself of the rest of her clothes. And as much as I was wanting to slam her against the wall, I couldn't. Because I was pretty damn sure the last person who had seen her that way had been Nixon.

I wouldn't take that memory away from her. I wouldn't replace it with pieces of me—that, in my heart, would be the final betrayal, so I turned around, took off my own clothes and showered with her.

We didn't touch again.

We didn't mention the kiss.

And in the end. I made her laugh twice.

Which basically meant I was badass. I needed her laugh more than she realized.

Her laugh told me that even though it hurt like hell…we were going to be okay…One day, maybe not today, we would recover.

Chapter Thirty-Five

Phoenix

So this is fun," I grumbled, wondering why I was literally sitting a foot away from the scariest mafia boss known to Sicily. He smirked and said nothing, while Frank, my father's murderer, kept a gun pointed at my head.

Low point. Definite low point.

"I never said thank you." I cleared my throat and tried not to sound as freaked as I felt.

"For?" Frank answered.

"Killing my father, of course."

Frank snorted. "I cannot tell if you are upset I beat you to the punch or if you truly mean what you say."

"Had he not done it, I would have," Luca piped up from the front seat. The driver was taking us through a series of subdivisions, almost making me dizzy as trees and perfect houses flew by the windows.

"Come again?" I asked.

"Your father, I hope he's burning in Hell," Luca said crisply. "And I hope when I meet him there, I'm able to experience his death by my hands for an eternity."

Shit. I really hoped Luca wasn't going to be the one to kill me. I knew I'd already pissed him off enough for a lifetime of torture—which begged the question why was I still sucking in air when he'd made it perfectly clear a few weeks ago that if I double-crossed him, or as much as talked—he'd end me.

"Why am I here—"

"Not now," Luca snapped. "It isn't safe."

"Right. Never is," I mumbled.

"You're lucky I need you. If I were you, I'd pray for my soul—because if this ends badly—yours will be damned right along with your father's."

"Can't pray for something you never had."

Chapter Thirty-Six

Chase

I always hated "family" meetings. For normal people, a family meeting meant a talk over curfew or maybe even game night.

Right. Our games included blood and guns. Pretty sure a family meeting at my house was like inviting the devil to dinner.

The only thing I couldn't really figure out was why we were meeting at my house of all places. I mean, I understood that Nixon was gone, but Mo wasn't, and since that family was *the* family, it just seemed strange.

At any rate, it was totally possible that my dad had thought it would be too hard to stay at Nixon's. I put on nice black slacks and a white button-up with a green tie. The other thing about family meetings?

You had to be respectful. My dad hated that I had tattoos, said they made me look like a punk, which only encouraged me to get more. He wanted me to cover them during meetings.

It had always been tougher for Nixon, considering he even had tattoos behind his ear, not to mention the lip piercing that pissed almost everyone off who met him.

He'd rebelled because it was the only control over his life that he'd had—what he did to his body, it was his and only his. Other than that, his life, the journey he'd been on, had been solidly planned out for him.

"Chase?" my dad called from downstairs.

"Coming." I grabbed my gun and sent a quick text to Trace for her to stay out of trouble and to keep the doors locked. The Abandonato house was like a freaking fortress—still it didn't make me feel any better about leaving her alone, especially in her emotional state.

The Abandonato family was huge. Everyone was present, at least all the men. Typically, the women would meet with us for a meal and then we'd all go our separate ways. The men went into a separate room to talk business and smoke cigars and the women gossiped in the kitchen.

You could tell it wasn't a typical meeting.

Everyone, and I mean everyone, looked like they'd had about an hour's sleep.

Hushed murmurs came from the living room when I walked in. Why was everyone staring at me? Shit, could they see my tattoos through my white shirt?

Feeling awkward, I nodded once, and walked over to the bar to make myself a drink.

I needed something strong if I was going to make it through the night. Just talking about Nixon made me feel sick.

"How's it going?" Tex appeared at my side.

"Oh, you know." I shrugged and took a sip of straight whiskey. "Fantastic."

Tex chuckled.

"What?"

"Nothing." He poured himself a similar drink, only he added more whiskey to his tumbler. "It's just that, maybe you and Nixon are more alike than you realize. It's like he's left his dark mood with you as well as the stick that was permanently fused in his ass."

"Thanks, man." I cracked a smile, not because I thought he was funny but because his words actually made me feel better. It made me feel like somehow Nixon was still with us.

My dad cleared his throat and tapped his glass. "Would everyone please get comfortable? We have much to discuss."

Tex and I took a seat by the fireplace and waited. A few men grumbled but everyone quieted down when my dad began talking again.

"While we mourn the loss of Nixon…"—he sighed—"we are thankful for the sacrifice he made in order to save our family."

A few men nodded in agreement while others made a cross over their chests and kissed their fingertips in prayer.

"God bless him." My father's voice was choked. "May God continue to watch over this family."

"Amen," we all said in unison, making a sweeping motion from our foreheads to our hearts and across our chests.

"Now." My father clapped his hands. "I hope we can move past the murder that took place so long ago. Nixon's death proves a life for a life. The Nicolosi family has made it right and we are not to continue searching into something that no longer holds any value in this family."

That didn't sit well with me because I still wanted to know who'd killed Trace's parents, and I knew there was no way that Nixon's dad had actually committed the murder. For one thing, he'd been a better assassin than that. He'd been set up, and if it wasn't by the De Lange family...then it had to have been by someone else. Someone who had reason enough to want to knock out not only Trace's family, but Nixon's as well.

"...it only makes sense to keep it in the family," my dad finished. I'd blanked out the first part, but I assumed he was doing what he did best. Taking control.

"Who?" My cousin Vin spoke up. "The only choice would be you, but—"

"Now let's not get ahead of ourselves." My dad put his hands up. "I do not want the job. My job is to be the right hand of the one in control. I like it that way and though it naturally would fall to me...I believe there is one who deserves it, dare I say, even more so than Nixon."

Confused, I looked around the room. Who the hell deserved to lead the family more than Nixon? His father had been the boss, as had his father and his before him? Pissed, I was about ready to storm out of the room when I heard my name.

"Chase," my dad ordered. "Please stand."

I wanted to say no thanks, but I couldn't disrespect my father in front of everyone. On shaky legs I walked to the middle of the room. Every eye was on me. I felt hot then cold all over. This couldn't be happening—it was too soon. I'd never wanted this.

My dad pulled something out of his pocket. "I nominate my son, Chase. Nixon's best friend and right-hand man. He's been here since the beginning; he watched the horrors of Nixon's childhood and stood by his side during the investigation, going as far as to enroll in Eagle Elite to flush out the murderer. He saved Tracey Alfero's life. There is no one that deserves this title more, not even myself."

Stunned, I stood there, hoping to God people would think my dad was drunk and spouting absolute nonsense. I opened my mouth to say something but was too late.

"I second." Vin raised his hand.

"Third."

"Fourth."

Men kept agreeing, and with each agreement I felt like I couldn't breathe. This couldn't be happening. I didn't want it. I'd never wanted it. I imagined what was happening to me felt a lot like slavery, like watching yourself getting sold to the highest bidder knowing your life would never be your own again.

"It must be unanimous." My dad cleared his throat and looked at Tex.

My eyes pleaded. I stared him down. Hard. I was going to kick his ass if he raised his hand. "I'm sorry, Chase." Tex closed his eyes and raised his hand.

Words wouldn't come. I couldn't think. Not with everyone staring at me, not with my dad holding my hand in the air.

And when he thrust a ring on my right hand, I almost puked.

Nixon's ring.

I'd said I wanted to be him.

And now I was.

I closed my eyes to keep the tears of rage in.

It should have never happened this way.

And now I was stuck just like he was, chained to the family in more ways than one, and poor Trace—history was on repeat.

Chapter Thirty-Seven

Chase

Y̶ou okay, man?" Tex brought me my fifth glass of whiskey and smacked me on the back of the head.

"Use a baseball bat instead of your hand and I'll let you know." I sipped the drink and let the alcohol slide down my throat.

"I'm sorry."

"You're an ass," I spat. "All you had to do was say no." My words were already beginning to slur but I didn't care.

"I know that." Tex took a seat next to me. "But your dad was right. He isn't the man for the job, you are. Maybe by taking his place, you'll set things right."

"I don't do well under pressure." I took another sip.

"Seriously?" Tex laughed. "Chase, you've always done well under pressure. Come on, out of the four of us, you were always the scary one. The one that never cried and laughed when we did. When you fell out of that tree at four you set your own arm before telling your ma you had to go to the doctor."

"This is a hell of a lot different than a broken arm." I cringed.

"Yeah well." Tex sighed. "At least now, you have the power to protect those you love—those we both love."

"Mo?" I asked.

He nodded. "She's not doing well. I mean, she lost her father—granted he was a jackass, but she never saw that side of him, he reserved all that for Nixon. And then her brother? Her twin? Can you even imagine what she's going through right now?"

"No." I licked my lips. "I've heard it's worse for twins, that they aren't ever the same...after."

"She won't talk to me." Tex smacked his leg with his hand. "She keeps saying she's fine, but I think she's just numb."

"You could always try the whole tough love angle."

"Yeah, and how did that work with Trace? You're lucky she didn't pull a gun on you or something."

With a laugh I took another sip of my drink. "True. But it was worth it. At least her fire's back."

There was a moment of silence and then Tex said, "I know you love her."

"So damn much," I answered honestly. Clearly the whiskey was having its effect.

"Kinda sucks."

"Yeah." I shook the ice in my glass and stared at the ground. "It feels so wrong. His girlfriend, his title, his money? It has to be some cruel joke, you know? I just can't help but wonder how this is going to play out with Frank and Luca."

"I was thinking about that, too." Tex scratched his head. "They said to just act normal and keep doing what we're doing."

"Yeah, they also said to kiss my girlfriend, meaning they clearly still don't know that it was all an act."

"Or maybe they did," Tex offered. "Maybe that was his way of giving you permission."

"Permission?" I snorted. "Permission to kiss a girl who, every damn time I touch her lips, will imagine I'm Nixon. Hi, Chase, welcome to a living hell. Oh wait, I've been camping there for months now."

"I was just saying."

"Yeah, well, stop saying." I rose from my seat. "Let's go check on the girls. I need to get out of here."

*   *   *

I found my dad and told him I was leaving.

"You can't leave." He grabbed my arm. "There are things we need to discuss."

"Then you should probably wait until I'm not this drunk." I jerked my arm away from him. "Tomorrow. We'll talk tomorrow."

"Fine." He slipped something in my pants pocket. "Do yourself a favor and tie up all the loose ends, sooner rather than later."

"Loose ends?" I shook my fuzzy head. "Everyone's dead, or haven't you noticed?"

"Not everyone." He grinned and slapped me on the shoulder. "Now, do your job."

Did he just threaten me? And who the hell would be a loose end?

"Ready?" Tex held out the keys and shook 'em. "I'm driving because I'm pretty sure if you did we'd be seeing Nixon sooner rather than later."

"Right." I followed him out the door.

Once I was in the car, I pulled the envelope out of my pocket. Inside was a picture of Mil with her face crossed off in red. And then a picture of Nixon and Trace. Both of them smiling with ugly red marks across their faces.

"Pull over!" I shouted.

"We're on the freeway! I can't exactly pull over!" Tex yelled right back.

"Pull the hell over or so help me God I'm going to jump out of this damn car!"

"Shit…" The car jolted as Tex pulled over to the shoulder, cursing the entire way.

I opened the door and threw up.

"Ah hell," Tex grumbled. "Did you have to drink that much?"

"Not the alcohol." I wiped my mouth. "We gotta get back to the house, now!"

I pulled out my cell and dialed Trace's number. *Pick up, pick up, pick up.*

"Hello?"

"Trace?" I yelled.

"Yeah? What's up? How did it go?"

"Lock the doors."

"They're locked."

"Trace, I…" I gripped the car door with my free hand. "Just don't answer the door for anyone, okay? I don't care if the Pope suddenly decides to come bless our entire family. You stay inside. You wait for us, okay?"

"Okay. You're scaring me, Chase."

"Good. You should be scared, because I'm about five seconds away from losing my damn mind."

"That's not good," she said just as Tex said, "Already lost it."

"Just...we'll be home in ten." I ended the call and slammed my hand against the seat.

"Calm down. What the hell has gotten into you?" Tex asked.

"He wanted Nixon dead."

"Who did?"

"My father."

"How do you know?"

"Because he wants me to kill Tracey."

Chapter Thirty-Eight

Chase

Tex slammed on the brakes, then must have realized we were on the freeway, because he sped off again.

"How would you know that?"

A bad feeling? I didn't know. Hell, all signs pointed to my father killing Nixon, but that would be impossible, wouldn't it? That would mean that Luca hadn't, and he'd admitted as much.

Shit, things were messed up.

What could my father possibly have to gain by me tying up the loose ends? What loose ends?

"I'll show you when we get inside the Abandonato house without getting shot at."

"That's fair." Tex exhaled and cursed again as we drove the rest of the way to the house.

Once we were inside, we pulled out our guns and gave instructions to the men that they were to double security until we said it was safe again.

I turned on all the alarms to the outside and made sure that my gun was loaded—twice.

Trace, Mo, and Mil were waiting for us in the rec room. All of them were sitting around the flat screen TV.

The minute Trace saw me, she ran into my arms. I'd be lying if I said I didn't need it more than my next breath.

"What happened?" She grabbed my right hand and tugged me over to the couch. She stopped suddenly and released my hand as if burned. "Chase?" She turned around, her eyes narrowed. She glanced down at my hand. I put it behind my back.

"They're going to find out why everyone's calling you 'sir' at some point, Chase," Tex said from behind me.

Mo began to cry softly into her hands. At least she was finally showing some emotion, too. Would our lives ever be normal?

Mil gave me the pitiful look girls give guys when they feel sorry for them but don't want to say it out loud, lest they make you feel like less of a man.

And Trace. Trace just stared at my hand.

Betrayal washed over her features and then understanding. "His ring."

"I had no choice," I whispered.

"The hell you did!" Mo screamed from the couch. "I'm so sick and tired of you guys saying you don't have a choice! This family, they don't own us! They don't own you, Chase! You can get away, you can run! This doesn't have to be our destiny!"

I scrubbed at my face with my hands and groaned.

"But it does," Tex said, pulling Mo in for a hug, "because we were born into it. When you're born into something like this, the only way to leave—"

"Is to die," Mil finished.

The room fell silent.

"Trace, I need to talk to you about that night, the night Nixon left."

Her face went red as she sat on the couch and she began fumbling with her hands. "What do you need to know?"

"Did Nixon say anything? Did he give you any hints about what he was doing?"

Trace shook her head. "He said good-bye, but I thought he meant that he was going away for a while. I had no idea. I mean how could I know he was going to do that?"

"Shit." I leaned back on the couch and played with the ring on my finger.

"He did ask for a favor."

Safe to say there was no chance in hell I wanted to know about the favor he had asked of her.

"My grandmother's journal." She squinted. "He said he needed to borrow it, but he also said he'd return it."

I jumped up from my seat on the couch and ran down the hall, followed by every other person in the room. I ran into Trace's room and began searching the different shelves for the journal. "Where would he put it?"

Trace ran in behind me and began searching where I had just searched.

"No, wait." I stopped her. "What else did he say? Think back. Did he give you any hints?"

Trace gasped and put her hands over her mouth. Her eyes welled with tears. She walked over to the bed and pulled back the covers.

Mil, Tex, and Mo walked into the room.

Trace sighed and threw the pillows off her bed.

And there it was.

The journal.

And it had a note on it.

Trace picked it up and held it to her chest. "He said he'd put it closest to my heart, to where he wanted to be."

"Your bed?" Tex said from behind us.

I knew. Even if Tex didn't. Her bed—he meant the night she gave him her heart—the night he took everything from her.

Only to give her something of hers back.

Why the hell did he have to go and die and be that noble even in his death?

Point, Nixon. "What does it say?"

She peeled the note from the journal and with shaking hands read it. "'Remember what I said, it's only good-bye for now. I need you to trust me. Listen to Chase. He'll protect you while I can't. And for the love of God read the damn journal. I had to pull some pages from it. More family secrets and all that. But be sure to read the journal with only those you trust. This cannot get into the wrong hands, because it's the only evidence we have.'"

"Well." I cleared my throat. "That wasn't cryptic, not at all."

"Why is he talking like he's watching us?" Trace whispered, tracing the note with her fingertips.

"Because he is," I answered. "He'll always be with us."

I'd be lying if I said I wasn't a bit suspicious. The note was written in the present tense. Then again he wouldn't have known he was going to die, and he could have ordered anyone to put the journal back if he couldn't.

But the thought plagued me. Because it had been a closed casket, and things were too messed up. What if…? I hated *what if* almost as much as I hated the word "regret."

Trace nodded and handed me the journal. "Guess we should get to reading. Don't wanna piss off Nixon."

"Yeah, he'd probably haunt us," Tex snorted.

Even Mo and Mil laughed.

We decided to change into comfortable clothes and meet in the rec room in a half hour. I put the journal back on the bed and sat.

"What are you doing?" Trace asked, closing the door so we had privacy.

"Trying to still my rapidly beating heart. I swear if one more thing goes wrong I'm going to hide in your closet and plug my ears."

"I need to change."

"So change." I shrugged.

Trace jutted out her hip and put her hand on it. "Fine." She grabbed her clothes, went into the walk-in closet and shut the door.

"You don't play fair!" I shouted.

She opened the door a crack and threw her discarded clothes in my face. Very funny.

After a few minutes (during which I swear I heard her fall down and curse), she emerged in a sweatshirt and black leggings. "I'm ready."

"I should probably go change, too."

She nodded and then bit her lip.

"What?"

"Nothing. It's nothing."

"Trace, it's never nothing with you. I swear I can hear your brain actually hurting itself. What's up?"

"Your tattoo?" She nodded to my chest. "What does it mean?"

I chuckled. "Which one?"

She pointed to the left side of my chest. "This one. The writing, it's in Italian."

I slowly unbuttoned my shirt and pulled it to the side. "It says blood brothers, *Fratelli per patto di sangue.*"

"Nixon." She caressed the letters on my chest. "He has one, too."

"In the same spot. But I think you already knew that."

She nodded.

"I should go."

"Okay."

I stood up and walked out of the room, knowing damn well that if I stayed, I would do something irreversible. She deserved better than that, and for once in my life I was beginning to think I did, too.

Chapter Thirty-Nine

Chase

It took us exactly one hour to find out what Nixon had written about. I stared at the writing and had to blink a few times in order to understand it. Could it be true?

"Shit." Tex sighed. "I really don't know what to say right now."

Mo's eyes filled with tears.

Mil didn't seem shocked at all, but the girl was impossible to shock. I mean, she was Phoenix's sister and all that. The girl was tough as nails.

Trace scooted away from me a bit. I didn't blame her. I would scoot away from me and I was me.

"How do we know this is true?" I pointed at the offending journal and cursed. "I mean, that's crazy, right?"

Mo lost it. She started bawling and then tackled me into the tightest hug I'd ever felt in my entire life.

I didn't blame her.

She'd been closer than simply a cousin—she'd been like a sister to me my whole life, and now I finally knew why it had felt that way.

Nixon's mom had had an affair with my dad. I was never my father's son. This meant my so-called uncle, Nixon's dad, was my dad.

The man I'd called a monster when I was a little kid...was my flesh and blood. How bad did that suck?

So basically my real father was dead.

Because both wives had cheated.

Both wives had done so to get back at each other.

When my mom had learned of Tony's betrayal, she'd gone to Nixon's father, who was my real father.

Nixon's mother had been in love with Tony. They had an affair for two years and then along came Mo and Nixon. Twins. Nobody would have ever known except Nixon's dad had suspicions and called for a paternity test.

The minute the truth was discovered both women were screwed.

And both of them died for it.

I released Mo and sighed. "It still doesn't explain how Trace's parents died."

"No." Mo wiped her eyes. "But it explains so much. Why would your father keep this from you? Why would he keep it a secret? Why would he demand Nixon call him Uncle Tony when he was really his dad? Why would he let his brother beat his son! And on top of that..."—she hiccupped—"we've been lied to our whole lives. How do we know who to trust?"

The more I thought about it the sicker I became. She was right. Nixon's real dad—my dad—Tony—had stood by and watched his son get beaten and did nothing.

He stood by and watched the woman he'd claimed to love get beaten, and did nothing.

One thing was for sure: My dad or uncle or whoever the hell he was, was a monster. And he was hiding something. I was going to either get it out of him or kill him with my bare hands. I'd never felt connected to him, never felt like we were close. And now I knew why.

Both men had kept secrets from us—but why?

"I need some air." I bolted from the room and ran outside. A few of the men looked at me like I'd lost it. To be fair, I was way past merely losing it and on my way to insanity.

"Chase!" Trace ran out of the house in one of my coats and stopped in front of me. "Are you okay?"

"No, I'm not okay!" I yelled. "How the hell am I supposed to answer that? He wasn't ever just my cousin!" The cold air nipped at my face. "He had always been like a brother to me—he gave me everything and I—"

"What?"

"I took it all from him. All of it!"

"Chase," Trace warned. "The men. We don't know who we can trust. We can't fight... not now."

"Shh." I pulled her close. "Someone's watching. I can see his shadow, stay close," I whispered. "And go with it." It could have been one of our men—but I was starting to become a paranoid lunatic when it came to everyone, especially considering my conversation with Tony. What if they worked for him? What if their loyalty wasn't mine? The shadow moved, and then disappeared behind the building.

I tugged Trace closer and kissed her forehead, speaking up. "I want you. I need to be with you, Trace. Having Nixon gone, it's killing me."

"Chase, you can't..." Trace shook her head. "You can't be like this. We can't do this!"

"We aren't doing anything," I said in low tones, reaching for

Trace's hand. "Don't you?" I looked directly at the shadow, hoping to God I wasn't hallucinating, I mean, two seconds ago I was pretty sure I had died or something. "Don't you feel the same way?" I looked above Trace's head at the shadow and then back at Trace.

She jerked her hand away from mine. "It doesn't matter what I feel. It's not about me, Chase."

"But it is." I reached for her again. This time her hand stayed firmly in mine. She needed to play along or she was going to die. She didn't know that, but I did. Because I'd just seen my father watching us from the side of the house. Meaning, he had to believe I'd bought it, I'd follow his assignment.

"It isn't." Trace sighed. "It never was."

I jerked her toward me again. She fell against my chest and looked up into my eyes. "What are you doing?"

I sighed. "What I should have done a long time ago."

I kissed her, hard, and then slid my mouth to her ear to whisper, "I'm going to shoot my gun. This is very important. I need you to collapse against me, okay?"

She nodded and clung to my shirt as I shot my gun into the side of the coat, making a muffled sound as it rang out into the night air.

Trace collapsed on me.

With a curse, I picked her up and carried her back inside.

The men were watching and hopefully so was my father. He'd think I'd tied up one loose end. Oddly enough, this might make him play perfectly into my hands. The sick thing was, that as much as I'd asked all my men to protect her, nobody ran to my side when I shot her—nobody blinked. My family officially sucked.

When we reached the kitchen I told her to crawl down the

hallway and into her room, locking the door until I came and told her all was safe. I closed the blinds to the windows, pulled out my knife and sliced down my arm so that I would have actual blood on my hands. Ripping my shirt, I sliced part of my side, using as much of the blood as I could, and then I bandaged myself up.

A knock sounded at the door.

If it was my father, retribution was going to happen a hell of a lot sooner than I'd first thought.

To my utter shock and surprise, and most likely bad luck, I was knocked to the ground by a fist to the face.

"You son of a bitch. I swear I'll kill you if you actually shot into her perfect body."

"Nixon?" I gasped.

"No. I'm an angel of death coming to take you to your maker, you ass. Yes it's me."

"B-b-but—" I stuttered.

"We don't have time. I just had to make sure she wasn't actually shot. You're lucky I saw Uncle Tony or I would have shot you on the spot. And ruined everything. Nice ring, by the way."

"Am I dead?" I checked my body for gunshot wounds and was treated to another punch to the jaw.

"Answer your question?" Nixon tilted his head to the side. "Or do I need to make things more clear?"

"Still an ass."

"Still more like a brother than your cousin, don't you think?"

I froze.

"Look, I can't stay. I shouldn't even be here. I just needed to make sure they made you boss... What did Uncle Tony say tonight?"

"That I deserved to take your place—oh, right, and he told me to tie up loose ends."

"Trace." Nixon cursed.

"Yeah, Nixon. What's going on?"

"Just act normal." He paced in front of me. "I'm already dead, all right? But you guys, you're alive, get it? If this goes badly..."

Aw shit. He was telling me what I didn't want to know. If it went badly, and he did die, then he didn't want Trace to mourn him all over again.

"But how are Luca and Mr. Alfero—"

"Sorry. This is where our conversation ends." Nixon raised his hand to my head and everything went black.

Chapter Forty

Nixon

He's lucky as hell I didn't beat the shit out of him." I pounded my fist against the table and cursed.

"Nobody ever said being dead was easy." Trace's grandpa chuckled.

"I hate this."

"It's the only way. Quite clever, too, might I add." He took a sip of coffee and drummed his fingers on the table. "It won't be long now."

"It's been too long," I grumbled. "If it doesn't work, if I'm wrong, if Phoenix and Mil are wrong…"

"If, if, if. Stop worrying; you'll give yourself an ulcer. At least I'd make it quick," Luca said, walking into the room. "Straight in the head, just like you asked."

"How…*kind*," I muttered.

"I aim to please."

"No, you aim to kill." This from Frank.

Luca chuckled. "That too. Now, what did you discover on your little spying mission? All went well, yes?"

If well meant I had to sit by and watch Chase take over my life and fall even more in love with my girlfriend then yeah, it had gone fantastic. I leaned forward and poured myself another cup of coffee. "He ordered a hit on Trace."

Frank gripped the table. "That lying piece of—"

"Quiet." Luca put up his hand. "And?"

"And, Chase knows that Uncle Tony isn't his real father. I left enough hints, and they've clearly read the journal."

"So..." Luca clasped his hands together. "All loose ends are tied, then?"

"Yes."

"So we wait." Frank took another sip of coffee.

"I hate waiting." I wanted to bang my head against the table a million times.

"Chin up." Luca pulled out a cigar and handed it to me. "If you're right in your assumptions, you'll be celebrating with your girlfriend by the end of the week." That was if she still loved me...loved me more than him. After all, I had left her again. And Chase, he'd been there the whole time.

"And if I'm wrong?"

"Then we go fishing in Lake Michigan." Using my body as bait, no doubt. I loved bleak futures. Truly, they were what got me through the monotony of life.

Hell, I needed a drink, but I had been pulling all-nighters just in case I was needed. Damn, but my body was completely exhausted. The only thing that helped was my cell phone.

Who knew I would be so addicted to technology?

Or her?

I'd turned it on airplane mode so that I couldn't receive calls. But I could look at my pictures.

My thumb hovered over the picture I'd snapped of Trace on our first date. I'd taken her on a picnic. Had she turned out to be just a normal girl and not the little girl I grew up with, I would have still fallen.

I would have still wanted her.

Because she was so damn special. She was...my other half. She didn't take my shit like most people and she seemed to genuinely care. When she touched me—well, sometimes it felt like everything was still in my world. And I needed that peace more than I'd care to admit.

Maybe I was just holding on to a fantasy. It was possible she would turn and walk away from me. And when that time came, if that was the choice she wanted to make, I'd let her. Not because I wanted to let her go, but because I respected her too much to keep her when she wanted to leave.

I truly believed that the greatest sacrifice someone could make in life was putting someone else's needs before your own wants and desires. Loving someone with such a passion that you'd suffer the rest of your life just so you could see them smile. You'd go to hell and back—if only it meant keeping them safe.

She was my Juliet—and damn if I didn't want the story to end differently. I wanted her to have a life, even if it was apart from me.

I saw a pair of boots and ripped jeans and looked up into Phoenix's eyes. "What?"

"Nothing." He sat. "I just..." With a heavy sigh he leaned forward. "I wanted to apologize again. I get it, I don't deserve your forgiveness and I sure as hell don't deserve your protection or anything else. I know that the only thing that's kept me alive so far is the fact that I'm a head of the De Lange family and even that didn't keep me from almost getting killed."

I set my phone down and leaned back. "No. We did."

"And my sister, don't forget her," Phoenix said.

"Couldn't even if I wanted to." I sighed. "Once she started telling me what you knew, what you saw…" I shook my head. "I knew there was no other choice."

"There's always a choice," Phoenix whispered. "You just happen to be one of the good ones."

"What do you mean?" My head snapped up.

"You know what I mean." He smirked. "As much as it pains me to admit it, and as much of a pain in the ass as you've been your entire life…you're the good guy. The one who runs headfirst into battle with your sword raised high above your head. You're like freaking William Wallace," he snorted. "And the rest of us? Well, if we aren't blinded by jealousy, we're blinded by something else entirely."

I swallowed and looked down at my hands. "Oh yeah? What's that?"

"Hope." He sighed. "Hope that it won't always be like this, that our families won't always be at war and that in the end, it's possible that the good guy wins."

"And if he doesn't?" I squinted at my hands. "Win, I mean."

"Even in your death you'd win, Nixon." He paused. "Because you fought, and regardless of the outcome, your success was in the journey."

I fought back the emotion in my throat. Damn if falling in love wasn't making me one of those guys that turned into a complete and total emotional loser when lives were on the line.

"Thanks," I muttered. "If you weren't such a complete ass, I might actually like you again."

"No problem. And if you weren't such a complete prick, I may actually accept a second try at friendship." He got up from his seat to walk away.

"Phoenix?"

"Yeah?" He stopped and turned to face me.

"If I die—"

"Nixon, don't do this now..."

"Just listen, damn it. If I die...make sure Chase doesn't kill you, all right?"

With a smirk Phoenix saluted me and walked off. "We all know Chase would rather torture me than kill me, but I'll be sure to sleep with one eye open."

"Right."

I was alone.

Again. I pulled out my cell phone one last time and looked at Trace's picture. I mumbled a prayer under my breath.

"It is time," Luca announced, walking back into the room. "Remember the terms of our agreement. I do not like killing such good prospects, but I will kill you to keep my name out of this little spat."

"Understood." I stuffed my phone back into my pocket and murmured one last prayer for Trace. I prayed that she wouldn't feel guilty for loving him, I prayed she could let me go, and most of all, I prayed that if it meant me dying to save her—that God would be just and take me.

Chapter Forty-One

Chase

Shit. Had I hallucinated the entire thing? I woke up on the couch with a blanket covering me. My eyes slowly adjusted to the darkness in the room.

Mil was sitting by me reading.

"What the hell happened?" I shook my head a few times to clear it.

"You passed out. Must be all the pressure." Mil shrugged. "You're lucky I was there to catch you."

"You caught me? All six-foot-two of me? Really?" I snorted and then groaned. My head pounded in protest.

Mil grinned. "Actually, the table caught you, and then you landed on my boot, which is still a catch, in case you were wondering." She stood and reached for a mug on the table. "Here, this should help."

I took a sip of the warm liquid and choked. "Is that straight whiskey?"

"With lemon." She shrugged and took a seat.

"I saw him, Mil."

"Who?"

"Nixon," I whispered.

"No you didn't," she said simply. "What you saw was your imagination conjuring up images of your dead best friend in order to alleviate you of the guilt you feel for wanting to get into his girl-friend's pants."

I squinted and said slowly, "Who *are* you?"

Great...No answer. She was officially back to reading and ignor-ing me again. I threw a pillow at her face. "And just so you know, I'm not feeling guilty."

Her arched eyebrows and snorting were enough to make me want to throw my drink in her perfect face.

What the hell?

Where did that come from?

Shit.

I looked down at my cup and shook my head for the third time. I seriously must have hit it hard if I was suddenly finding Mil attractive.

"You feel guilty," she said without looking up from her book. "You feel like you're stealing his life, but don't worry. Things always have a way of working out."

It was my turn to snort and roll my eyes. "Yeah, I highly doubt there will come a day when I won't feel like the worst friend in the world for living while he didn't."

Mil licked her lips and closed the book. "Chase—"

"Oh my gosh, what happened to your head?" Trace ran to my side and ran her fingers over my temple. "And your eye?"

"My eye?" I repeated.

Mil snickered behind her book.

"What the hell is wrong with my eye?"

"It's turning black and blue." Trace's brown eyes filled with concern as she touched the tender flesh.

"Care to explain, Mil?"

"Nope." She got up from her seat and threw the book back onto the couch. "I'll see you guys in the morning. It's going to be...a busy day."

"It's Thursday. Why would it be busy?" Trace asked. "I'm the only one with lab."

"Just trust me." She gave us both a weak smile and walked off toward the bedrooms.

I scratched my head. "Raise your hand if you think she's up to something."

Trace and I both raised our hands and smiled. I grabbed hers midair and pulled her onto the couch with me. We lay like that for probably ten minutes before her heavy sigh begged me to ask the question. "How was your near brush with death?"

"Great." She sighed. "How was my acting?"

"Too good." I groaned. "You almost made me believe I shot you."

"Why did you shoot?"

And there it was.

I didn't know how much to tell or how little, but the problem was she was involved. She needed to be on her guard.

I reached into my pocket and pulled out the picture that my father had given me earlier that evening.

"Look." I pointed at the red marks across Nixon's face as well as hers.

She took the picture from my hands and then thrust it back into my face as if it was burning her fingertips. "Why? Why would he want me dead?"

"Loose ends," I whispered. "You're a flight risk? I don't know, had I been conscious the past hour I would have probably gotten further than asking myself the same damn question."

"Right, and why were you unconscious?" She was still in my arms but she turned to face me. Our lips were only a breath away from each other.

I knew what I'd seen was real. I knew I'd seen Nixon, but for some reason both Mil and Nixon needed me not to know. And for reasons I knew I had to keep secret—Trace could never know there was a chance Nixon was alive, because if she did, and he died again...

Shit, she wouldn't make it through.

I wasn't sure *I* would make it through.

Panic seized my chest as she reached up and traced my lips with her fingertips. How horrible did it make me that my first thought was if Nixon lived I would lose this. I would lose her. And not just for now—but forever.

Time wasn't on my side. I had no moment but now.

Every person panics when they realize all of a sudden, their lives are going to change, that they're going to go in a direction they never saw coming. I felt like my whole life had led up to this moment.

Nixon's destiny didn't just define our family or Trace's; it also defined me. The outcome of whatever happened would define the rest of my existence.

I closed my eyes and swallowed as Trace's fingers fell to my jaw, lightly caressed my five-o'clock shadow, and then dipped into my hair.

Groaning, I leaned forward. Our foreheads met.

"I love you," I whispered.

There. I'd said it.

"I love you, too." She said it too fast, too simply. It wasn't the same love. She needed to understand.

"Trace." My voice cracked as I reached for her hand and brought it to my fingertips. "You don't understand; you never have."

"What?" Her eyes filled with tears. "What don't I understand?"

"You. Me. Us." I sighed and kissed the tip of her finger and then sucked on the end before moving to her next finger and her next. She gasped but said nothing. When I finished my assault, I kissed the top of her hand, and sighed against it. "When I say I love you. I don't mean it the way you do. I'm not...capable of loving you in that way."

Her eyes narrowed.

Here went nothing.

"When I say I love you, I mean I love you so much it hurts to be close to you, it hurts to be away from you. I hurt all the damn time because my stupid heart has decided for one reason or another that it can't survive without being next to yours. I don't know what the hell you've done to me, but I'm a disaster. I'm broken for you and I never want to be fixed. And it hurts like hell because when you kiss me, I know you think of *him*. When I kiss you, all I see is *you*, all I feel is *you*."

A tear slid down her cheek.

"When you touch me, a part of my heart breaks off, because in the back of my mind I'm always aware that the way you define the touch and the way I feel it are two totally different things.

Trace, I love you. I love you. I"—my voice cracked—"I am in love with you."

"B-but all those times…" she stuttered. "I thought you were kidding, acting! I mean, you're Chase! You're never serious when it comes to that stuff. And Nixon—Nixon would *kill* you—"

"He's already threatened to shoot me in the head…believe me. I know that loving you will be the highest price I'll ever pay for anything. But, Trace, you're worth the cost."

"What are you asking?" She licked her lips and stared into my eyes. "What are you saying?"

I was going to do it.

Even though I knew he was alive.

I was going to ask.

Because she deserved to hear the question, regardless of what her answer might be.

"Choose me," I whispered. "Because my heart? My soul? My damn existence? Has already spoken, and it wants you, and only you—forever."

I felt like I'd just run a marathon without any food or water. My chest heaved with exertion as her eyes searched mine for a minute longer. Then her lips touched mine.

In a real kiss.

She was kissing me the way I'd always wanted to be kissed by her—she was consuming my darkness, and replacing it with her light. And in that instant I knew—nobody would ever compare to her. For my entire life I had been lost, and now I was found.

I molded my lips to hers and wrapped my arms around her. Every plane of her body was touching mine—causing me to burn with need for more of her. I growled low in my throat when our tongues collided. With a jerk, I was on top of her, pressing her down into the couch as sensations of her taste, and her lips, etched themselves onto my soul.

Everything was us. Nothing else existed except for her kiss, her taste, her hands on my body. I pushed my body harder against hers. The need to show her all my pent-up frustration, all my feelings, was so overwhelming I wasn't sure I could control myself. I was bruising her mouth with mine and I didn't care. She had to *feel* me. I needed her to feel *me* and only me.

Trace suddenly broke, or something broke—it was as if all the frustration, all of what she'd been holding on to—released. And it was like I could physically see Nixon pried from her existence.

In kissing me, she was letting him go.

But she felt too right for me to feel guilty. I knew that the very person she was letting go of was still breathing.

My knee hit the TV remote, turning it on and causing me to jump back and look into her eyes. "Trace?"

She reached for my head, pulling me into another hot kiss. Her mouth crashed against mine. I pulled away slightly. "Trace?"

"What?" she breathed.

Shit, I was going to be that guy, the one that just had to know the truth… "I need to know something." I played with a piece of her fallen hair and dug my hand into the depths of it as it cascaded through my fingers.

She closed her eyes and rested her head on my hand. "Anything."

"If he was here, if Nixon was here… would it still be me? Would you be letting me kiss you, and touch you? Would you want this?"

Trace's eyes opened slowly and then a blush appeared on her face. She slowly licked her lips and squinted. "Chase, that's not our reality."

"I can see you letting him go—" I sighed. "You want to. I can feel it. But damn if my curiosity didn't just ruin everything." Shaking my head, I rose to my feet. "I still love you. It changes nothing. I guess..." Hell. "I guess I just want it all."

Her eyes were sad when she lifted her head and sighed. "Me too, Chase. Me too."

I held out my hand and pulled her to her feet and walked with her down the hall. We didn't say anything as we both passed each other by and got ready for bed.

I turned the lights off and crawled into my makeshift bed on the floor, placing my gun underneath my pillow.

Yeah, no way was I going to sleep after all that kissing, talking— freaking bleeding my heart all over the place only to find out I'd always be second.

Trace's breathing became heavy, but my damn eyes wouldn't close.

About an hour later, as I was contemplating whether or not I should just stay up all night, she stirred.

"No! Don't!" Thrashing in the bed, Trace let out a whimper. "Please, Nixon. No! No! Don't leave! Don't!"

My heart broke. I quickly jumped onto the bed and pulled her into my arms. "Shh, Trace, it's okay. You're safe. It's okay."

For a moment she tensed and then relaxed into me. "It's not okay." Her voice was weak and gravelly. "The only thing that would make it okay would be Nixon still living." She turned in my arms and kissed me briefly across the lips. "But you're right."

It was my turn to tense.

Trace gripped the sides of my face with her hands. "It's not fair to be second." Her eyes filled with tears. "He's gone. You're here, Chase. You've always been here."

I swallowed.

"You." She placed a tender kiss on my mouth. "First, Chase. I want you to be first. I choose you."

Chapter Forty-Two

Chase

The moonlight outlined Trace's tearstained face as she sat in my lap on the bed. "Say something, Chase."

"Sleep." I touched my forehead to hers. "We're both tired and emotional. We'll sleep and go to lab tomorrow...get you coffee and try to go about life as normal."

"What about you and me?" Trace outlined my jaw with her index finger. Her eyes were heavy with exhaustion.

"We'll talk in the morning." I gently lay down on the bed and held up my arm for her to rest on me. She sighed and laid her head on my chest. Within seconds her breathing had deepened. And I was stuck staring at the ceiling, wondering how the hell I was going to explain to Nixon—that is if he survived—that I had taken from him the one thing he was actually living for.

Sunlight peeked through the windows. Trace's arm was draped over my chest. I traced little circles along its length, content with merely watching her as she slept, knowing that in my arms she was safe—from everything.

The door burst open.

There was Tex. I thought he'd better have a damn good reason for barging in on us. His eyes scanned the bed and then the floor where I usually slept and then went back to the bed. He swallowed and blinked a few times, still saying nothing, but words weren't really necessary. He had to know. It was evident from the way we were holding on to each other. Everyone was moving on; damn if it didn't hurt like hell to keep growing, to keep going.

Tex took a step into the room. "I just wanted to know if you guys wanted coffee. Mo's making breakfast and...well, it just seemed like it would be nice for all of us to eat together—like we used to before..." His voice trailed off.

Guilt gnawed at me all over again.

But I was unable to say anything to put him at ease. "Sure man, just give us a few minutes, okay?"

"Okay." He backed out of the room. "If it's any consolation. I know you love her."

His words made my hand freeze to a stop. The guilt grew and grew. "I do. I love her."

"So did he." Tex nodded and walked out of the room. And I was officially exhausted. I was on borrowed time either way. And so was Trace; she just didn't know it.

"Hey," I whispered into her hair. "Sleepyhead, we've gotta get up. You've got lab with Luca, and maybe I'm too hopeful that you'll burn down the entire building."

"I don't burn things," came her grumbling response. "What time is it?"

She lifted her head and blinked a few times, as if trying to make the image of my face less fuzzy. The breath hitched in my chest. She was so beautiful. Her golden brown eyes bored into mine as a lock of hair fell across her face. I couldn't find the words. I seriously felt like an idiot because I was totally gawking at her like I'd just lost my mind.

"Chase?" She squinted. "You all right?"

No. I was dying. Seriously dying inside…How could I go on without her in my life? Knowing what it was like to wake up next to her? To hold her in my arms. The familiar pain streaked across my chest, weighed on me as if I'd just been buried under the ocean.

"Um, yeah, just tired. You snore, by the way."

She scowled. "You sound like Nixon."

The room fell silent. I didn't know what to do to make it better, so I simply shrugged and laughed. "Well, we were more like brothers."

And shit. It was like I hadn't actually thought about that until now.

Hell. Cousins with some messed-up parentage that almost made us look like brothers. Both in love with the same girl. Weird, because it was like we shared parents, too, or they shared each other— however you wanted to look at it. There had to be some law about that, or something in the Bible that said you'd be condemned to Hell for coveting your cousin's girlfriend. The same cousin who technically looked a hell of a lot more like your brother and who your real dad parented. Shit, it was messed up. On the bright side, at least Nixon and Trace weren't married. Right, because that somehow made it less horrible.

"I'm just going to go shower, okay?" Trace interrupted my dark thoughts and walked over toward the bathroom. I grabbed my stuff and went to the hall bathroom. Within fifteen minutes I was ready to go. I threw on my Eagle Elite uniform, black slacks with a white button-up shirt, red sweater vest, and jacket—and made a beeline for the kitchen. The smell of sausage and eggs assaulted me.

"Hey, Harry Potter, glad you could make it," Tex called from the table.

"You've been saving that one for four years, haven't you." I shook my head. "Lame, and this looks nothing like Harry Potter. Don't be an ass just because you don't have to go to class on Thursdays."

He smirked.

I snatched a glass of orange juice and sat down.

Mil was reading the paper in the corner, still in her pj's. "Your eye's healing up," she pointed out without actually looking up from the paper.

"No thanks to you." I snatched a piece of toast. "I'm lucky I survived."

"Survived what?" Mo asked from the kitchen and then looked at me. "Holy crap! What happened!"

"People really should learn not to drink and walk at the same time." This from Tex.

Glaring at Tex, I answered Mo. "Apparently, I fall on tables and shit."

"You should be more careful." Mo put a plate of food in front of me.

"Right," I answered. "I'll be more careful next time I'm around tables named Mil."

"Huh?" Mo asked.

"Nothing." Mil smiled sweetly at my sister and then sent me a seething glare. I smiled and took another bite of toast.

"Oh my gosh, that smells amazing." Trace walked into the kitchen and immediately I started choking.

"Dude, chew your food." Tex patted my back and handed me a glass of water but I waved him off. Water wouldn't help. I needed freaking CPR.

Beautiful. Damn, she was so incredibly beautiful that it hurt to look at her. Her soft brown hair was in a high ponytail and for the first time in two days her uniform looked ironed, clean, perfect on her body.

And the killer?

The part that had me ready to jump out of my chair and slam that perfect girl into the wall and kiss her senseless?

She was wearing the boots.

My boots.

The ones I gave her.

I smiled as she stuck out her leg for approval.

With a wink in my direction she grabbed a plate from Mo and took a seat next to me. The smell of coconut wafted off of her and into my airspace. I was starved for it. I leaned closer to her and placed my hand on her bare knee.

We ate with the rest of the group.

Things were almost normal.

Except they weren't. Which I was reminded of the minute I opened the door to go outside, only to find every single one of the men I had placed to guard the house—gone.

"What the hell?" I dialed my father's number. We needed those men to get us to school without anyone seeing Trace. My father would have been the only one who suspected she was dead and I was taking a huge risk by even allowing her to go about life.

We needed a driver. And we needed to be able to sneak her in and out of classes, not because a college education was that important but because Nixon had specifically said to go about life as did Luca. Besides, the last thing we needed was for Tony to show up at the house now that my men were missing. School was probably the only place he wouldn't go snooping around.

The phone rang and rang.

Finally my father picked up. "Chase, I'm a bit busy right now."

"My men," I barked into the phone. "Where are they?"

"Son, I have no idea what you're talking about."

"Right," I snorted. "Let's try this again. You work for me. I'm your boss. If I don't have my men back within the hour I will personally drive my ass over to your house and slam my fist into your head. Got it?"

My father made a choking sound as if he was laughing at me. "To be young again."

"Yes." I hissed. "To be young and actually able to get shit done rather than staying at home being completely useless. I mean it. I did what you asked last night, but this is the final straw. You either want me in power or you don't."

He sighed heavily on the other end of the line. "It's complicated, Chase. I'm not safe, not at the house, I needed extra security. Just in case."

I was silent for a moment. "Did someone threaten you?"

No doubt Nixon was poking around.

"Not exactly." He cleared his throat. "I just…you know what happens when you drink a lot and…"

"And?" I prompted.

"Nixon." My dad laughed. "I could have sworn I saw Nixon, but instead it was the De Lange kid. He wants to make a deal."

Things had just gotten interesting. "Oh?"

"I was going to speak to you—"

"It's your lucky day. You're speaking to me now. What does Phoenix want?"

"Money," my father blurted. "He wants money and then he's going to disappear for good. But the thing is, Chase…I don't have access to the funds we use for bribery. I'm going to need you to make the withdrawal."

Son of a bitch. My own father was going to betray me. Did he think I was that stupid? The boss never made the withdrawal. Not unless he wanted to get A) shot, or B) flagged by the Feds.

"Hmm." I paused and mouthed to Tex to get the car. "You do have my permission. When does Phoenix need the money?"

"Tonight."

"Of course he does," I said. "Fine. I'll get the money. We'll put all of this behind us and live like one big defective family. Sound good?"

"I never did get your sense of humor."

"I wasn't being funny, Dad."

"Fine. Tonight then?" Damn if he didn't sound ridiculously pleased with himself.

"Sure. Oh, and remember." I cleared my throat. "If anything goes wrong, if for one second I smell a rat, I'll shoot you."

"You'd shoot your own flesh and blood."

"Of course not." I hung up and threw the phone against the ground. It shattered into a million pieces.

Tex pulled up and got out of the car. "Shit. You didn't have to take it out on your phone."

"I need a new one." I released Trace's hand and flexed my fingers.

"I'm on it." Mo ran back in the house. We always kept extra phones around. Mainly because we needed lots of lines open for business, but also because Nixon and I had always had a tendency to break phones when we got upset. Expensive habit.

I paced in front of everyone. "He wants us in the dark for a reason. Damn you, Nixon." I realized I had slipped. Trace looked at me curiously, as did Tex and Mil. "Sorry, that was uncalled for." I cleared my throat. "Normal. Everything has to go normal today. Trace, I'll go to class with you; maybe we'll find answers there. If not...Shit, I'll have to get the money myself."

"Money?" Mo repeated. "What money? What's going on?"

"Apparently we need to pay someone off." I clenched my hand into a fist. "And good ol' Dad wants me to be the one to make the transfer."

"It's a setup," Tex interjected. "No boss does the business himself. He pays someone to do it for him. What Tony's asking is not only ridiculous, it's stupid. He knows you aren't stupid enough to go do it yourself."

"Which is exactly why I have to." I scratched the back of my head. "I'll go to the bank after classes and make the withdrawal with Sherry. She's family so she won't blink an eye when I take that much money from the accounts. Just know that if a bomb goes off it's probably not an accident."

At Trace's sharp intake of breath, I paused. "Shit, I'm sorry, Trace. I was being sarcastic."

Her hand flew across my face so hard I nearly fell. "Well, stop being sarcastic or I'm going to kill you myself!"

Mo had just returned, holding out my new phone, but she snatched it back from me.

"What the hell, Mo, I need that!"

Mo stuffed it in her purse. "Not until you're done looking like you want to shoot the first thing that looks at you funny."

Tex grinned sheepishly and batted his eyes.

"What the hell are you doing?"

"Looking at you funny. Is it working? You wanna shoot me?"

"No." I shoved my hands in my pockets.

"Cool. Mo, give him the damn phone."

"Men!" she shouted and handed me the phone, then got into the running car. Mil stood on the stoop and waved good-bye.

I paused. "There aren't any men here to protect you."

She lifted her coffee cup in the air with one hand and pulled a pistol from her bathrobe with the other. "Do I look like I need protecting?"

"No." I chuckled.

"That would be a hell no," Tex called from the front seat. "Play nice, Mil."

"Always do!" She walked back inside and shut the door.

"She scares me," Tex announced once we were on the road.

I laughed. "Yeah, well imagine what she was like before reform school."

Chapter Forty-Three

Nixon

So?" I took a long swig of coffee and leaned against the tree. "Fifty-fifty it's going to work?"

"I'd say..." Phoenix shrugged. "Thirty-seventy."

"Chase will do it because he knows it's not a normal call to make. We can bank on that." I replayed the plan in my head over and over again until I wanted to puke. "I told him to go about business as normal. He'll do it."

"Good." Phoenix nodded. "Because if he doesn't your entire plan goes to hell."

It would be fine. It had to be. "How was Tony?"

"Oh, you know." Phoenix shrugged. "Pissed, but when you make an angry man an offer he can't refuse—"

"He's evil," I interrupted. "Pure evil. No doubt about it."

"As am I," a voice interrupted us. "The danger does not come in the evil, but in the person. Evil is everywhere, but in the end it is always a choice."

"And you choose it?" I asked Luca. "You choose to make life hell for everyone?"

"Absolutely not," he scoffed. "I keep order in a world full of chaos. I am perceived as evil, but true evil? The type that people fear—it masquerades as something far more worse than darkness."

He sighed and put on dark sunglasses. "It makes you believe it is light itself, and that is where you find your danger. Be ready tonight, gentlemen, or you will both be waving at me from the bottom of Lake Michigan."

Phoenix swore. "Such a charmer."

"I never thought—" I laughed. "I never thought that in the end it would be me and you. Old friends, sworn enemies."

"Yeah, God has a great sense of humor."

I watched Trace walk into class. She was holding Chase's hand and they were laughing. The knife went deeper into my chest as I tried to look away but it was like I couldn't. I was so damn happy she was healthy, alive, safe. Shit. I'd spend my life watching her from afar, as long as I knew she would still be smiling, as long as I knew she would be safe from the evil around her.

Phoenix slapped me on the back. "If it's any consolation, she clearly loves you."

"How would you know?" I snapped.

He removed his hand from my back. "The way she looks at you. It's different than how she looks at Chase."

"And how does she look at Chase?"

"Like he's her savior," Phoenix said softly.

"And me?"

"Like you're her oxygen."

I didn't say anything.

The problem was that I didn't just see how they reacted to each other. I could tell by her body language that slowly, piece by piece, she was willing to let go of me. I wasn't sure what hurt worse: how fast she was able to do it, or knowing the person she was actually doing it for.

Last year I'd practically branded her as mine.

And now I wasn't so sure. No matter what anyone told me, I knew what I saw. She was slipping like sand through my fingertips and I had no one to blame but myself. I wanted to punch Chase until he bled, but he wasn't the real villain, not in this story. No, I only had to look in the mirror to see that guy.

I was forced to be the bad guy so that she could have a chance.

But damn, how I wanted, just for once in my godforsaken life, to be the hero, the knight in shining armor, the guy she deserved to have. The guy who'd rescue her at all costs, the guy who'd damn his family to hell in order to keep her.

But I couldn't forget my family.

My blood.

My damn code of honor.

I envisioned myself standing with Trace in the end, but lately, her face had started to disappear, right along with my future.

Phoenix slapped me on the back. "She needs you man; just give it time. And do me a favor: When this is all over and we aren't waving to Luca from the bottomless pit of Lake Michigan, give her a chance to process through stuff, okay?"

I snorted. "Never took you for one to spout out wisdom."

"Yeah well, impending death has a way of doing that to a person."

"You aren't going to die." I turned around to face him. "Neither of us will. Now, let's go wait back at the house. If memory serves, you're supposed to be helping Tony get the gang together."

Phoenix laughed. "Mass killings are my specialty."

"I still can't believe he'd go along with it."

"He wants to silence everyone and he's a bastard. Of course he'd go along with it. He double-crossed the most powerful mafia boss in America, and then spat in the face of one of the Originals in Sicily. If that wasn't bad enough, he tried to wipe out Trace and set up his own family. I'd say he deserves what's coming to him."

"Right." I had a sinking feeling things weren't what they seemed but I didn't voice my opinion aloud. I didn't want Phoenix to hesitate; hesitation could mean death, and after seeing Trace again I very much wanted to stay alive.

Chapter Forty-Four

Chase

And there he is," I said under my breath as Luca waltzed into the classroom, clipboard in hand.

"Good morning, class." He smiled in every direction but ours. "Today I'll be handing out a study sheet for next week's test. I trust all of you have been diligently studying. The test will be in lab format. You'll need to go through a series of three labs for a chance to gain 150 points toward your midterm. Any questions, please do not hesitate to raise your hand."

I itched to raise my hand and say something along the lines of, "Why the hell would you pretend to kill my best friend? What game are you playing?" Instead, I bit down hard on my lip and turned in toward the desk. Papers were passed back until they reached us. They were one short. Great. Now I really did have to raise my hand.

I raised my hand but Luca was looking down.

I waited, and then finally with a huff I pushed back my chair and approached his desk. "I need a paper."

Luca looked up briefly from his desk and smiled. "It seems you do, Mr. Winter." He slid a note over the paper and winked.

"Memorization is the key, Mr. Winter. Wouldn't you agree? After all, it is easier to know what to look for once you have obtained the answers up here." He pointed to his head and then looked back down at his desk.

I followed his eyes to see something written on a paper.

Do not fail.

The message could have so many different meanings, but in that moment, I knew it was pertaining to me. I couldn't fail.

I stuffed the note into my pocket and took the sheet of paper. "Thanks, Mr. Nicolosi, great talk."

"Agreed," he murmured without looking up.

I walked back to the desk and noticed Trace was already working hard on her sheet. I pulled out the note that Luca had placed on top of my worksheet and read it.

There will be five men there to shoot you. Go alone. A ghost will be there to watch your back, as ghosts tend to do. It will be next to impossible to get that much cash at once. Obtain the account number and bring the piece of paper with you with an empty briefcase. You will need to bring it to Nixon's house. He will be waiting—casualties are expected. Whatever you do, do not trust anyone. No one but the ghost.

Quickly, I switched on the Bunsen burner and held the note over the flame. It erupted quickly. I pretended not to notice. Trace lifted her head. "Holy crap! You're on fire!"

I shrugged and pulled the paper away then stamped it out with my hand and threw it into the trash can next to our work table. "Whoops."

Her eyes narrowed.

I shrugged. "So, what problem are you on?"

"What was that?"

"A love note."

"Liar. I don't write love notes."

I smirked. "Who says you're the only one interested?"

"You're being an ass."

I cleared my throat and tucked a piece of her hair behind her ear. "I thought you were used to that by now."

"One doesn't get used to assiness, one just learns to cope with its many faces."

"Are you calling my face an ass?" I tilted my head and leaned forward. "Because I kind of dig it."

"What's up with you?" Trace laughed. "We're supposed to be working."

"Screw work." I pushed her paper onto the floor, earning a glare from the students at the table next to us. "Let's leave early. The way I see it, Luca has to let us go. Plus, I need to make that really fun errand after school and we both know how fun that's going to be."

She seemed to think about it.

I grabbed her hand. "Just follow me, it'll be fine."

We grabbed our stuff and approached the desk hand in hand.

"Mr. Winter, Miss Rooks, what can I do for you?"

It hadn't occurred to me until now that both Trace and I were hiding our identity, our bloodlines with our last names.

With a heavy sigh I answered. "It's kind of loud in here. May we study in the library?"

Luca's eyebrows knit together. I gave him a firm nod. I was hoping my mafia mojo was going to work. Hoping he'd see the underlying issue, not the work or the noise excuse. Shit, it was dead silent in there. But I needed to get away. I slowly tilted my head toward Trace and then mouthed *please* to Luca.

Wow, I must have been desperate. I never said please.

"Brilliant idea, Mr. Winter." Luca waved us off. "Remember not to be tardy."

"I'm always on time," I responded, gripping Trace's hand with mine as we exited the classroom and walked hand in hand all the way down the hall.

The day had officially caught up with me—the seriousness of the situation, the realization that what Trace and I had would never be permanent. Ridiculous that with all the chaos going on around me, the planned death of my best friend, all I could think about was making her mine. My emotions were in hyperdrive. Part of me wanted to put Trace into hiding just to keep her safe—but the selfish half of me craved having her near. Just one more kiss, just one more touch and I'd gladly walk off to the executioner.

When we reached outside I couldn't take it anymore, I jerked her behind one of the buildings, dropped my bag, threw hers on the ground, and pushed her against the wall. I don't know what touched her first—my body, my lips, my hands. I was all over the place, needing to taste her.

Because in the pit of my stomach I knew—it would probably be for the last time. I was desperate for her to see me, not him. I needed her to feel my lips, not his. I know she'd made a choice; she'd said as much last night, but my heart was aching with the possibility that we only had today—we had now, and that was it.

"Chase." With a push, Trace put some distance between us. We were both breathing heavy. Her lips were swollen from my assault. "What's going on?"

"We're skipping class."

"Why?"

"So I can kiss you." I grazed her lower lip with my tongue and gave her a slow agonizing kiss, then pulled back. "Is that a problem?"

Her smile didn't reach her eyes. "No, except it seems like you're upset or something."

"Not upset." My hands shook as I placed them on her shoulders and exhaled. "Just a little...sentimental."

"Chase Winter." She laughed. "I never thought I'd see the day."

"Please." I had to touch her. My hands went to her neck as my thumbs grazed her lower lip. "I've been nothing but sentimental with you."

"You have two autopilots. Jackassery or sentimental sap. Why can't you just find some middle ground? Hmm?" She teased.

"Go big or go home, I guess." I leaned in until our lips were touching again.

She pulled back.

Shit.

"I..." Her cheeks stained red. "Chase, I like you, I love you, but Nixon's only been dead a few days and I just—" Tears welled behind her eyes. "I'm not saying no. I'm just saying not right now. I need time. And the way you kiss me, the way you touch me..." She choked on a sob. "Sometimes it makes me forget him and I hate myself that I would do that after everything he's done for you, and for me."

Never in my life had I ever felt like a bigger bastard than in that moment. I jerked away from her and picked up both our bags. "You're right, Trace. I'm sorry, I don't know what came over me."

"Hormones?" she joked.

I laughed with her, but inside I was a bit crushed. Maybe for her…but for me? It was instinct. It was love.

Chapter Forty-Five

Phoenix

I knew something was wrong the minute Tony answered the phone. "Yes?" He was too calm, too patient, not his usual self.

"So we doing this or what?" I snapped.

"Patience." Tony chuckled. "Don't you just love when everything goes according to plan?"

"I freaking live for it. Seriously. Oh look, I almost shit my pants with happiness at your excitement."

"You're a pain in the ass, you know that?"

"Yeah, well." I rolled my eyes and managed to keep my tone even. "It's my marker; what can I say?"

Tony was silent for a minute and then said quickly, "My house. We'll meet there and do the exchange."

"If you double-cross me—"

"You're the one getting the better end of the deal. My silence. My loyalty. And my money. You'll shut the hell up if you know what's good for you."

I laughed.

"What's so funny?" Tony snapped.

"You."

"Don't push me, boy, or I'll—"

"Do nothing. That's right. Nothing. You may have the money, you may pull the strings, and you may think I'm a dumbass puppet, but I have one thing you don't."

"What's that?"

"Every damn card stacked against you. So if I were you, I'd start talking a little nicer before I rain a hellstorm on your freaking parade."

I hung up the phone then threw it across the room.

Luca clapped behind me. "Well played. Perhaps I do have use for you in my family."

I shook my head. "More family is the last thing I need."

"Redemption." Luca's eyes narrowed. "Would be a first."

"How the hell do you redeem the damned, Luca? A shit's still a shit even when you put a rose on it."

"And blood is thicker than life." Luca slowly lifted his cigar to his mouth and took a puff. "You may say you don't want a family, you may say you want out, but you're forgetting one tiny thing."

I looked away, hoping he wouldn't go on.

"I. Own. You."

"Everything ready?" Nixon said as he came into the room.

I quickly hid my expression and shrugged. "Of course." My eyes darted to Luca and he gave a slight nod. "Everything's going perfectly according to plan."

"Good." Nixon's mouth relaxed as he took a seat in the chair and looked at his phone again. I knew what he was doing; he was memorizing her face. Hell, if I had a girl I'd be doing the same damn thing. Made men were no different from soldiers headed off to war—in the end we all wanted something to fight for—whether it be a pretty girl or a cause. When facing death—every human being needed something that, if the worst happened—would pull them through.

And maybe that's why I was beginning to feel more terrified than anything—because I knew—I had nobody worth pulling for, and it hurt like hell.

Chapter Forty-Six

Chase

After my make-out session gone wrong, I called for Tex to pick up Trace. We didn't talk about it any further and it kind of pissed me off that something I wanted so badly was so close I was able to taste it, but could not fully have it.

I was confused by my own feelings and definitely not on my A game, which meant it was possible I was going to get murdered in my own bank if I didn't get my shit together—fast.

Checking both of my guns for the third time, I put both of them in the back of my pants and pulled my shirt over them.

I was a big fan of brass knuckles, so I had one of those on my left hand. It also had a knife that would snap out and slice someone if I needed it. I did all my business with my right hand anyway.

After taking a few deep breaths, I approached the large building. It was white with large spikes protruding from the top. Tony had built it to look like more of an artful fortress than a business building. His office, and the offices of the family, were all in the bottom of the building. The basement.

They were down there for a reason.

No windows to jump out of, no escape.

If you went down there and had done something to piss off the Abandonatos, you should record your good-bye on the little security video on the elevator, because it would take an act of God for you to make it out alive.

Funny thing is, we'd had several people do just that. It was like they knew by pushing *basement* that it was their final descent.

It was their hell.

I waved at the secretary, and she smiled and waved back. With an exhale I walked toward the back of the building where the elevators were located. I pushed the button, it dinged, and I walked in and looked up at the camera as the silver doors closed.

Basement. I pushed the glowing B button and waited as the elevator descended to the bottom floor. With a ding, the doors opened. Complete silence greeted me. I walked directly toward the basement-level secretary.

Her eyes revealed her fear.

That was the first and last thing I noticed before a gun went off. A bullet whizzed by my head. I ducked and reached into my waistband for a gun. I turned to the right and saw a guy stalking toward me. The secretary started screaming and hid in the corner. I fired two shots directly at his forehead and rolled behind the desk, where the secretary was seated. Releasing my brass knuckles I grabbed my other gun and held it out in front of me. One gun was pointed to the right, one to the left.

And then I felt something touch the back of my head.

"Not so smart for a boss, eh?" a man's voice said.

I didn't panic. It wouldn't make anything better. "I'm smart."

"Oh, yeah? Then why do you have a gun pointed at your head?"

I shrugged. "You tell me." I looked down at his shoes.

Not boots. He was wearing tennis shoes. Brand-new tennis shoes. Not name brand. I closed my eyes and inhaled. He smelled like fast food.

Paid. He was a hired hit man. By the looks of his shoes he'd already gotten half his payment, too.

He also wasn't used to the mafia, used to our kind.

I laughed.

"Stop laughing!" He pushed the gun harder against my head. "I'm gonna enjoy this."

I sighed and stepped on his foot then quickly leaned over to the right as I pulled his arm forward and smacked it against the marble countertop. His gun toppled to the ground. I turned and kicked him in the stomach, and he stumbled backward, hitting the copy machine.

"I'll enjoy this much more, I guarantee it." I pulled out my gun and shot him in both knees. He fell to the ground with a loud crack and swore in agony.

Three more. There were three more guys.

Footsteps neared me.

I ducked under the desk and motioned for the secretary to be quiet, but her hands were shaking. Shit. With one swift movement, I knocked her to the floor and pulled her underneath the table with me.

"Thank you, thank you." She shook in my arms.

I hit her across the back of the head, rendering her unconscious. She wouldn't thank me when she woke up with a killer headache, but at least she'd be alive.

The footsteps got closer.

And then three shots rang out.

A man walked in front of the desk. His shoes were—white.

His hand reached down to me. "Come on. I don't have all day," he whined, sounding genuinely irritated that he'd had to shoot someone.

I grabbed his hand but kept my finger on the trigger in my left hand.

Once he pulled me out from underneath the desk I was face-to-face with the last person I thought I'd see.

"Sergio?" I gasped. "Man! I thought you moved!"

"Nah." He unloaded his gun. "I like to dabble every now and then when I see a damsel in distress."

I snorted and put my gun away. "Same ol' Sergio. Thanks, by the way. You must be—"

"The ghost."

"Didn't think you were a man for hire these days."

His brown eyes narrowed. "A man does what he can do, to help family." Sergio tucked his gun in the back of his pants and leaned against the marble countertop.

I swallowed and looked away. "Yeah, well…think you can help me get the account information?"

He snorted. "I could do it blindfolded. Let's get this done. You've got more guns waiting for you."

"I wait with bated breath." I swore and followed him into Tony's office. It suddenly felt wrong to be calling him Tony instead of Dad. But there was no love lost, and that was damn tragic. Parentless kids, all of us. Nixon, Trace, Mo, Mil.

"So." Sergio sat behind the computer. "Word on the street is you need ten mil."

"Word on the street? What are we? In a gang?"

Sergio chuckled. "What else would you call it?"

"Valid point." I leaned against the glass desk and watched him log in to my father's computer. "How do you even know his password?"

"I'm a ghost. I know all." His hands sped across the keyboard so fast that it made me dizzy. "This may take a few minutes." He motioned to a seat, but I refused to sit down. Not after having five guys shooting at my face and knowing it was my own family that had sent them.

This was only the fifth time in all my life that I'd been in my "father's" office. I walked over to the minibar on the far right and poured myself a whiskey.

"Think you should be drinking, all things considered?" Sergio asked from the desk.

Ignoring him, I took a long swig and looked at the table next to the minibar. There were pictures. But they weren't of me.

They were of him and Nixon.

With a curse I turned away. Was it always about him? Would it never be about me? How selfish could I get that I would even ask that, but…I wanted something that was my own, someone that was my own, and it seemed as of late I was either stuck with second best or picking up someone else's pieces.

"Almost there, just keep your pants on," Sergio called.

Again, I ignored him and searched more around the room. There weren't any more pictures on the tables he had set up. Two chairs were in the corner with a closet toward the main door. Curious, I walked over to it and tried the knob.

Locked.

I pulled out one of my picks and had the door open in seconds. Shock wasn't an adequate word to describe what I was seeing. Shock would have been a normal response. My response was anything but normal.

Horrified? Now that was better.

A shrine.

With prayer beads.

And a picture of Nixon's mom. I could stomach that, I could deal with that amount of crazy, but the picture had Trace's parents in it. I'd seen them only once when I was little but I'd also seen pictures. From what Nixon had told me, they were unmistakable.

There were red marks across every face in the pictures. My stomach heaved as I numbered how many faces had the red mark. Both of Trace's parents...and my dad. My real dad.

Which could mean only one thing.

Tony had been snuffing out the entire family for over eighteen years.

And today would be his day of reckoning. His finale.

I hoped to God it would be a massive disappointment. I'd even tell him that to his face, right before I pulled the trigger.

"Done!" Sergio announced. I turned around and walked toward the desk while he scribbled something on a piece of paper. "So, the wire transfer will go to this account." He handed me the paper. "Did you remember to get a briefcase?"

"In the car already." I stuffed the piece of paper in my pocket and shrugged. "How are you in on this? Who are you actually working for? Me? Luca?"

Sergio's eyes darted behind me. I turned and saw a camera nestled quite nicely in the corner. Great.

When I turned back around he was already walking toward the door.

"Wait," I called. "If this goes badly...thank you, for what you just did."

"We're family." He shrugged and pulled out a pair of sunglasses. "Try not to end up with a bullet in the head, eh?"

"I'll do my damnedest." I cracked a smile and took a seat on Tony's plush leather chair.

How long? How long had he been planning this, and why the hell were Trace's parents involved? I wracked my brain but couldn't come up with any solution other than pure insanity.

I waited another five minutes then left the room and walked down the hall to the elevator.

I was more pissed off than scared; I didn't really get scared anymore. Impending death never scared me. Hell, it was a reality. But now? Knowing that Trace could lose both me and Nixon? At the same time? All over again? Yeah, that sucked. I refused to leave her. Even if I had to go to hell and back and beg to be brought back to life—I refused to leave her. I couldn't.

The elevator dinged. I walked out and dialed Tony's number. "I got the money."

"You did?" The ass sounded surprised.

"Yeah."

"Complications?"

"A few minor ones. Nothing to get upset over."

"I'm impressed."

"Don't be," I snorted. "Now, where am I meeting you?"

"Our house, of course."

I paused. I thought we were supposed to meet at Nixon's, which meant he was changing things. Why was he changing things? "Fine. See you in ten."

I hung up and got into my car. Shit. Things were already going sideways and I had no idea what to expect. Would he put a gun on me when I opened the door? Would he take the money, confess, and then shoot me?

I contemplated all the ways I could die the entire way to the house. The minute I got there, I jumped out of the car and grabbed the briefcase. Birds chirped and the sun was shining, just as if something huge wasn't going down.

And then I heard a gun click. "We've been expecting you."

I turned around. "Phoenix?"

His smug grin made me want to rip his head from his body.

"Who else were you expecting?"

Chapter Forty-Seven

Chase

Phoenix nudged me in the back with his gun. Holy shit. I would kill him. End him. If he as much as sneezed on my back. I walked in front of him and opened the door to the house.

Tony was standing in the living room, smoking his usual cigar and looking out the window.

"Ah, you've made it."

"Nice greeting," I said dryly. "Can you please call Phoenix off of me before I put a bullet in his head?"

Tony nodded and Phoenix backed off, walking over to Tony and slapping him on the back. "See how easy this was?"

"Easy?" I repeated.

"He needed money." Tony shrugged. "How would it look if our family simply gave the De Langes ten million dollars? It would look like a handout. Besides, I need Phoenix to be silent, and we've come to a sort of agreement. I pay him to keep my secrets and he finishes the business I don't wish to finish."

"What business?" Dread pooled in my stomach.

Tony puffed on his cigar. "You and a few others…"

I opened my mouth to speak when all of a sudden I heard a whimper. I walked farther into the living room. My eyes fell on the couch.

Mo, Mil, and Trace were sitting there. Hands tied behind their backs and duct tape over their mouths.

"You sick son of a bitch!"

"Kids!" Tony spat. "You're all children! Did you think this was a game? Did you think I was working underneath a *child* for the past four years to simply hand over all the power I've had? Do you think I like having to listen to a child order me around as if I was nothing? A child that did not even deserve to be boss in the first place! Blood relation, Chase! You are the blood relation!"

"I know," I mumbled. "That doesn't mean you needed to kill Nixon. Your actual son, you dirty bastard."

"Lucky for me, I did not have to. I simply provided the information to the Nicolosi family. I knew they would not be pleased that their golden family, the chosen Abandonatos, were falling apart at the seams all because they could not let go of the past."

"Let go of the past?" I stepped closer to the couch. "Calling the kettle a bit black, aren't you? Considering you killed Trace's parents in cold blood and set up your own family to take the fall."

"He deserved death and much worse." Tony puffed on his cigar again and looked out the window. "He was weak so he beat on his wife. But she loved me. We loved one another; she was going to leave him and he—"

"Killed her," I finished. "And my mother?"

Tony laughed. "The stupid bitch found out about my affair, went to Nixon's father and had her own little affair; only she never loved him. When he discovered she was using him, he had the Nicolosi family take care of her for him…didn't want her blood on his hands. Though he wasn't opposed to take his own wife's blood—or even a boy who wasn't his son. Perhaps that's why he kept her alive so long? He wanted to watch her suffer, wanted to watch his bastard son suffer while his mother was beaten."

I stole a glance at Trace. Her nostrils flared. Damn, in the past five minutes she had gone from looking terrified to completely pissed.

"So…" I moved closer, into the room. "Why kill Trace's parents? They weren't involved in your little melodrama."

"Mario, Tracey's father—he discovered us one evening. Said his loyalty was to the Alfero and Abandonato family. He was going to ruin everything."

"So you eliminated him, and pointed at the one man everyone would suspect." I shook my head in disgust. "You're a pathetic excuse for a human being."

Tony threw his cigar into the nearby fireplace and stalked toward me. "I survive! I keep the family together! I may be heartless but at least I know what it costs to keep our blood strong!"

He stopped directly in front of me, his chest heaving.

I shook my head. "You. Are. Nothing."

His fist flew across my jaw. I knew he was going to hit me, so I let him. The minute I fell to the ground I scooted away from him like I was afraid and dug a knife from my pocket.

"And I'm pathetic," Tony snorted. "Yet you crawl away from me like a little bitch. At least Nixon died with honor, whereas you—" He reached for his gun. "You'll die shaming everyone."

Ignoring him and his raised gun, I slid my knife underneath the first pair of feet I touched and then quickly slipped my hands away.

Chapter Forty-Eight

Phoenix

Things were going to hell fast. What was worse—I'd been given the job of tying up each of the girls. Luckily, I was able to make the knots loose enough so they could at least wriggle free without too much trouble.

Tony was clearly insane. He pointed the gun at Chase while I took another step into the living room.

"Are the theatrics really necessary?" I tried to sound bored as I examined my fingernails.

Trace shouted at me through her covered mouth; by the fiery look in her eyes I could tell she wasn't exactly singing my praises at the moment.

Tony threw his head back and laughed while I mouthed, *Forgive me*.

I'd never asked anyone to forgive me before—never had to. My dad had always said our calling was above forgiveness, that we were above reproach because of what we did—who we were.

Tony wiped at his eyes. "How proud, Chase, do you think it makes me to see you... my bastard son, on your knees?"

"Here we go again," I muttered, trying to distract everyone.

Tony took a swing at Chase, knocking him to the ground again, and that's when I saw the knife. He was going to get himself killed to save the girls—my sister, Trace, Mo. Acting fast, I rushed in front of them and knelt.

"What the hell are you doing!" Tony spat.

"The knots. They came untied. I'm fixing them, you bastard!" I yelled back then slid the knife slowly up Trace's leg, knowing it was probably scaring the hell out of her. But instead of flinching, she focused on my eyes the entire time. I imagined that would just make it worse—staring into two soulless holes, but she wasn't staring at me like I had no soul. Instead, she was staring at me like I was her only hope. My heart pounded a bit harder as I finally got the knife into her hands. I stood up and turned around so that she could undo her ropes without Tony seeing.

Tony kicked Chase in the stomach over and over again. I knew Chase was tough, so I didn't stop it, even though I wanted to. Chase would rather suffer a few broken ribs, knowing the girls were safe, than save his pretty face and be responsible for their deaths.

Blood trickled down Chase's chin. His eyes had started to swell shut, and he glanced behind him and saw that the girls were free then looked up to me in confusion.

I made a move to help him to his feet just as Tony cocked the gun.

"I'm not sorry." Tony tilted his head and aimed in between Chase's eyes. "Say hello to Nixon when you see him."

"Or you can just say hello now," a voice said from the doorway.

Chapter Forty-Nine

Chase

I heard girlish whimpers from behind me as Nixon made his way into the room, gun pointed directly at Tony's head. He was followed by Luca, who was clapping.

"Beautiful performance," Luca said. "Do you think we got everything we needed, Nixon? Or should we make him suffer."

"Do I get a vote?" I asked from the ground, still pissed.

Nixon looked around at me and rolled his eyes. At least he looked like he was still in good humor.

Tony jumped over my body and in front of the girls on the couch.

Shit.

"How are you alive, Nixon?" Tony trained his gun on Trace. "Hmm? How is that possible?"

Nixon shrugged. "I'm like a cat. I have nine lives. Besides, God said he doesn't want me."

Tony chuckled. "So, what happens now? You kill me?"

Luca nodded. "The idea has some appeal."

"How do you suppose you will be able to do such a thing?" Tony asked. "I have all your precious women at my fingertips. One pull from this trigger and Tracey dies, or how about Mil? Phoenix, you've always hated your sister. Why don't you help me? The way I see it is it's only three against two."

"Right." Phoenix moved to Tony's side, the bastard.

Luca nodded and rubbed his chin. "I believe, Nixon, that I've had enough." He pointed his gun in Tony's direction and fired at the same time Tony fired at Luca.

Luca fell to the ground, still shooting. Tony cringed and held his arm.

I made a move to grab the girls and pull them to the ground with me just as a bullet grazed my shoulder.

With a wheeze I fell. Well, that sucked. At least it felt like it went straight through. Guns were firing everywhere until finally everything was silent.

I looked up to see that Tony was leaning against the wall holding his arm. Phoenix was next to him, bending over. Nixon and Luca walked across the room, both of them uninjured.

"You will have my blood on your hands, Nixon," Tony spat. "You will both be blamed for bringing down an entire family!"

Nixon shook his head. "You can't blame a ghost, right, Luca?"

"Correct." He nodded to Nixon who lifted his gun toward Tony.

A shot rang out, but it wasn't from Nixon's gun.

Panicking I looked up to see Tony on the ground and Phoenix with his gun still aimed, shaking.

"I'm sorry," Phoenix said. "After everything, Nixon. I can't...I can't let you have his blood on your hands. It's me. I deserve it."

"Phoenix—" Nixon moved to catch him, but Phoenix fell to the ground, blood spewing from a wound in his stomach. "It wasn't supposed to be like this. You were supposed to let me shoot him. Damn it, Phoenix! Why didn't you listen!"

Phoenix coughed up some blood and smiled. "It was supposed to happen exactly like this. Maybe in my death…" He coughed again. "Maybe God will forgive me. Maybe…" He heaved. "Now all of you are clean. Every last one of you. And I can die—in peace."

Nixon's eyes welled with tears. "At least it's not the bottom of Lake Michigan, right, man?" He reached for Phoenix's hand and squeezed it.

Phoenix let out a weak laugh. "Yeah, at least it's not Lake Michigan. Nixon, say the prayer, say it…"

Nixon knelt over Phoenix and made a cross, then in Sicilian said, "Our code of honor has been met. God, take his soul, forgive the sins committed against you, against humanity—receive Phoenix—then and only then, may he die in peace. Amen."

Phoenix's eyes fluttered closed as he took his last breath.

I'd seen death my entire life.

But it wasn't until now that I felt myself holding back tears.

I had to look away.

Feeling like I was going to be sick, I leaned back against the couch and closed my eyes.

"It is done," Luca said in a sad voice. "Bless the father, the son, and holy spirit."

"Amen," everyone said in unison.

Chapter Fifty

Nixon

Trace's eyes met mine and in that instant I had to become indifferent. I had to focus on my task—otherwise it wasn't going to end well. Hell, I hadn't meant for all of it to happen this way. I wasn't supposed to show up, but I couldn't help it; not after hearing what the bastard had done to my family, to Trace's family. I wanted vengeance. So I took a leap of faith.

I put my gun on the table and leaned against it as a few men walked by and readied Phoenix's body for funeral arrangements and Tony's for burial. He would get no funeral, no honors—nothing. But Phoenix? As long as Trace was all right with it, I wanted his funeral to honor him. What he'd done for us was...beyond what I had asked of him. In those last few days I'd had one of my best friends' back. Possibly one of my only remaining friends considering I was ready to shoot Chase where he stood.

He couldn't leave it alone—he couldn't leave her alone. Did he really think I wouldn't be watching him? Watching her?

Their stolen kisses destroyed me.

And the fact that he'd made her choose?

Their room was bugged. I'd at least thought Chase would be intelligent enough to know that. Or maybe he'd wanted me to hear.

Maybe he wanted my heart to rip into two.

"Nixon?" The warmth of Trace's hand scalded my back. I jerked and turned around.

"Yeah?"

"Y-you're alive." Tears streamed down her face as she stepped into my arms. It was the one thing I'd been looking forward to. Going back to normal. But I didn't know how. Didn't know how to fix it.

I gently pushed her away. "Why don't you go see to Chase? We don't want him passing out from his wound."

"But—"

"Go," I urged. "I have some stuff to take care of."

Hands shaking, I wiped off both Phoenix's and Tony's guns and put them in a plastic bag, handing them over to Sergio. He'd arrived shortly after to help clean up.

Another one of his specialties. Making things go away.

"Anything else?" he asked examining the room. "You're going to need a crew to come in."

"Yeah." I couldn't get my anger and hurt under control. "Could you just take care of it, Sergio? I need to—"

"It's fine," he interrupted me. "Go."

I nodded and stalked out of the room. The last thing I heard before the door slammed was my name on Trace's lips.

*   *   *

I didn't know where I was going or what I was doing. So I just drove. I drove by the place Trace and I had had our first date. Drove by the school and ended up stopping at the curb and turning off the car.

I hit the steering wheel over and over again until my fingers bled.

How the hell did things get so complicated? I'd thought I could handle it. I lied to myself. I'd forced myself to believe that I could exist in a world where Tracey and Chase were together. But I couldn't.

It would slowly kill me inside, until I wished for death.

With a curse, I put the car in drive and made my way back to my house. Time to face the music. And tell everyone good-bye.

Chapter Fifty-One

Nixon

I opened the door to my house and walked in.

The girls were sitting at the table as if they were waiting for me. Tex's eyes widened when he saw me. Quickly he pushed from the table and embraced me.

"Dude, I thought you were dead."

"Yeah, everyone did." My eyes fell on Trace. It wasn't her fault. I'd pushed her into Chase's arms. I'd given her my damn permission. What the hell was I thinking? Was I high or something?

"I'm glad you're back, man, things have been crazy... and no bullet wounds. Nice."

"Yeah, nice," I repeated. "Luca take off?" My eyes fell to Chase, who was sitting far away from everyone in the corner. A bandage wrapped around his shoulder.

"Yup." He nodded. "Everything's been taken care of."

My eyes fell to Chase's hand. It was like my ring was glaring back at me.

"I missed you." Mo reached across the table and grabbed my hand.

"Thanks Mo, I'm sorry I—"

My sister slapped me across the face and then beat my chest, collapsing into my arms. "Never again, Nixon, or I swear I'll kill you myself!" Sobs wracked her body as I held her.

"It was the only way—"

"To hell with your damn excuses, Nixon!" Mo pulled back and slapped me again. Holy shit, the woman was strong. "You may be the devil but I'm kind of used to having your annoying ass around here!"

I smiled. Probably the first smile I'd had in a few days. "Sorry, Mo. I love you."

"I swear you're the evil twin." She pushed against my chest and slumped back into her chair.

"Anyone else need to take a shot at me?" I joked.

Trace kept her head down, staring at the table. I walked a little closer. Her head jerked up, followed by her gun-wielding hand.

A shot rang out and then I felt severe pain in my left arm. "What the hell?" I touched the outside of my tricep and examined my fingers. Blood dripped off of them.

"Holy shit!" Tex pushed away from the table. "She just shot you!"

Mo and Mil snickered and covered their mouths. Even Chase cracked a smile.

"What the hell is wrong with you?" I directed my yell to Trace. "Last time I took you shooting you couldn't even hit a damn target. You could have killed me!"

"Good!" She pushed away from the table and threw the gun onto it, making a clattering noise. "It's what you deserve!"

The room fell silent as she crossed her arms.

"I deserve to be shot at? To die?"

"Yes." Her lower lip trembled. "Because you destroyed me! Don't you get it? You ruined me! You wrecked me! There is no going back and it's all your fault! You and Chase! I'm so pissed I don't even know what to do! I have nothing! I have no one!"

"But—"

"No!" She yelled, "I-I have nobody. Chase lied to me, you lied to me, and in the end you both ripped my heart in half! Yes you deserve to be hurt, because then maybe you can feel even a sliver of what I feel right now! I have no heart left. The pieces are gone. You've left me with nothing. And I hate you for it. I hate both of you!" With one last sob she ran down the hall, leaving the room blanketed in an awkward silence.

After a few seconds Mo spoke. "You're getting blood on the floor."

"Not the time, Mo," Tex hissed.

Mil stood. "We'll just be—going."

They trickled out of the room, leaving me and Chase staring at each other. I didn't know what to say, what to do. I don't think he did, either. Shit, we'd made a mess of things.

Chase rose from his chair and slowly approached me. With a single nod, he swallowed and then walked over toward the bar and poured us both drinks.

Wordlessly I followed him as he opened the doors to outside. We walked in silence to the end of the property. To the place where we had first made our pact. He held out the glass of whiskey.

We drank in silence.

"I can't bring myself to apologize," Chase finally said.

"I wasn't asking you to."

"I took her." Chase looked down at his glass. "I have no excuses other than I thought you were dead, and then when I found out you weren't"—he laughed humorlessly—"I panicked. I saw her slipping through my fingers—the life I wanted, our future—everything."

"My fault." My voice was hoarse, like there were jagged pieces of glass etched in my throat, making it hard for my words to come out smoothly. "I pushed you guys together. In so many ways I thought it would help. I don't know what the hell I was thinking, I just...I was—"

"You were thinking about her, Nixon." Chase shook his head. "And that's where we differ. Because toward the end, when I was forcing her to choose"—he sighed—"I wasn't thinking about her. I was thinking about me."

I exhaled and closed my eyes. "I won't fight for her."

Chase threw down his drink and punched me in the jaw. "The hell you won't! You piece of shit! I deserve to be shot! And you're going to sit there and just give up."

My drink clattered to the ground as I swayed on my feet. "What the hell, Chase? You're the one who took the most precious thing in my life from me. You're the one who, even though you knew I was alive, kissed my girlfriend, my forever, my reason for living. And you're yelling at me?"

"Damn right I am," Chase spat. "She loves you!"

"She loves you too." I massaged my jaw. "And I'm not gonna do that to her."

"Do what?"

"Make her choose."

Chase hung his head and rubbed his temples. "Stop being the bigger man."

I sighed. "It's not about me, man. It's about her. I'm not going to put her between us. Hell, I'm not even going to let it get between you and me. It's *her*, it's always been *her*, it's about *her*. Hell if I'm going to sit here and throw a fit for wanting something that doesn't want me back. She loves you? Fine. Because, Chase. It's never been about my wants or my needs. I can't live if she's unhappy. I can't breathe if she's upset. If being with you brings her that peace, then I want you to have her. I'll be your best man at the wedding. I'll babysit your kids when you want date night. Chase—" I swallowed the emotion in my throat and shook my head. "It's about *her*."

Chase's eyes welled with tears. I'd never in my life seen the guy cry, but I knew he was close. The man was tough as shit. And I hated that we had been brought to this, that after a lifetime of friendship it would be something like fighting over a girl that would bring us back to the spot where we'd made our pact.

His eyes glazed over as he straightened his spine. "I don't know if I can let her go. How do you let her go? How did you do it? I can't—" He shuddered. "I can't, Nixon. I'm sorry, but if she wants to be with me, I won't say no. *I can't.*"

I sucked in a deep breath and held out my hand to him. He took it. I pulled him in for a hug. "I wouldn't expect you to, Chase. I would never ask that of you."

"I want to hate you."

I released him from my grip and laughed. "Yeah, well, sorry to disappoint you."

"You wanna go apologize first? Or should I?" Chase asked.

"Let's give her some time, all right? She did just shoot me. I wouldn't put it past her to do it again."

Chase chuckled. "Hell of a lucky shot. I'm surprised you're still walking straight, a foot to the left and you would have been—"

"Thanks, yeah, I know what I would have been. Dying."

We picked up our drinks and walked back to the house.

I opened the door to see Mil, Mo, and Tex all back in the room watching us pensively.

It was as if they had all taken in a huge breath and were waiting to see if me or Chase needed to go to the hospital.

"It's fine." I waved my hand in the air. "Nobody's going to die."

They exhaled in unison.

"Not to rain on anybody's parade, but we gotta call the men together tonight. Let them know what happened." Tex shoved his hands in his pockets.

It was awkward. A few weeks ago I'd been the boss. I'd been the boss for years and now I had to look to Chase. After all, his blood was the boss's blood, the man I used to call father.

He clenched his right hand, and light bounced off the ring. "Make the call, Tex."

"Right away." Tex pulled out his cell and started making arrangements.

"And the funeral," I said. "We can't forget about Phoenix."

"No." Chase nodded. "We won't forget him."

Chapter Fifty-Two

Nixon

I watched as the men slowly began trickling into my house. Most of them were so damn happy to see me alive it was as if there wasn't this giant elephant in the room—Chase being boss, and me being...what? What was I? I grabbed a glass of wine and took a seat.

Chase called the meeting to order just as Sergio walked in.

The men began to whisper between themselves.

And then Frank Alfero walked in, with Luca.

It hadn't occurred to me until now how much power was sitting in that room. The head of the Nicolosi family from Sicily, the Abandonatos, and the Alfero mafia boss. Frank nodded at me and took a seat opposite on the couch.

"Gentlemen." Chase cleared his throat. "Please welcome Luca Nicolosi and Frank Alfero. They've been gracious enough to attend our meeting."

Luca nodded at Chase. "Someone has to clear the air."

Over the next hour Luca explained in great detail the plans that had unfolded over the past few weeks. How I'd gone to him and staged my own death in order to snuff out Tony. How I needed more proof and how, in a moment of clarity, the De Lange boss, Phoenix, had redeemed himself by not only helping us, but by finishing off the rat that put us in that situation in the first place.

I watched as men, the ones I had grown up with, the ones I had looked up to, shook their heads, slapped backs with one another and began mumbling prayers under their breath.

Yes. We were the mafia.

But when family died? When lives were uselessly lost in our tight-knit family? That wasn't business. No, it was tragedy and each and every one of them knew it.

When Luca was finished, Frank stood. "I'd like to say something." He cleared his throat and looked around the room. "I'd like to thank your family. Not only did you put me into hiding, but you protected my granddaughter at all costs. It's because of you that I may finally let go of the death of my son and daughter. It is because of you that I am able to hold my head high once again. I owe you my allegiance. This fighting, between us, it ends. It ends now." He took his seat.

Chase stood. "There is one more thing to discuss."

I knew how uncomfortable it would make him, so I stood and walked over to his side, giving him silent encouragement with my presence.

"Nixon and I…" He looked to the ceiling. "Well, we discovered some things about our pasts—things that really shouldn't matter anymore. Regardless of my own parentage, and regardless of his, I motion to reinstate Nixon as the boss."

"Chase," I growled. "What the hell are you doing?"

He turned to me and grinned. "My damn job, like you ordered me to."

It was unanimous. Chase slapped me on the back and left the middle of the room. I wasn't sure how I felt, but for some reason it was right. Even though I wasn't blood related to my father, even though normally that was how things worked. I was good at what I did. And I wanted it. Sadly, I couldn't bask in the glory of it that long, not when I realized that now things were once again backward. If Trace wanted to end up with Chase, he was once again the safer choice. Damn.

"One more thing." Luca stood. "Since I am here, it is imperative that we notify the De Lange family of the happenings. It is also crucial that the next boss be appointed."

"Did Phoenix have any brothers?" Sergio asked.

"No." I chuckled and looked at Chase. "But he has a hell of a stepsister."

"A woman?" a man asked.

"It has been done before," another answered. "Is not the most peaceful city in Sicily run by a woman?"

"True." Luca seemed to think on it. "Shall I bring it up to the family?"

I laughed. I couldn't help it. "Bring it up?" I nodded. "Seems to me your way of bringing things up includes threats with death and Lake Michigan."

Luca shrugged. "I cannot help that I am one for dramatics."

Frank rolled his eyes in my direction.

"Fine." I nodded. "Notify the family and Emiliana. I want it to be done before you leave, Luca, and the funeral, too."

"Done," he said. "Now, let us make a toast."

Each man raised their drinks.

"A toast," Luca said, "to family."

"Famiglia!" Everyone cheered and drank.

Chapter Fifty-Three

Chase

Things were set to rights. I knew Nixon was probably thinking in the back of his mind that I'd handed the job back to him so I could have Trace—he couldn't be more wrong. I gave him the title because I knew I didn't have what it took to pull it off. Nixon was a badass, he was...ridiculously loyal and selfless. In the end I knew that I would choose me over someone else.

And that's why I didn't deserve Trace.

Because in the end, I chose myself—not her. Had I chosen her, I wouldn't have put her in the position I did.

In the end, I was selfish in my pursuit of her. I loved her... and maybe that was the problem. My love for her overshadowed everything else. I would have run away with her without looking back.

The men dispersed.

I sat at the table twirling a glass between my hands.

All the lights were off.

It was just me and a vintage bottle of whiskey.

Good lord, I was depressing.

I felt a hand touch my shoulder and looked up. Trace was

standing over me, her eyes sad. I couldn't look at her. I had to look away; my breath hitched as her hand slid down my arm and then touched my hand. I gripped it, I held on for dear life.

"Chase, I—"

I closed my eyes and just listened to her voice. "Say my name again...please."

"Chase." She choked a bit. "Chase, Chase, Chase..." She released my hand and grabbed my face between her palms. "Chase."

I opened my eyes and looked directly into hers, holding her with my gaze, begging her with my soul...*Me, choose me. Because I need you. More than I want to admit.*

Her mouth met mine in a gentle kiss. For a brief moment, I was relieved, I thought maybe she was choosing me, maybe it was just going to be us, maybe there was a happy ending and we'd ride out into the sunset. But she pulled back too soon. I leaned forward, our foreheads touched.

She spoke so softly I almost didn't hear her. "I'm so mad at you."

"I know." I sighed.

"You lied to me, Chase. You made me..." Her eyes closed. "You made me choose. I relied on you for everything. You were my survival and you betrayed me, you betrayed what we were, what we had."

Nodding, I tried to pull away from her but she wouldn't let me. Her hands were like a vise grip on my head.

"You made me love you—made me rely on you...Because of you, I don't know if I'll ever be whole for him. I don't know if I can be that girl that he first loved. And I want to hate you for it, except you've made me love you so damn much that it hurts."

"Trace, I—"

Her lips silenced me, again, a brief kiss, a brief velvet touch of her lower lip and then she pulled back again. "I do love you...but..."

"But?" I knew it was coming. The hairs on the back of my neck stood up. I broke out into a cold sweat.

"Chase." She pulled away and wiped a tear from her eye. "You have my heart, but Nixon...he owns my soul."

I shuddered; it felt as if she had just grabbed a knife and rather than stab me in the back, told me that she was going to cut me deep through the chest. In the end I would have preferred the sneak attack, because maybe then I wouldn't have to watch those gorgeous brown eyes well up with tears as I nodded and felt my chest constrict until I thought my body was going to explode under the pressure.

The cold knife went straight for my heart—it pierced the muscle, ceasing it from beating, but didn't end there. Had she been merely rejecting me, the pain would have stopped, but she wasn't just rejecting me, she was *disappointed* in me, and still choosing another. So the knife twisted; it twisted until I went numb and then... I closed my eyes as I savored the feeling of everything in my world stopping.

It was me and Trace, stuck in a time warp. I reached for her face and sighed when my hand came into contact with her cheek. A single tear met my fingers. I pulled back and rubbed the tear between my thumb and forefinger and then got up.

"Chase, wait..."

"No." I grabbed the bottle from the table. "It's fine." I managed a tight smile. "This was always how it was supposed to be, Trace. Believe me, we're better off as friends."

"Can we still go there? After...everything?" Her eyes were hopeful.

"Sure," I lied and stumbled away from her, seeking the darkness of my room and the bottom of the bottle in my right hand.

The minute I walked into my room, I slammed the door behind me and locked it. Shit, did everything have to smell like her? Numbly, I walked over to the bed, the same bed we'd shared less than forty-eight hours ago. Her smell was so deeply etched into the fibers of the sheets that I couldn't bring myself to do anything except take a swig of whiskey and allow her scent to overwhelm the pain.

I don't know how long I sat there on the bed. Drinking and sniffing like some lunatic.

That's the thing about love—you'd do anything to secure it—except when you finally have it, you're so damn worried about losing it that your choices are no longer selfless but selfish. That's what happened to things with Trace and in the end that was how I lost her.

I refused to pack away the memories of her kiss.

The way we fit together perfectly.

I held on to those memories because in that moment I was pretty damn sure that no girl would ever be able to fully wipe them from my consciousness, and hell if I'd let them to begin with.

I drank half the bottle.

Not a proud moment for someone who doesn't normally drink. Shit, she'd turned me into an alcoholic over the course of two weeks! What the hell did that say about my self-control?

The room spun. I put the bottle down and rubbed my eyes.

It was late.

You'd think I'd be too drunk to even think.

Clearly, I had a way higher alcohol tolerance than I would have preferred for the current situation.

Someone knocked softly on my door.

I refused to answer.

The knock came again.

With a curse I stumbled to my feet and opened the door. Mil stood on the other side. Her hair was pulled into a messy bun and she was wearing really short black workout shorts and a tank top.

"Shit, Mil, I'm not in the mood." I moved to close the door but her hand stopped me. She pushed against my chest.

"Chill. I'm not here to take advantage of your drunken state." Rolling her eyes she stepped past me into my room.

"What part of I'm not in the mood don't you get?" I slurred and stumbled over to my bed.

Mil held up her hands. "Again, not here to steal your virtue and I'm pretty sure if the opportunity did present itself you'd be asleep in a pile of your own puke within thirty seconds. So, thanks but no thanks."

I groaned into my hands and lay facedown on the bed. "What the hell do you want?"

Muttering a curse, she walked over to my bathroom and turned on the shower. I heard a few things clattering around before she was back, standing in front of me.

Somehow my shoes were off, then my jeans. Damn, it was cold. Mil pulled me to my feet and lifted my shirt over my head. I swayed against her.

"Chase Winter, I swear if you puke on me or try to hit on me in any way, I will cut you. Clear?"

"Am I in Hell?" My teeth chattered as the cold from the room seeped into every bone in my body.

"Close." She muttered, grabbing my hand and walking me into the bathroom. The steam billowed out from the shower. "Get in."

"Why?" I croaked.

"Because you smell like whiskey."

"Maybe I like smelling like whiskey."

She didn't say anything, just stood there, arms crossed.

"You checking me out?" I took a step closer to her and stumbled. I steadied myself on the granite countertop and cursed.

Mil snorted. "Believe me, you couldn't be any less attractive to me right now if you tried."

"Is your plan to make me suicidal?" I closed my eyes so the room would stop spinning.

"Nope, although I think at one point it was yours. You do know that drinking that much vintage whiskey could get you killed?"

"I have a stomach of steel." I belched and then ran over to the toilet and began showing her just how steely-like my stomach could be.

A cool cloth was placed on my neck as I continued to puke. "Why the hell are you being so nice to me?" I wiped my mouth with the same cloth and cursed.

Mil helped me to my feet and managed to look at me in the eyes as I stripped off the rest of my clothes and stumbled into the shower. She was behind me, helping me, like I was some sort of elderly person.

Apparently she wasn't going to answer the question.

I don't remember much of the shower, just that somehow I managed to get back into my bed—and that I was dry. Weird. Had she toweled me off?

Hello rock, meet bottom.

"I'm helping you…" Mil whispered as she pulled the covers over my shoulders and patted my head like a small child, "because even though I think you're an asshole…getting your heart broken sucks. Besides, I have a proposition for you."

"Okay." I turned over and lifted the cover. "But make it quick."

"Yeah, you need to stop flashing me." She put the blanket back on me. "Drink some water and we'll talk in the morning."

"Why talk when we can—"

She placed her hand over my mouth. "I don't think I like drunk Chase."

"Me either…" I grumbled.

"Go nighty-night, sleeping beauty. The morning will come soon enough." Mil left the room and I fell into a peaceful darkness.

Chapter Fifty-Four

Nixon

How did it go?" I asked once Trace was back in my room. Her eyes were red from crying. Shit. I didn't think it would go that badly. I mean...what am I supposed to do with that? Comfort her for loving someone else? Say it's going to be okay even though my own damn heart was on the verge of breaking?

"Awful. Pretty sure he's passed out drunk somewhere." Trace walked past me and sat on the bed.

I opened my mouth to speak but she interrupted me. "If you say it's going to be okay I'm going to stab you."

I backed away from her. "I'll just keep standing over here then and pray you don't find my knife," I joked trying to lighten the mood.

"You suck." Trace refused to look at me. "Both of you suck. I feel like a plaything. Old, dirty, used..." Her breath hitched. "Damn it, Nixon!"

Whoa, when did she go from sad to pissed? I backed up again, and was against the door when she charged toward me, beating my chest with her fists. "Damn you!"

"Trace—"

"I give you everything and you have the audacity to go and ask to be killed! Who are you? Romeo? What the hell is wrong with you!"

"I—"

"No!" She pushed against my chest again. "What if it had been me?"

"Trace." I shook my head. "That's hardly the same thing..."

Her hands froze in midair as her face contorted. "But it is, Nixon. How can you not see it? I understand why you did it, but you..." She turned away from me and crossed her arms. "I gave you my heart... What if you would have truly died? Do you think I would have recovered from that? Ever?"

I came up behind her and wrapped my arms around her. "I knew you had Chase, knew if I pushed you toward him, you'd be fine. Sooner or later you'd forget me, Trace. You would have been fine."

"Amazing." Trace shook her head.

My arms tightened around her. "What is?"

"You can outsmart even the nastiest of mafia bosses and yet when it comes to love you have the intelligence of a flea."

"Ouch."

Her body slumped against mine. "I feel lost."

"Let me find you."

"I feel sick."

"Let me heal you." I kissed her head.

"I feel sad."

"Let me be your happiness."

She turned in my arms. "And if you truly die? You gonna expect me to follow you into death?"

"No." I tilted her chin up. "I expect you to live a damn good life. I expect you to listen to me when I tell you there has never been anyone but you. No one. Only you, always you, forever you. And I'm sorry, but I won't take back what I did."

Her eyes widened as she tried to jerk free from me.

"Listen," I commanded, tightening my grip around her body. "I wouldn't take away one moment with you. I wouldn't take away my decision to leave you, because in the end, it was the right thing to do. I will always save you. You need to know that...I will always choose you over me. Even if that means walking away, even if that means letting you and Chase be together. Trace, if it means that for the rest of my life all I have to live off of are the memories of your kiss? I would do it. Because it's never been about me, but you and what I can do for you."

She exhaled.

"When I wake up in the morning...I don't think, wow, how can I make her love me more? How can I have my way with her? I, I, I? Not in my vocabulary. In fact, I'm a big fan of the letter *u*. I eat, I think of you. I drink, I drink to you. I cry, so you don't have to. I'd die, for you to live. And I'd survive with a broken heart only if it meant mending yours."

Her lower lip trembled as her eyes got glassy. "When did you get so romantic?"

"Been reading lots of *Romeo and Juliet*." I winked. "Besides, romance isn't something you work at—not when you find the right girl. When you fall in love, when you take that leap, it's as natural as breathing; it's as simple as that. I'm romantic because my heart demands I be nothing less than one hundred percent, for you, day and night."

Trace sighed. "I don't know what to do with that. When you're an ass at least I can threaten bodily harm, but now..."

"Now?" I placed a feather-light kiss across her lips. "What do you want to do now?"

"I think..." She pressed her hands against my chest. "I think I want to start over."

"I like fresh starts." I grinned. "Firsts are good, too."

She blushed. "Yeah about that...I was kinda caught up in the moment, and you looked so sad and—"

"Are you apologizing for sleeping with me?" I chuckled.

"Yeah. I think so." Trace's face took on a light pink as she covered her face with her hands. "Holy crap, I'm so lame."

I kissed her nose. "You're forgiven."

"For?" She didn't remove her hands.

"Taking advantage of me."

She pulled her hands away from her face and opened her mouth, most likely to yell, but then my mouth was pressed against hers, muffling the words between our lips. In a frenzied kiss, I picked her up off her feet and slammed her onto the bed.

Her tongue tasted like home. I groaned in frustration as she grabbed a few tufts of my hair and tugged. Hell, I needed to calm the crap down before I lost complete control.

A knock sounded on the door.

I got up but Trace pulled me back down on top of her. "Ignore it." Her teeth nipped my lip ring.

"Damn, that felt good."

Grinning, she licked my lower lip and then kissed me again.

The knocks kept coming.

"Shit, don't..." I got up from the bed. "Don't go anywhere."

"What am I gonna do? Hide under the bed?" she asked, breathless.

"Right." I opened the door a crack and barked, "What?"

"It's Luca. Arrangements have been made and he needs to speak to you." Tex peeked around my body and gave me a thumbs-up. Would it be totally inappropriate to strangle him?

"Go," I heard Trace yell from behind me. "I need to get ready for bed anyway."

I groaned.

"You'll be fine." She patted my ass and stepped around me. "See ya, Tex."

"Boots." He grinned.

"Stop staring at her ass." I pushed past Tex and managed not to punch him even when he didn't deny that was exactly what he had been doing.

*   *   *

Luca was sitting at the dinner table with a glass of wine. He held the stem between his thumb and pointer finger, twisting and turning it on the table in annoyance.

I pulled out a chair and sat. "Make it fast."

"You need a drink."

"No, I'm fine."

"I said"—Luca nodded to Tex—"you need a drink. Believe me, you'll want one."

"Aw shit." I took a glass from Tex and licked my lips. "Bad news?"

"Do I ever bring good news?"

Valid point.

Luca took a long sip of wine. "It has been decided that Emiliana will step into the position of boss for the De Lange family. The families are asking that peace be reestablished between the five families here in Chicago."

"So?" I shrugged. "We knew that would happen."

"However…" His eyes darted between Tex and myself. "Not everyone is convinced she will do an adequate job. Therefore they have appointed your family as a type of…"—he lifted his hand into the air—"babysitter, if you will."

"Babysitter?" Tex repeated. "What the hell does that mean?"

"You will teach her your ways," Luca stated blandly.

"It's not freaking *Star Wars*," I spat. "I'm not Obi-Wan Kenobi and she sure as hell isn't Luke Skywalker."

"My thoughts exactly. You have too much on your plate as it is, Nixon. I would not ask this of you if it was not of the utmost importance."

"Can't Frank do it?" No way did I want to help Mil learn the ropes. She either knew how things worked or she didn't. You can't just *learn* how to be a boss.

"The rest of the families, Frank Alfero included, believe you're the best for the job. All of you are young; you are the new generation."

"Thanks, I think." He was right, I did need a drink. I took a long sip of wine and stared at the wall. "That isn't all, is it?"

"I've always liked you."

I chuckled. "You gonna shoot me now?"

"Nah." Luca poured himself another glass of wine. "The De Langes were involved in a few inappropriate business dealings."

"Shit." I exhaled. "You mean for me to help clean up the mess."

"I mean for you to make it go the hell away," Luca stated. "The girl... She may not have the stomach for what needs to be done."

"Do I have a choice?" I asked after a few moments of silence.

"There is always a choice." Luca rose and slapped my shoulder. "But remember, there are always consequences."

"Yeah, yeah." I finished my wine and stood. "Does Mil know yet?"

"Yes." Luca buttoned his coat and straightened his black tie. "She is not happy."

"When has she ever been happy?" Tex mumbled behind me.

"I trust I will hear of your glowing progress over the next few months?"

I shook Luca's outstretched hand and kissed him on the right then left cheeks. "You can count on it."

"I hear Lake Michigan is lovely in the spring," he joked as he made his way toward the door. "I shall see you at the funeral tomorrow evening."

"Yup."

After he left, Tex and I sat in silence at the table.

"He's an ass," a female voice said from the kitchen.

"Ah, Mil." I grabbed a spare wineglass. "Happy you could join us. And Luca isn't an ass, he's just... a man with a lot of power."

"Oh, I know." She took the glass. "I wasn't talking about him. I was talking about Chase."

I raised my glass. "Then we are in agreement. Cheers."

She closed her eyes and drank a deep sip from the merlot. "I need you guys, now, more than ever."

"Wow, that was the nicest thing she's ever said to us, Nixon." Tex winked at her, and she scowled and took a seat.

"We'll help as much as we can." I stared out the dark window and concentrated on the day in the future when we wouldn't have impending death hanging over our heads.

Chapter Fifty-Five

Chase

It was official.

I hated funerals.

Cremation. That was my future. No chance in hell was I going to put my friends and family through hours of torture only to relive all the memories and then get buried in the ground.

I adjusted my black tie and put on my aviators to hide my bloodshot eyes. I'd been on edge ever since I woke up, to remember Mil and her word. Proposition. Damn, that couldn't be good. Since when did that girl ever need a favor from anyone?

The sermon wasn't long.

Nixon and I were the first to put flower petals on the casket, followed by Tex, Frank, Luca, and then the girls.

Nobody really cried.

My stomach was in knots as the casket was lowered into the earth. Then it started raining.

Wow, it was as if God was aware of my mood and had decided to make it worse. We sang in Sicilian and then the pastor mumbled the benediction.

I heard sniffling next to me and looked over as Trace hid her face in Nixon's jacket.

Ten seconds. I stared for all of ten seconds. I even took a step in their direction. I was so damn used to comforting her that seeing her cry caused a knee-jerk reaction in me. I wanted to be the one to catch those tears.

She pulled off her dark sunglasses and wiped her eyes, and then looked in my direction.

I should have looked away.

But I couldn't.

I was frozen.

In ten steps, she was in front of me.

My jaw clenched as she very slowly stepped into my arms and hugged me. I put my chin on her head and wrapped my arms around her body.

Nixon looked in our direction, gave me a small nod, and walked off.

I don't know how long we stayed like that. Minutes? Hours? People began conversing. Some drove away right after the funeral ended; others stayed and shook hands with Nixon.

But me? I was hugging the girl I loved.

"I'm sorry I was angry with you," Trace whispered. "I just...I don't know, I don't want this to be awful but I think it's going to be, isn't it?"

"Yeah." I managed to say, "It's gonna suck, but..." I looked over at the hole Phoenix's body had just been lowered into. "You need to know something." I kissed the tip of Trace's nose. "I will always be here for you. Always. I promise I'll try to move on, if you promise me one thing."

"What?" Her eyes twinkled.

I nodded to Nixon. "Give him hell."

Her face broke out into a grin. I felt my expression matching hers and then we both laughed. She gave me one final hug and then ran off into Nixon's waiting arms.

Thank you, I mouthed to him.

He nodded and walked off with her.

"Hey, sleeping beauty. Dream of me?" Mil said from behind me.

Well, no time to mourn my broken heart when I had to deal with the devil and a hangover all in the same morning. "Thanks for your, uh, help, Mil."

She crossed her arms, forcing her dress to tighten around her little body. Damn, but she was a tiny little package of rage. From her dark hair to her really pretty long legs and bright blue eyes. If she wasn't so hostile I'd have half a mind to be attracted to her.

But she was like a damn tiger.

And I was fond of all my parts, thank you very much.

"So?" I put my arm cautiously around her. "What's this proposition?"

Mil tensed underneath me. "Don't laugh or I swear I'll shoot you. Don't think I won't do it. After all, we're at a cemetery."

"Have I ever told you how lovely you were?" I tilted my head. "No?"

"Ass. Do you want to hear it or not?"

"Okay, you've got me." I stopped walking. "What do you need?"

She exhaled and looked up into my eyes. "I need you to marry me."

When you compete against the ruthless, all is *not* fair in love and war…

See the next page for an excerpt from

ELITE.

Prologue

Whoever told me life was easy—lied. It's hard. It sucks. The crazy thing is—nobody has the guts to admit the truth. Everyone, and I mean *everyone*, has a secret. Everyone has a story that needs to be told. Hurt is everywhere; as humans we practically drown in its essence, yet we all pretend like it doesn't exist. We make believe that everything is fine, when really, everything within us screams in outrage. Our soul pleads for us to be honest at least once in our lives. It begs of us to tell one person. It forces us to become vulnerable to that one person, and the very second that we do, everything seems better.

For a moment, life isn't as hard as it seems. Effortless. It's effortless, and then the gauntlet falls.

When I met Nixon I had no idea what life had in store for me. In my wildest dreams, I could have never imagined this.

"Everything…" He swallowed and looked away for a brief second before grabbing my hand and kissing it. "Everything is about to change."

Chapter One

I can feel you breathing down my neck, Trace." Grandpa gripped the steering wheel and gave me a weak smile before he reached back and patted my hand.

Yup, patted my hand.

As if *that's* going to make me feel any less nervous.

I closed my eyes and took a few deep breaths, trying to concentrate on the excitement of my situation, not the fear. I refused to be scared just because it was new.

I mean, sure, I'd never ridden in an airplane before last night, but it wasn't as if I was freaking out...yet.

I missed my dogs and everything about our ranch in Wyoming. When my ailing grandma suggested I enter the contest, I obeyed to make her happy—anything to distract me from her illness. Besides, it's everyone's dream to go to Eagle Elite, but your chances of getting in are slim to none. One company did a study and said your chances were only slightly higher than that of your body morphing into the body of a whale.

Guess that made me a big, giant, fat whale, because I got in. I'm pretty sure the company did it as a joke, but still.

Out of millions of applicants, they drew my number, my name. So fear...it really wasn't an option at this point. Going to Eagle for my freshman year of college meant that I was basically set for life. I would be placed in a career, provided for in every way possible. Given opportunities people dreamt of.

Sadly, in this world, it's all about who you know, and my grandpa, bless his heart—all he knows is the ranch and being a good grandpa. So I'm doing this. I'm doing it for me and I'm doing it for him.

"Is that it?" Grandpa pointed, snapping me out of my internal pep talk. I rolled down my window and peered out.

"It...uh, it says E.E. on the gate," I mumbled, knowing full well that I was staring at a steel gate that would have made any prison proud. A man stepped out of the small booth near the entrance and waved us down. As he leaned over the car I noticed a gun hidden under his jacket. Why did they need guns?

"Name," he demanded.

Grandpa smiled. He *would* smile. I shook my head as he proceeded to give the guard the speech, the same one he'd been giving all our neighbors for the past few months. "You see my granddaughter, Trace." He pointed at me. I bit my lip to keep myself from smiling. "She got into this fancy school, won the annual Elite lottery! Can you believe it? So I'm here to drop her off." How did Grandpa always stay so completely at ease all the time? Maybe it was because he was always packing a gun, too, but still. He and Grandma were the coolest grandparents a girl could ask for.

I swallowed the tears burning at the back of my throat. It should have been him and Grandma here with me, but she died of cancer about six months ago, a week after I found out about the school.

They were my world, Grandpa and Grandma. Being raised by your grandparents isn't all that bad, not when you have or had grandparents like mine. Grandpa taught me how to ride horses and milk cows, and Grandma could bake the best apple pie in the state. She won at every state fair using the exact same recipe.

My parents died in a car crash when I was really young. I don't remember much except that the night they died was also the night I met my grandparents for the first time. I was six. Grandpa was dressed in a suit. He knelt down and said something in Italian, and he and Grandma took me away in their black Mercedes. They moved their whole lives for me, saying it wasn't good for a little girl to live in the city. Chicago hadn't seemed that bad to me, at least from what I remember. Which wasn't much.

I gave Grandpa a watery smile as he reached across the console and grasped my hand within his large worn one. He'd sacrificed everything for me, so I was going to do this for him, for Grandma. It may sound silly, but as an only child I felt this immense need to take care of him now that Grandma was gone, and the only way I could see myself doing that was getting a good job and making him proud. I wasn't sure about his retirement, or about anything, and I wanted to be. I wanted to take care of him, like he took care of me. He was my rock, and now it was my turn to be his.

Grandpa winked and squeezed my hand again. He was always so perceptive. I could tell he knew I was thinking about Grandma because he nodded his head and pointed at his own heart, and then pointed at mine as if to say, *She's in your heart. She's in mine. We'll be okay.*

"You aren't from around here, are you?" The man interrupted our exchange and directed the question at me.

"No, sir."

He laughed. "'Sir'? Hmm...I have to say I like the sound of that. All right, you check out. Drive straight down the road for one-point-five miles. Parking is on the right and the dorms will be directly in front of the parking lot. You can drop her off there."

He slapped the top of the car and the gate suddenly opened in front of us.

My heart was in my throat. Large trees lined the driveway as Grandpa drove the rental toward the dorms.

Nothing in my life had prepared me for what I was seeing. The buildings were huge. Everything was built in old stone and brick. I mean, I'd seen pictures, but they did not even come close to reality. The dorms looked like ritzy hotels.

Another security guard approached the car and motioned for Grandpa to turn it off. My mouth gaped open as I stepped out of the car and leaned my head way back so I could look up at the twelve-story building.

"New girl's here," came a voice from behind me. I flipped around and my mouth dropped open again.

"So squeaky clean and innocent. Like a little lamb. Right, Chase?" The guy tilted his head. Dark wavy hair fell across his forehead; he had a lip piercing and he was dressed in ripped jeans and a tight t-shirt.

I backed away, like the little lamb/whale that I was.

My grandpa stepped forward protectively, reaching inside his jacket, probably for the gun that was usually present. I'm sure he was just trying to freak the guys out. "A welcoming committee? This place sure is nice." Anyone could see the guys standing in front of us were not here to welcome us and certainly weren't part of any committee, but Grandpa was making a point, marking me as his to protect. I stepped behind him and swallowed at the dryness in my throat.

"Is there a problem?" Grandpa asked, rolling back his sleeves. Whoa. Was my seventy-two-year-old grandpa going to get in a rumble or something?

The guy with the lip ring stepped forward and then squinted his eyes in Grandpa's direction. "Do I know you?"

Grandpa laughed. "Know many farmers out in Wyoming?"

The guy scratched his head, causing his shirt to rise just above his hips, revealing a lovely view of his golden tanned abs. I swallowed and grabbed my grandpa's arm.

The guy named Chase smirked and hit the other guy on the back. He glared in my direction and then stepped right up to me, reaching out to lift my chin, closing my gaping mouth.

"Much better," he whispered. "We'd hate for our charity case to choke on an insect on her first day." His eyes flicked to Grandpa's and then back to mine before he walked away.

His friend joined him and they disappeared behind the dorm. I could feel my face was heated with embarrassment. I didn't have much experience with guys. Okay, it was safe to say my first and only kiss had been with Chad Thomson and it had been awful. But still: Something about those guys warned me they weren't good news.

"I don't like those boys. They remind me of . . . Well, that doesn't matter." Grandpa scratched his head then went to the trunk of the car to pull out my few things. I was still trying to get over the fact that I had embarrassed myself when someone walked up to us with a clipboard.

"No parents allowed in the dorms. Sorry. Rules." She popped her gum and winked at my grandpa. Was she flirting with him? What the hell kind of school was this? The guys had piercings and treated people like dirt, and the girls flirted with old men?

My grandpa shot me a concerned look and sighed, placing his hands against the rental car as if trying to brace himself for the emotional turmoil of the day. "You sure you'll be okay here?"

I sighed heavily and looked up at the intimidating building. I needed to do this for him, for us. It was why I had applied.

Taking a deep breath, I stepped away from him and gave them both my most confident smile. "I'll be fine, Grandpa, but I'll miss you so much." Warm tears streamed rapidly down my face as I stepped into his embrace.

"I have some things for you. I know..." Grandpa coughed and wiped at a few of his own stray tears. "I know she would have liked you to have them, Trace."

Wordlessly, he walked away from me and pulled a small box from the back of the car, then returned and handed it to me. "Don't open it until you're in your dorm. Oh, sweetheart, I'm going to miss you so much."

I hugged him again and closed my eyes, memorizing the way his spicy scent filled my nostrils with all the comforts of home. "I'll miss you more."

"Not possible," he said with a hoarse voice. "Not possible, sweetheart."

He released me and folded some cash into my hand. I looked

down into my clenched fist, where a few hundred dollar bills were rolled with a rubber band. "I can't take this." I tried to give it back, but he put his hands up and chuckled.

"Nope, your grandma would roll over in her grave if she knew I was dropping you off at some fancy school without an emergency fund. You keep it. You hide it in your pillow or something, okay?"

"Grandpa, we don't live in the Depression anymore. I don't need to go hiding money under my mattress or in my pillowcase."

He narrowed his eyes and laughed. "Just keep it safe."

I hugged Grandpa one last time. He sighed heavily into my shoulder. "Be safe, Grandpa. Don't let the cows out and keep milking the goats. I really will miss you."

"And I you... Just, do me a favor." He pulled away and looked into my eyes as I nodded. "Be careful. There are people out there who..." He cursed. Grandpa rarely cursed.

"What is it?" Okay, he was starting to scare me.

He looked behind me and pressed his lips together in frustration. "Nothing. Never mind. Just be careful, okay, sweetheart?"

"Okay." I kissed his cheek.

Grandpa grinned and got into the car. I waved as he drove off, then turned back toward the girl with the clipboard.

"Okay." I took a soothing breath and faced my future. "So where to?"

"Name?" she asked, sounding bored.

"Trace Rooks."

The girl smirked and shook her head as if my name was the most amusing thing she'd heard all day. Was everyone rude here?

"It's your lucky day," she announced, motioning toward the building. "You are in the United States."

I looked around just to make sure I wasn't getting punked. "Um, yeah, I know. I'm American."

"Gee." She put the pen in her mouth and sighed heavily. "I didn't know that. You seemed foreign to me. Where did you say you were from? Wyoming? Do they even have electricity there?"

I opened my mouth to defend myself, but she interrupted me… again.

"I know where we are, New Girl. Rooms are themed based on countries. Don't ask me why; it's just how it's done. Your room is the United States Room. Go make yourself at home. Oh, and welcome to Elite." She eyed me from head to toe twice before finally spinning around and returning to the building.

How was I supposed to get all my stuff in the building? Wasn't there some sort of welcome packet or directions or something?

I vaguely remembered some information that had come in the mail the week before. It had my student ID card, amongst other things. I rummaged through my purse and found the packet and quickly began scanning it for the schedule.

"Are you lost?" a deep voice asked from behind me. I turned around and quickly came face to face with the same guy I'd seen before. Only this time he had three friends with him, not one. Lucky me.

"Nope. Apparently I live in the United States." I gave him my best smile and tried to lift my heavy suitcase with my free hand. It didn't budge and I almost fell over. Awesome.

"I'm Nixon." He moved to stand in front of me. His icy stare did weird things to my body. I'm pretty sure what I was experiencing was called a panic attack. Every part of my body felt hot and then cold, as if I was going to explode any minute.

"Tracey, but everyone calls me Trace." I held out my hand.

He stared at it like I was diseased.

I quickly pulled it back and wiped it on my jeans.

"Rules."

"What?" I took a step back.

The guy from before named Chase left the waiting group and approached us. "He's right. As cute as you are, Farm Girl, someone needs to tell you the rules."

"Can it be fast?" I asked with an overwhelming sense of irritation. I was tired, jet-lagged, and about five seconds away from crying again. I'd never done public school, let alone a private Elite school where the guys were tattooed, pierced, and better looking than Abercrombie models.

"You hear that, Chase?" Nixon laughed. "She likes it fast."

"Pity." Chase winked. "I'd love to give it to her slow."

I gulped. The two guys behind them laughed hysterically and high-fived each other.

"The rules." Chase began circling me slowly, making me feel like one of those carcasses vultures feed on. Fantastic.

"No speaking to the Elect, unless you've been asked to speak to them."

"Who are the—"

"Nope. You've already broken a rule. I'm speaking, New Girl." Chase smirked. "Geez, Nixon, this one's going to be hard to break in."

"They always are," Nixon replied, lifting my chin with his hand. "But I think I'll enjoy this one."

Okay. It was clear someone had just dropped me into a horror movie where I was going to be offed at any minute.

"If an Elect talks to you, never make eye contact. Because, technically, you don't exist. You're just a pathetic excuse for a human being, and at this school, you're a real tragedy. You see, while one of the Elect is out running for president and basically ruling the free world, you'll be lucky to be working for one of our companies. You follow the rules, and maybe we'll throw you a bone."

Furious, I glared at him, ignoring their second rule. "Is that all?"

"No," Nixon answered for Chase. This time his touch was smooth as he caressed my arm. I tried to jerk away. His face lit up with a smile, and honestly, it was like staring at a fallen angel. Nixon was gorgeous. He was an ass, but he was a gorgeous ass. "You feel this?" His hand continued moving up my arm until he reached my shoulder, and then his hand moved to my neck and his thumb grazed my trembling lips. "Memorize it now, because as of this moment, you can't touch us. We are untouchable. If you as much as sneeze in our direction, if you as much as breathe the same air in my atmosphere, I will make your life hell. This touch, what you feel against your skin, will be the only time you feel another human being as powerful as me near you. So like I said, feel it, remember it, and maybe one day, your brain will do you the supreme favor of forgetting what it felt like to have someone like me touching you. Then, and only then, will you be able to be happy with some mediocre boyfriend and pathetic life."

A few tears slipped down my cheek before I could stop them. I knew I needed to appear strong in front of Nixon and Chase. I just...

I didn't have it in me, not when he would say such cruel things. I choked back a sob and stared them down, willing the rest of the tears to stay in. I didn't care who these guys were. They had no right to treat me like this, though it still stung. I so desperately wanted to fit in.

He jerked his hand away from my face. "Pathetic. Are you going to cry? Really?" Nixon scowled and held out his hand to Chase. Chase handed him some Purell.

"Don't want to get farm on my hands, you understand." Nixon smiled such a mean smile that I literally had to clench my hands at my sides to keep from punching him in the face and getting expelled.

"Don't even think about it, New Girl. You touch me, I tell the dean, who just so happens to be Phoenix's dad. We control the teachers because, guess what? My dad pays for everything. Now, if you have any questions about what we talked about here, please direct them to Tex and Phoenix, 'kay?"

The two guys who had been standing back from us waved and then flipped me off.

"That's how they say hello," Nixon explained. "All right, Chase, it seems our job here is done. Oh, and Farm Girl, don't forget. Classes start tomorrow. Welcome to Hell."